Shoes for an Imaginary Life

A work of fiction except for the parts that are true.

LINDA LEWIS

DEDICATION

This book is dedicated to my mother,
Christel Rostek Mattern,
with love.

ACKNOWLEDGMENTS

Who would dare to dream of reconnecting with a kid from high school marching band thirty-five years later, falling in love, adopting four adorable rescue dogs (Simon, Henry, LucyGirl, and Olivia), and making our home in the old neighborhood.

Me. That's who.

Endless thanks and all my love to Tim Lewis... my husband, my hero, and my best friend ever.

Nea Kameri

Miranda carried a Turkish serving tray with a crescent star motif out to the patio, careful not to spill her husband's coffee. Time and a soft patina had dulled the sparkle and fizz of its former beauty. Potted palms and flowering trees surrounded the infinity pool overlooking the caldera, their pale reflection promising serenity. (*Stop. That is a lie! It was NEVER like that, and far from serene.*) Blue canvas lounge chairs were neatly arranged poolside, and twelve place settings of Royal Copenhagen waited in the dining room for guests who never came. (*It makes you wonder where a man would be without an ocean view, his hand-painted china, and a beautiful young wife to prove he's not gay...*)

Dominic Manos lived on the island of Santorini in a traditional villa overlooking the Aegean Sea. The house resembled the others at the top of the giant crater, with its simple flat roof, white plaster façade, and a cobblestone courtyard draped in Bougainvillea. (*Not the worst place in the world to be held captive, but when life*

1

gets dark enough, the view doesn't matter.) Not so typical was the stunning blue dome on top of the house, made by a local craftsman according to Dominic's design. On the Island of Santorini, however, this architectural detail was reserved exclusively for houses of worship, not for vanity or decoration. Those living nearby were aghast that he would show such disrespect for the church, and even less regard for his neighbors. But Dominic Manos had little use for the Father, Son, and Holy Ghost, and even less interest in the commoners who lived nearby.

Miranda served Dominic his coffee with an uncomplicated breakfast of homemade bread, a slice of watermelon, and a fresh peach cut in half. She placed a pressed cloth napkin in his lap just as he trained her to do. *"Quality people don't use paper napkins, Miranda. Remember that!"* Quietly and obediently she sat at his side looking out at the sea, wondering about Nea Kameri. The smallest of the lava islands, Nea Kameri is actually the mouth of a dormant volcano that brought massive devastation when it erupted three centuries ago. The tourists who visit every year to take pictures perceive no threat. But under the surface, active tubes of molten lava were boiling and screaming to come out. One immediate threat of a volcano is death by suffocation. And even if you do survive, the lasting damage can be even more painful, leaving scars and emotional wreckage that never heal. Volcanos and angry husbands are alike that way. You never know when one is going to blow.

The only way off the island, at least for now, was in her imagination. If she was discreet, she could go anywhere in the world without being caught. Miranda poured Dominic another cup of coffee and placed the breakfast dishes on the tray. But instead of heading for the kitchen, she closed her eyes and sensed a familiar chill. Cautiously, she stepped down onto the wharf at Pier 33, a decade into the past. Harry Stowe was waiting for her on the pier with two tickets in his hand! She had on her best L.A. Gear jeans and matching denim jacket, the one with the blue cursive logo on the back. Her white high-top sneakers came with laces in every color to coordinate with all her outfits. Miranda glanced back over her shoulder. Dominic was having a drink by the pool and reading his morning papers. She ran to meet Harry and nearly tripped over her blue shoelaces!

The dock was wet and slippery. Miranda stayed close to Harry as they inched their way toward the ferry. He always smelled so good... like oak moss and lavender. It was windy that day, and the water splashing onto the dock was getting dangerously close to her new sneakers. They reached the front of the line without getting wet, and were greeted by the boat's captain. When he took Miranda's hand to help her down the gangway, she noticed she was wearing a mood ring on one hand, a big, gorgeous diamond on the other. Harry always had exquisite taste, (in diamonds, not mood rings). Miranda was her youthful, spirited self again, the girl she missed terribly. But for now, she was just glad to be a million miles away from the man drinking vodka at 10:00am.

She threw on a pair of sunglasses and boarded the ferry, giggling and dancing like a child when a wave came over the bow and splashed her face. They were on vacation in San Francisco and on their way to Alcatraz! In her thoughts she ignored the fact that Harry had been dead for years, and that the accident was her fault— a detail that may have inspired her to jump into the San Francisco Bay had she acknowledged it.

Miranda's imagination took her straight to her favorite place on the tour. She could smell the musty dampness and hoped her hair wouldn't frizz. This was D Block— solitary confinement, also known as the "treatment unit," where the worst of the worst criminals were locked up 24 hours a day! When she was at Santorini with Dominic, she revisited this decrepit space again and again but could never understand why. Prison life was depressing, so why did she keep going back? The recorded narration on the Sony Walkman that visitors wore on a lanyard around their necks, stopped when they reached the cell of Robert Franklin Stroud, the Bird Man of Alcatraz. Stroud was the notorious prisoner who murdered a bartender over a spat with a prostitute, assaulted a hospital orderly, and stabbed a fellow inmate and some guards. His biography states that Stroud was hard to manage, so after serving time at Leavenworth he was moved to The Rock where his bird breeding privileges were revoked. He was imprisoned there for seventeen years. Miranda secretly hoped Dominic would drink himself to death sooner than that.

She listened to the narrator tell the story about how Robert Straud used to bite the buttons off his prison shirt, toss one up into the darkness of his cell, then crawl around on his hands and knees in the pitch dark trying to find it. He did it over and over again to entertain himself and pass the time. Miranda envied his freedom.

On New Year's Eve, the recording went on, through dingy, east facing windows high on the opposite wall, prisoners in D-Block could hear the sounds of people in downtown San Francisco celebrating. The voices and music travelled freely across the water. For Straud and the others, the festivities seemed close enough to touch, though forever beyond reach, beyond hope for the prisoners. Mouth-watering smells of grilled barbeque made their way to the island, teasing Robert Straud about his grim fate. And while the holiday promised a night of champagne, parties, and kisses at midnight for men and their dates, the prisoners of D-Block would mark the New Year cold and alone.

Miranda stepped into the cell. The darkness was heavy like death and it was strangely comforting. The door slammed shut and oxygen was sucked from the room, squeezing air from her lungs while an imaginary elephant climbed on her chest, crushing her in the blackness of imprisonment. She was back at the villa with Dominic.

Linda Lewis

Charlie Fine

The sun by the pool was calming, and much nicer than the mist over San Francisco Bay. Miranda smoothed her hair, dabbed her cheeks, and tried to collect herself. Dominic would be outraged if he saw her tears or the memories she was hiding.

"I thought you might be ready for another drink and a cold bottle of water." She placed them on the table, kissed his forehead, and stretched out in a lounge chair beside him. "Another beautiful day," she said through a smile, "I never get tired of living in paradise."

"You've been gone awhile. What were you doing?" Miranda was ready with a response, since her husband grilled her with the same questions every day.

"I was picking out a pair of earrings to wear and decided to polish some of my David Yurman... and then I rearranged my jewelry box, and decided to get out some of the necklaces I hardly wear... you know, so I can create some different looks when we go out. I was thinking about the pearl choker from his Hampton Collection... you know which one I mean?"

"I remember that it cost me a fortune. For some reason Claire always finds a way to sell me the most expensive pieces. I don't suppose you know anything about that..."

"I just know that Claire has wonderful taste," she replied. *(Stop. That's all you have to say. No need to oversell it. Dominic is like a German Shepherd. If he senses fear he'll know you're lying.)* "I'm going to get a towel and something to drink... I'll be right back."

"Five minutes, Miranda."

Miranda recalled her first date with Dominic Manos, the night he revealed the photos of her taken by Neil Lipman, the lame brain detective with an assignment to capture her pretty life on the old Marinette. She restored the boat herself and lived aboard on Michigan's west coast at the Charlevoix Boat Basin, and later at the city docks in Petoskey. She named it Seeking Miranda and cherished the memories of the people and adventures she once had. Of course, there was a lot more to the story than that— there always is. *It wasn't the end of the world,* she told herself on that first date with Dominic. *Worse things can happen than a wealthy, handsome man having you tailed and paying someone to take your picture!* She told herself she was flattered, like a starlet being followed by the paparazzi. *It was a compliment that he wanted to know her so intimately and went to such great lengths.* Miranda always tried to convince herself that things were okay, even when things were terribly wrong. She recalled that Harry Stowe had her followed once, too. It was a bad time in their marriage. She was at a hotel with a friend from the Mallard Point Yacht Club, a man named Charlie Fine.

She recalled her last night at the club, the night of the annual clambake. Miranda, Harry, and all their friends were together celebrating another great summer of boating on Lake Michigan. Miranda was happily married to Harry Stowe. *(Another lie. If she was happy, why was she thinking about Charlie Fine?)* There was a football game on the big screen TV in the bar... Michigan verses Michigan State, the most exciting game of the year! Harry, of course, was not drinking. He had a bad experience with alcohol once, but that's another story. Miranda had one hand on a glass of scotch, the other digging around in her new handbag, searching for the right lipstick. She liked to look her best.

A grisly rogue with coarse red hair and a scar below one eye was watching her from the end of the bar. Miranda knew better than to encourage friendships that might compromise her integrity. After all, she was the former editor-in-chief of the Providence Orchid Society newsletter and had an image to maintain. So when she picked up her drink and walked over to the corner bar stool that night, no one was the wiser. There was purpose in her step, and confidence in the look she shot back at Charlie Fine. With her back arched and head tilted a certain way, her message for him was clear. The friends watching the ball game may have noticed but suspected nothing, certain Miranda couldn't possibly have an interest in such an unkempt man. She set her drink on the bar and sat down beside him. Despite his rough manner, Charlie excited her.

There are lies and there are true stories. So here is the actual series of the events that started everything between Miranda and Charlie, a true story you might not believe.

Weeks before the clambake there was one especially hot Saturday afternoon when all the friends gathered on Charlie's boat, one of the most prestigious boats in the harbor, a yacht called *Hook.* They took a cruise to a harbor town an hour away where they would enjoy a nice lunch at a steakhouse with outdoor seating, patio umbrellas, and plenty of cocktails. It was windy and rough with four to six footers crashing over the bow. Charlie turned on the weather radio as a precaution. Weather conditions, however, were not a concern for the people onboard, whether inside the salon or high up on the bridge. A boat this big could handle much more. On the Great Lakes, size matters. Miranda stood at the helm next to Charlie, with Harry watching close by. Charlie whispered in her ear. "Watch. Watch what these boys are gonna do." Two teenagers, apparently the sons of a couple on board, pulled off their tee shirts and stepped out the door of the wheelhouse. Miranda noted the mischief on their faces and wondered what they were up to.

The boys stayed low and held onto the railing, inching their way forward to the bow pulpit. The first crouched down and ducked his head to avoid the spray as the water crashed onto the windshield. Taking small, measured steps, he inched his way along. One step at a time, he made it all the way out to the end while the other boy lagged behind. The only thing beneath the bow was the rushing fury of Lake Michigan, opening wide and eager to swallow him up. The boy was suspended over the water, the boat bouncing and leaning each time Charlie cut through another wave. He appeared to be teetering at the edge of the universe, perched at the very tip of the bow. With treacherous Lake Michigan winds pressing against him, he was poised for heroism or disaster. The second boy, the younger of the two, crept out behind his brother on his hands and knees, grabbing onto the railing, squeezing tight. He was scared to death, but he was too close to go back, and too cocky to admit defeat. When he made it to the end, the boys stood straight up on the bow pulpit, one behind the other, laughing and cheering like victors while the friends on the deck looked on.

Charlie leaned in close and whispered, "You should do it, Miranda." Miranda didn't react, even though she knew she wanted to. Not because the boys did it and had such a great time, but because she wanted to show off for the crowd, and more than anything, she wanted to impress Charlie.

Oh my God, she thought. *What would Harry say?* The boys rushed into the wheelhouse, soaking wet and shivering, grabbing for a beer and a towel. Their tan skin was peppered with goose bumps, their nipples hard against the cold.

The oldest called out, "Who's next?"

Charlie never looked away from the helm. He took a drink of whiskey and a long drag on his cigarette. He tapped her once on the back, and shouted, "Miranda!" She pretended to decline, said she was way too scared, that someone else should go. It was extremely dangerous. Even in her new Sperry dock shoes, the deck was soaked. She could easily slip and fall. The drop from the bow pulpit to the waterline was at least twenty feet given the rough seas. If she fell and landed in a trough the distance would be much greater, and the next wave would submerge her completely. She could be hit by the boat and get caught in the propellers where she would be sliced to bits! Ignoring any inkling of common sense and throwing caution to the wind, Miranda stood up and made her way to the wheelhouse door. She ignored Harry's reaction; his lips pursed tight as they always did when he was angry. She stepped past him and out onto the gunwale, eager for the show to begin. The friends, well into their third round of drinks, whooped and cheered.

Miranda held the bow rail and inched along, just like the boys had done. The first wave came crashing over, blinding her. The water was colder than she expected and drenched her completely. She swallowed a mouthful, choked, coughed, and wished she would have ducked her head. The sting of the spray hurt her bare skin. She needed to push her hair out of her face to see, but also needed both hands to hang on. The lake was angrier than she imagined, possibly a foreshadowing of events to come. Her swimsuit was a tasteful white one piece by La Blanca— classic and sexy, something Marilyn Monroe might wear. But now that it was soaked and clinging to her skin, it was nearly transparent. Miranda was too scared to be self-conscious. Like the second boy, she was too far out on the bow to go back. Her eyes were fixed on the horizon, looking away from the water, and away from the pounding seas two stories below. "Miranda... it's okay. You made it!" She heard Charlie's gravelly voice, the smell of cigarettes and whiskey on his breath. He was shouting in her ear! As she ducked her head to avoid the next wave, she felt his body press hard against her from behind, his fingers laced purposefully over hers, pressing them firmly onto the rail. Miranda was no mind reader, but his intentions were clear.

They stood there on the bow pulpit, his hot breath on her neck. The engines roared, the propellers gaining traction. Charlie's dockmate who took the helm didn't have the skill to handle a boat this size in rough seas, and Miranda wanted to go back in. *(A total lie! She would have stayed out there with Charlie through a typhoon and a hurricane combined just to see what would happen next.)* The danger, the painful coldness, and thoughts of Charlie Fine's plans for her— maybe not for *that* day on his boat, but surely someday— brought a level of tension that never went away after that. Miranda thought about him when she was trying on pretty dresses in a fitting room at Nordstrom, and when she got undressed at night. She thought about the strength of his hands as she soaked in her big bathtub under the glow of the Russian chandelier. She was living in that moment all the time— the forceful waves, her soaking wet swimsuit, and Charlie's firm grip. That's what was on her mind when she approached Charlie at the bar that night.

For the rest of the summer they acted like the incident on the bow pulpit never happened. Charlie always gave Miranda a lot of compliments and attention when he saw her at the club on the weekends, but no more than before. When Miranda walked hand in hand with Harry down B-dock and past the pool to the clubhouse for dinner, Charlie sat at the dock looking down from the privacy of his wheelhouse— watching, waiting, and doing whatever else he was inclined to do while thinking sexy thoughts about her. When the day finally came and she met him for lunch at a cozy bar and grill, it was never intended to be a friendly lunch at all, nothing like the lie she pretended when she took out his business card and called him that rainy November day. And when she looked in the rearview mirror on the way home, it wasn't because she regretted what happened and needed to see if she looked guilty. It was because she wanted to look at her cheeks, still burning.

Miranda knew there would be consequences when she walked over to Charlie that last night at Mallard Point, the night she stepped away from her charmed, pretentious life into the flames that waited on the corner barstool. The pages of a fairy tale turned; a chapter closed. She could learn to live without a castle and a prince, she could always find a way to get money, but she would not go on without knowing Charlie. There would be an affair; sparks would fly. The attraction between them was palpable when the Mallard Point friends met up for the Miami Boat Show in January, and again the following month at Deer Valley. People would whisper and say, *could it be? Why is a lovely girl like Miranda with that unkempt, rakish Judas?*

Miranda's imagination ran wild with daydreams about Charlie Fine; rough, urgent thoughts about a pirate taking a wench for his pleasure. Their afternoons together were little more than a bottle of whiskey and a squeaky mattress at a roadside motel. Could it be that this appealed to Miranda because for once, somebody took away her tiara, tore off her expensive bra and panties, and stripped away her sense of entitlement and control? She pretended to resist, scowling at him for taking advantage of her innocence. Charlie, though happy to play the role of the aggressor, found his greatest pleasure in pleasing her. Miranda wondered why, as Charlie's captive, she was finally free. There was no question that she loved him and felt safe with him, and she knew he felt the same. But love was dangerous territory for people whose connection was born in depravity and deceit. Except in the privacy of each one's own heart and mind, the word was never given a voice.

No one could say how much of Miranda's behavior was the result of her illness. At what point do poor judgment and selfishness become a clinical diagnosis? While never entirely faithful to her medication, Miranda always convinced her doctors she was fine. *(Another lie.*

Does she seem fine to you?) Mania is a lifelong game of truth or dare that you play with yourself... a badly behaved alter ego who shows up with a case of beer and insists you go skinny dipping, or perhaps make out in a public place where you're sure to get caught.

Healthy people might say they're on top of the world. Mania, on the other hand, is on the other side of the sky, ruling the planets, sipping scotch, and setting off M-80's in a full parking lot. *(Have you known anyone with bipolar disorder who voluntarily goes to a psychiatrist for medication so they'd give up shopping, alcohol, and sex? Me either...)* It's been said that people with bipolar disorder are smarter than most, or so it has been romanticized by the great thinkers, artists, and creators who freely eat from the tree. One doctor was so enamored with Miranda's sparkle and fizz, that he wanted to be bipolar for a day, just to bite into the apple and taste the unbearable sweetness.

Shoes for an Imaginary Life

The Dominic

There was something strange about Hanna, Dominic's personal chef and bartender aboard his boat, *Neptune's Hammer.* Miranda recalled the strange dynamic between the two the night she joined him for dinner on their official first date, also known as "Number 30". There was a familiarity between them that overstepped the bounds of a professional work relationship. Hanna poured his drinks with curt efficiency, as if serving him were a bother. And when he replied, *thank you, Hanna,* his tone was disingenuous. When she served dinner, Miranda detected an eye roll under Hanna's sandy blond bangs, pushed loosely to the side and tucked behind one ear, the same way Miranda fixed her hair when it got windy. As a matter of fact, Hanna almost resembled an older version of Miranda in certain ways. Her tall frame was lean but without the curves and muscle tone of a younger woman. And while she was plenty attractive and impeccably groomed, her beauty had seen its prime and faded. Maybe it was the look of resignation in her eyes, the drawn cheeks of an older woman who was too thin, or that she had spent too many years doing what she hated. Miranda wondered about Hanna's life and her secrets when she wasn't fixing drinks for her boss. Their resemblance was curious, but she let it pass.

That first date with Dominic was the foolish final scene, a regrettable game to find another rich husband to replace the late Harry Stowe. With *Thirty Dates in Thirty Days*, Miranda inched one step closer to accomplishing her goal, which was to never do yard work again. But *Thirty Dates in Thirty Days* brought huge consequences. Without that charade she probably would be sleeping in the strong arms of Drew Becker at night, instead of being cussed out by a drunk. Miranda ignored her inner voice that told her to run. Instead she had too much scotch and slept on Dominic's boat, just as she had done with so many men, on so many boats, on so many nights in the past. But a lot of girls did that. In harbor towns where there are yachts and big shooters everywhere, it's perfectly common for beautiful girls to meet men, have some drinks, and spend the night. Morning would bring sunshine and a hangover, brunch someplace nice with Bloody Marys, and a casual goodbye. But this night with Dominic would not end that way.

On that first date, when the alcohol had served its purpose, Hanna walked Miranda down a spiral staircase to the staterooms below. She showed her to the end of a narrow hallway to a room on the port side with twin beds, made up with navy and white striped bedspreads, and a stack of thick, coordinating towels. Two navy throw pillows were monogramed with a gold crest and a large cursive letter 'M'. "What about Dominic? Is he going to bed, too?" Miranda thought that was a reasonable question, and was glad she had not been shown to the master stateroom. Hanna grinned and laughed softly. Actually, it was more like a purr.

"You won't see Dominic again until brunch. He won't bother you tonight. He's not interested in that anyway." Hanna touched Miranda's shoulder and let it linger there a moment too long. That's all Miranda could remember from her first date with Dominic.

On their second date, Dominic took her to a tiny French restaurant in Petoskey. Miranda had never noticed it before, not even when she was working in town for Jim Tiller. Just the thought of his name was a punch in the stomach, another reason to beat herself up for losing her job and destroying a cherished friendship. Tiller was the one person who gave her a chance at a good future when she was at her worst. The sexual deviance she explored that night at Castle Rouge wasn't anything she hadn't already done in bed with Charlie. It was only the fact that Tiller found out about it that made it so bad. Oddly, once she married Dominic, she had no interest in any of those things and he didn't seem to either. Strange that a man recently wed to a beautiful young wife would have no physical desire to be with her. On the rare occasion they went to bed at the same time, he was eager to show off some crude skills he learned in his youth that were noteworthy only in his ego and imagination. It was a routine that brought Miranda nothing but boredom and disgust. Dominic refused to take cues, both subtle and overt; like an untrainable dog with no interest in learning to fetch. He was never wrong about anything. She started to sleep in the guest room, and it stayed that way for all the years she was with him.

Aux trois Capitaines had only six tables, each draped with a starched, rose colored tablecloth, and adorned with fresh cut flowers. There was a wall of solid glass that overlooked Little Traverse Bay. The glare of the setting sun was the only thing lighting the restaurant, except for some tall candles scattered about. Miranda could see the city docks below and wondered why she was so eager to sell her boat and leave there. Even with the commotion of kids and drunks on the weekends, it was a good life. Nostalgia followed her everywhere. Something about the intensity of bipolar disorder, whether manic or depressed, gave life an edge that was always begging for drama and change, an adventure or a cure. It was an itch that could be scratched but never to full satisfaction.

A tall, gaunt man in a tuxedo took their order. He called Manos by name, acknowledging he had been there before. It reminded Miranda of a movie she and Harry liked to watch, *Pretty Woman,* with Julia Roberts and Richard Gere. There was a scene where he takes her to a fancy restaurant with some important business associates. There were no prices on the menu, and there was so much silverware Julia Roberts had no idea what to do with it all. Everyone finally orders, and the waiter brings a plate of escargot. When she uses the special tool to pry one of the snails out of its shell, the tool snaps and the snail flies across the room. Miranda didn't want to chance it, so she skipped the escargot and ordered steak tartare instead.

Dominic loved to talk about himself, a shameless self-promoter. He talked about his companies, his cars, his homes here and in Greece, and various household staff he deemed horribly incompetent, Hanna, for one. Nothing about a wife and kids, although after the mess with Charlie Fine she would be sure to check on that. He asked if she had been to Santorini. Miranda said she had not. Dominic took her hand across the table, looked out over the water, and said he would take her there someday. It sounded so romantic. More than anything, Dominic talked about his boat, *Neptune's Hammer.* He loved his boat the way Harry loved his cars. For all the times Miranda fumed at him about washing and waxing his Porsches all weekend long, then tidying up the bottles on the chrome shelves in the garage, she wished she would have just smiled and kissed him. She was so impatient and critical, even though Harry was so perfect. She sighed at the thought of it. Her regrets chased each other like mice on a wheel, scrambling to exhaustion and dread.

The waiter brought a bottle of wine and Dominic made a show of sniffing and swirling, sticking his prominent nose into the glass as if he were an expert. They drank it, then ordered another. Dominic really was a bore. He was a drunk, much too old for her, and clearly not interested in her beyond a dinner companion. There was no sexual chemistry, that was for sure. Miranda decided not to see him again. She would find another job, enjoy her little home, and hopefully find out why Drew stopped calling her. She had a life to live, and this odd man would not be a part of it. Dominic excused himself to the men's room. In his absence the waiter brought the check. She turned it over. Chateau Lafite-Rothschild, $1200— per bottle? Plus all that food? On the way home he asked her to join him aboard his boat for Fourth of July weekend in Harbor Springs. She said she had to stay home and do yard work. Dominic said he would send a man to take care of that, and Miranda accepted.

Linda Lewis

Bar Harbour

Early on the day of the fourth under clear skies, Captain Daniel Bering and his crew motored *Neptune's Hammer* up from Mallard Point Club in Traverse City, north past Charlevoix, and east into Little Traverse Bay where he dropped anchor just inside Harbor Point. The grand Victorian cottages were tucked discreetly between clumps of mature trees, looking auspicious and quaint at the same time. Adirondack chairs sat in neat rows along the shoreline awaiting the fireworks display, and colorful beach towels were scattered around the private boat docks. Wood boats with names like *Althea, Knotty Lady,* and *Wigwam* were washed and polished to a high sheen, begging to go for a ride. The stately porches were adorned with crepe paper streamers in red, white, and blue, while potted geraniums and American flags lined the sidewalks.

Fifth generations of the original Harbor Point families— the nation's early industrialists with names that were easily recognized— sipped Manhattans prepared by a distinguished gray-haired bartender,

known only as "the black man." While most of the
domestic help on the Point were African American, the
residents would have been apoplectic had anyone of
their ilk been branded a racist.   While the maids,
groundskeepers, and caterers fussed to make things
perfect, the old guard— the Nanas, the Pappaps, and
their friends— were gathered on the lawn, drinking and
boasting. The men wore khaki pants, polo shirts in
pretty colors, and loafers with no socks.   The ladies
dressed in expensive coordinates by Lily Pulitzer with
cardigans draped neatly over their shoulders. Even in the
hottest months it was chilly at night, so much so that
many of the prestigious homes on Harbor Point didn't
have air conditioning. On the beach, local teenagers
gathered in the grass playing cards and listening to
music, while kids vacationing from downstate did
cannonballs off the swim platform, screaming on impact
when they hit the cold water. The weather was calm,
and the fireworks would begin as planned just before
10:00pm. By nightfall, smaller boats and some woodies
were anchored around the bay. Date number three was
set to begin.

Dominic and Miranda sat on the bridge of Dominic's
boat alone, sharing a joint. Daniel Bering, Hanna, and
the crew changed out of their uniforms and took the
dinghy into shore, tied up at the guest dock, and walked
up through the park to the Bar Harbor, a dive bar at the
corner of E. Bay and Main. Despite its block façade and
dingy interior, the town's beautiful vacationers couldn't
resist its tradition and charm.

Bering and the crew drank beer at the bar. Bering was an alcoholic. They waited, had another drink, and then finally got a table near a window. On the clearest day it was dark inside. They never spoke casually when Dominic was aboard the boat and they liked getting caught up. Hanna asked Bering about the young woman Dominic was seeing. She had to be at least twenty years his junior. Hanna stirred her drink, tapped the straw on the edge of the glass, and placed it on the cocktail napkin. Her nails were long and pretty with a neat French manicure. While Dominic certainly still had the looks, the toys, and the bank account to attract a much younger woman, Miranda didn't seem like his type— although neither did she when she met Dominic a lifetime ago.

Hanna was the oldest of six, the only daughter of a corn farmer down state. No one in her family had ever gone to college. A straight 'A' student in high school, Hanna received a scholarship to study at Michigan State. There was an on-again-off-again romance with a young man her parents liked very much. He was a year younger than Hanna and was studying for a degree in education. He planned on being a physical education teacher and high school football coach when he graduated, hoping to settle close to where his parents still lived in Midland.

He may have been a good catch for other girls Hanna's age, but she had bigger plans than a life with a common schoolteacher and a house full of kids, stretching their paychecks to make ends meet. She couldn't see herself in the role of a small-town wife, raising a family in a disgusting place like Saginaw. Hanna was beautiful and poised, a track star with a long lean body, a perfect smile, and a sprinkling of freckles across her nose. But growing up in a house full of brothers and their friends left her insecure. They ganged up on her, teased her about being too skinny, and swore she would never get a boyfriend. In the privacy of her dorm room she imagined nights on the town, dressed in designer outfits on the arm of someone important, someone who would make her feel special. She would be the glamorous wife of a successful businessman who could indulge her with expensive gifts, a life of sophistication and prestige. She intended to leave her farm community roots behind, dab some make-up on her freckles, and never look back.

Her senior year, Hanna was invited to spend the weekend on a boat in Traverse City with a college friend and her family. Friday night they went out for drinks at Tommy's Gotcha. That's when Hanna met Dominic Manos. Far from the distinguished gentleman Miranda noticed the first night she saw him there, "The Dominic," was a loud, pompous drunk, handsome as ever with his silver ponytail, Greek accent, and crystal blue eyes. He had a foul mouth that never stopped insulting the waitresses, and Hanna glared at him in disgust. He was everything Hanna's future husband would not be."

Dominic was surrounded by pretty girls in tank tops with deep tans and too much make-up. They were laughing at his jokes and pressing their breasts against him. Hanna leaned in past him, motioned the bar tender, and ordered a drink. Dominic grabbed her breast and squeezed hard. It was his churlish way of getting a girl's attention. Too shocked and embarrassed to scream, she tried to pull herself away. The other girls giggled, rubbing her arms and inviting her to join them. Hanna wasn't nearly as confident as she let on. Even with her looks, she was still the awkward, skinny girl her brothers made fun of. She secretly considered Dominic's groping a compliment. After that, when Hanna and Dominic became a couple, of sorts, they considered that night their first date. Hanna wondered if Miranda was a lesbian, or at least bisexual. That would certainly explain Dominic's use for her.

Daniel Bering took a long drink of Sam Adams. He was a graduate of the University of Virginia and spoke with a slight southern drawl. Bering went into the U.S. Navy after college, hurt his back, and received an honorable discharge. He lived on a steady diet of whiskey, weed, and pain pills, which may have explained his ambivalence about pretty much everything. Or maybe that was just his way. He had a nice girlfriend, who he rarely saw, but he spoke of her as a bright spot in his otherwise dreary existence.

Bering was close to the same age as Dominic, and often wondered why he hadn't achieved the same success in life as his boss. He was well compensated to pilot *Neptune's Hammer,* but he never aspired to anything more, and spent every penny he earned. Running boats was what he was good at, so why push himself? Besides, he didn't expect to keep working for Manos much longer. There were always opportunities for experienced yacht captains. Soon Bering would take the helm of a Hatteras owned by a family in Wequetonsing. The boat was called, *"Good Shepherd."* Bering hated Dominic Manos... was tired of his bullshit, hated the way Dominic looked at him. Their relationship had changed over the years. Bering was tired of keeping his boss's dirty secret.

"Her name is Miranda, and that's all I know," said Bering. He wasn't protecting Dominic's privacy. He was simply too drunk and tired to weigh in. "Dominic had her aboard for dinner that night a few weeks ago." Hanna recalled having his best navy blue blazer ready for the occasion. The crew laughed. Dominic was always overdressed. The handsome dockhand, Colin, was the youngest and best looking of the crew. He nodded and said Dominic told him to shine his shoes, put out the best bar ware, and make sure the liquor cabinet was fully stocked.

"She got drunk," Hanna scoffed. "I think she was already wasted when he brought her back to the boat. I knew what was coming when Dominic told me to have the port stateroom made up for a guest." Hanna reached in her bag, took out a Lancôme powder compact, studied her image in the mirror, and retouched her lipstick. "He reminded me to put out a bunch of those little soaps and shampoos that he steals from hotels everywhere he goes. Cheap bastard."

"If I didn't know any better, I'd say someone is jealous."

"Fuck you, Dan."

"Yeah, that's right, Hanna. And you would know 'cause you've been there." The men laughed and ordered another round.

The dock hand, Colin, was only on Dominic's payroll for sexual favors and everyone knew it. Other than that, he was useless. "So how was it, Hanna, sleeping with Dominic all those years? Did he ever actually touch you? I mean, I know what the boss likes, heh, heh. So how was it, Hanna? Did you pretend to enjoy it?"

Hanna took a drink and rolled her eyes at the young dockhand. "Just for the record, you ass, there's a big difference between sleeping together, and sleeping together. When you grow up someday, you'll know that, or maybe you won't. Maybe you'll make a career of taking care of old gay men, the way you take care of Dominic. Given your lack of ability to do much else, I'd say you've got a good career ahead of you." *Neptune's Hammer* was not given that name with the intention of attracting girls.

"When you first met Dominic, did you ever think the two of you might get married?" Colin was twenty-four and had been on the boat three years. As Dominic's boy toy he knew more than the rest of the crew about his boss's personal life than Hanna thought appropriate. If she could fire him, she would. "I mean, he is a great catch, what, with all the parties, fancy friends, the money? He could have gone on having sex with his male friends, and you could have continued spending time with the girls... if you know what I mean."

Though it was none of anyone's business, that's exactly how it turned out, but without the big diamond, and without the financial advantages of being his wife. Hanna may have preferred men earlier in life, and probably should have married the gym teacher. Dominic used her. For years he passed her around to his political acquaintances in exchange for preferential treatment in his business dealings. When he entertained on his boat it was Hanna's job to line up dancers and prostitutes from Detroit to entertain the men. Dominic always made a show of bouncing the half-naked girls on his lap, groping them and snapping their G-strings while everyone watched. It was imperative that his business cronies see him as a real man's man, strong and straight, always surrounded by beautiful friends of the opposite sex. He went one step further and had Hanna take pictures of those nights, not just of himself with the prostitutes, but of his associates half undressed with the girls dramatically grinding away on their laps.

When the guests left, Dominic picked a few of the prettier ones and put them in bed with Hanna. They smelled like sweat and cheap Giorgio perfume, dirty and tired from entertaining all night. Hanna stopped asking herself whether she liked it. Sex with girls wasn't that much different than sleeping with men. After a while, she didn't much like being in bed with either. Dominic didn't care what she enjoyed, as long as she acted like she was into it and he could watch. He never proposed.

Hanna didn't care. *(That's a lie. All she ever wanted was to be his wife.)* The pictures from those wild nights were arranged into colorful, pornographic collages, framed, and displayed in the library of Dominic's Winter Palace in Miami. A small brass plaque on the door simply said, *DWM GALLERY.*

"I think Miranda is going to be *the one*," taunted Colin. She's got everything to offer that you do... college degree from Michigan State, panache, charm, beauty. Only she still has a great ass. Don't tell me that Dominic hasn't thought about that. I think he's gonna ask her to marry him. She will be the perfect beard."

Hanna thought about the gym teacher, the kids, and the imaginary house in Saginaw she would never live in. She secretly always hoped that things would turn into more between her and Dominic. They loved each other, to be sure, but not as husband and wife. She was his accomplice, his administrative assistant, and his cover for whenever he needed to appear respectable. And while Hanna had all the designer clothes, and cars, and trips she could ever wish for, life was as empty as it could be.

She used to tell the story about how she broke a nail on the way to the airport where Dominic's jet was waiting to fly them to Miami. She went straight to the salon for a repair while the crew had to wait. Whatever power she had, she liked using it. Now she was bitter; too old to start again. She had given her life to a man who offered her no life at all. She wished she could hate Dominic, but he's all she had.

Bering finished his beer and ordered another. Colin spotted a group of men from the sailing club come in and take a seat at the bar. He grabbed his beer, smoothed his hair, and ran off to greet them. Bering leaned in across the table and Hanna did the same. "Apparently, Miranda was seeing someone. You remember the guy that installed the navigation system two summers ago? The guy that Dominic stiffed for the bill?" Hanna nodded. She remembered Drew Becker but wasn't aware that her boss didn't pay him. It explained why the project was left unfinished. Bering hired a man to complete the install when they got to Florida that winter.

"He and Miranda were dating, apparently... might have been more serious than that." Hanna recalled Drew Becker working on the bridge, lying on his back, stretching to reach up behind the dashboard. His tee shirt was soaked with sweat, riding up in the front so she could see his tan belly and toned abs. "Anyway, Dominic had me go over there. He lives in the old boathouse out on Lake Charlevoix. He was some relation to old Hank Becker. I'm sure you've heard the stories." Hanna nodded. "I was supposed to rough him up, tell him that Dominic Manos gets what he wants, and that Miranda was no longer available, you know, the usual line of B.S. that Dominic likes to lay on people. I said that Dominic has men who would be watching him, that he would get beat up or worse if he tried to see her. And I mentioned that she had been seeing Jim Tiller the entire time they were dating... told him it was really no great loss, that she was never his girlfriend in the first place." Bering hung his head. "That's all I know. Becker hasn't been seen around town or at her house since. Whether Miranda really likes Dominic or has something else in mind, I have no idea."

"Holy crap, you told him that? Told him she was with Tiller?" Hanna wouldn't put anything past Bering, but this was low, even for him.

"I didn't want any complications. Didn't want to have to go back to Charlevoix and deal with this guy again. He obviously bought the story, or he'd be back in town on his motorcycle looking for her."

"Oh my God," she stammered, "what did he say when you told him?"

Drew was out in the driveway at the boathouse when Daniel Bering showed up. He had uncovered his grandfather's old HackerCraft and was tossing around the idea that he might restore her someday... now that he had someone to enjoy it with.

Bering ordered another beer. "I have no idea. I said what I went there to say, and I left. There was nothing further to discuss."

The Bar Harbour was packed. It was getting dark, and the fireworks on Little Traverse Bay would soon begin. A large commercial barge was anchored offshore, with men walking purposefully to their stations. The bursts would explode right over the water, over *Neptune's Hammer,* and would end with a boom.

Linda Lewis

The Sisters Upstairs

This was the night Dominic Manos told Miranda his story. Whether entirely true or not, she believed every word. They sat companionably beside each other on the deck. The air smelled like sulfur and a haze lingered. The smaller boats had motored back to their docks and *Neptune's Hammer* sat gently rocking, the bay nearly flat. The crew wouldn't be back till late. Dominic had spent years keeping track of Hanna, her comings and goings, the people she spent time with. There were occasions when he hired a private eye to take pictures. Manos was an important man, after all, and had his reputation to consider. But lately he didn't much care where Hanna went or what she was doing. Their relationship had come to an end in every way, except for her duties on his boat. He would provide her with a nice stipend for her service when the time came to let her go. She had no skills to speak of, having spent her best years serving him and entertaining trashy girls and his boyfriends.

Dominic poured two glasses of champagne, handed one to Miranda, and lit another joint. "I don't usually go back into the past because it's history now and it doesn't mean anything. The past is the past. Anyhow, my parents gave me away when I was three. I was an orphan, but never a ward of the court. My parents wouldn't sign the papers for that. If they had things might have been different. I don't remember where I lived when I was really young, nothing about my life until I was six or seven. The school I went to was Clark Elementary on Harrison Street. Sometimes I stayed in a foster home, but when nobody would take me I got sent to a camp in the country where I lived with other boys.

"In the cottage where I stayed there were twenty bunk beds, so forty kids in all. There were ten cottages and each one was named after a river. I usually got assigned to North Ten Mile or Saint Clair, and the older kids stayed in Wester Creek and Ford. We weren't supposed to go over there but we did anyway. There was school in the morning, then lunch, then in the afternoon we picked up stones, and that's what we did every day. They liked it when you worked hard. If you tried your best they left you alone, and if you didn't you got paddled. The people in charge were fat and wore gray uniforms, but they were slow and could never catch me. If you stole or set anything on fire, the judge could keep you there, maybe forever. The worst thing I ever did was run away, and I had my reasons. If anybody had booze or cigarettes, I did that, too."

Miranda knew that Dominic grew up in Flint, Michigan, in a predominantly Greek community there. He still had business interests in the area, including a plant that made parts for General Motors, giving him an arm's length relationship with the auto giant. It was hard to believe he grew up this way.

"Back in the days after the war, there were stamps you could use to buy gas. I think people got extra stamps for taking me in but I'm not really sure. When it got too crowded at the Mobile station on W. Bristol, they made me go and wait. I hated standing in the long lines, especially in the summer when it was real hot. I didn't want to go back to North Ten Mile so I stood in line and never complained." He was telling the story in the voice of a child.

"When I was around nine or ten, I don't remember exactly, I went to live with a family by the name of Studt. Their house was at 357 West Wellington, close to the school. There were two teenage daughters. The oldest one was named Dorothy, and I can't remember the other one. I liked living there. There were two bedrooms upstairs. The first room is where the girls slept, and to get to my room, you had to walk through their room first, down the side opposite the bed by the window. While I was living there, the sisters sometimes told me to come into their bedroom. They wanted to teach me about hugging and kissing. They showed me what to do and they liked it.

"Until the girls got a little older, that's pretty much all they wanted. Then the younger one started having boyfriends. They were a lot older than me, and they reminded me of the boys in the cottages. There were two black boys that came to the house a lot. I never found out their names. We would all meet upstairs in the bedroom to do some hugging and kissing, and the girls told them it was okay to do some things with me. It started out pretty easy. They told me what to do. But later, they wanted to do other things and it hurt. I wanted to scream and I wanted them to stop but I couldn't tell anyone. I knew if I caused trouble the Studt's would send me back. I didn't want to leave, so I never said no."

Miranda felt a tear on her cheek, then another. She blinked hard, dabbed her nose with a Kleenex, and looked up at Dominic. She wondered how a man could be so strong to live his young life this way and grow up to be so normal and kind.

"Around this time, Mr. Studt decided the family would move to California so he could get a better job, because the GM plant where he worked had gone straight to hell. He said they wanted me to go with them, but since I wasn't a ward of the court, I wasn't allowed to leave Michigan. When I said things could have been different, this is what I was talking about. My aunt and uncle, who I never knew I had, owned a small grocery in Burton Township. There was an apartment upstairs where they lived. Somehow, they found me and my aunt said I could stay with them. To me they were strangers, but it didn't matter. I was just glad someone would take me. There were two small kids and a black cocker spaniel I really liked. His name was Buddy. During the day I delivered groceries on my bike to the rich people who lived along the river. The houses had long driveways and sat way back from the road. I'd never seen anything like that! The lawns were green and smooth. Some had expensive bikes like Schwinns and Western Flyers parked in the driveway. I couldn't believe anyone could have enough money to pay for all that. After I finished my deliveries I restocked shelves at the store. My aunt said my mother's name was Alice, and my dad was George Demosthenous from Marquette in the U.P. I wondered if he changed his name so I couldn't find him.

"I was older now, fifteen to be exact. I remember this because I was almost old enough to drive. There was a priest who lived in Flint. I don't remember how I knew him. The way we worked it, was that he would let me drive around in his car if I did certain things for him. I already knew what to do. I liked driving his car. People noticed me and it made me feel important. I also knew most of the police in town, and some of them used to give me rides if I was out too late. One night they dropped me off to see a friend of theirs. I had to climb up an outside stairway to get to her apartment. It was dark outside and there was no street light. She was a lot older than me. One of the cops said she was a professional. When she wasn't working, she let me have sex with her whenever the police dropped me off. She was always tired; I never found out her name."

Miranda watched as Dominic Manos relived the stories of his childhood, if you can call it that. He was matter of fact and without emotion, the way Miranda told the story of her childhood summer vacation in Saint Augustine, as if narrating from a video. She wondered how often he replayed those old tapes in his head and how much pain was still in him. They sat quietly on the bridge of Dominic's boat, his battleship, perhaps, to show the world his strength, a trophy in place of his sorrow. They drank Champagne and walked in silence as the taillights slowly found their way out of Harbor Springs. The kids from the beach were shooting off bottle rockets on the side streets where their parents would never find them. Miranda decided to love Dominic. She could never change his past, but she could make sure he was never abused or abandoned again. Still unsure about God the Father, the Son, and the Holy Ghost, Miranda decided she was Jesus Christ and she would save him.

Shoes for an Imaginary Life

Wequetonsing

The next morning, the morning after she heard his long, sad tale, Dominic told Miranda about a place he was thinking about buying in Weque, the same lakeside community where Tiller moved all that heavy furniture when he was a boy. Bering, Hanna, and the crew had returned late in the night, and Dominic suggested they take the tender across the bay to see the cottage by water. He was bright and chipper, with no apparent ill effects from all the alcohol or reliving his tragic past.

The dinghy turned gently to port. A cold spray came over the bow and Miranda screamed— it was cold! She dried her face with her shirt, opened her eyes, and there it was— a shining Victorian castle with a sprawling back lawn, bordered by mature shrubs and Petoskey stones. Pom Pom geraniums in pink and choral filled huge planters along the seawall, their scalloped leaves and bright faces smiling back at her. The cottage was wide as it was tall, not quite as big as its mammoth neighbors, but charming in design and detail. Miranda imagined the two of them waiting for next year's fireworks, relaxing companionably in Adirondack chairs, with Frank Sinatra drifting down from the porch speakers. She imagined all the fun they'd have redecorating a few rooms at a time, shopping in Alanson for antiques, and having afternoon cocktails with the neighbors.

Dominic asked Miranda if she liked it. He said he already made an offer... wasn't sure if the owners would take it. The cottages were almost always passed down through families by generation, but he said he had connections and was optimistic. He told her in a most convincing tone that they would make a life in Weque together, a summer home they would share. The tender met a small wave and Miranda choked on her bottled water. They had known each other for such a short time yet Dominic was already planning their future. Miranda coughed, smiled, and sighed.

Maybe she should have asked more questions, followed up on the details that fell between the cracks. But Dominic quietly charted a course for a future that wouldn't be hers at all, and Miranda subconsciously relinquished control. He was older, wiser, more experienced, and probably knew what was best. Why would Dominic Manos have anything but good intentions for the girl on the old Marinette, the girl he would soon marry?

Gazing out at the Agean Sea, Miranda sat on a tufted bench in her dressing room, sipping scotch and regretting the choices that landed her on Santorini with Dominic. It was her private D-Block, only bigger and better appointed. Beyond the rows of rods and hangers, glass cases held carefully stuffed handbags. Cabinets and shelves of polished burlwood were accented with chrome and subtly backlit, and each Louis Vuitton sat in its own little cubby, just like at the store. Looking at the bags made her sad. It was the same collection Drew spotted in her bedroom in Petoskey the night she disappeared. He thought they were ghastly and questioned why anyone with half a brain would spend thousands of dollars on a monogrammed piece of plastic. Even the antique LV trunk in the living room at his boat house didn't impress him until he opened it and saw what was inside. Miranda knew the trunk was extremely valuable, but didn't stay with him long enough to learn about all the money inside.

Every handbag held such fond memories. She recalled her first ride in Harry Stowe's Porsche 911 Turbo when she was practically still a girl, and got makeup all over the interior. He was horribly neurotic and drove her crazy trying to make everything perfect, but he also adored her and would have done anything to make her happy. What Miranda saw as an overbearing desire to control her, may have really been love and concern. Decisions she made during their time together certainly gave him reason to worry. Even without all the exciting trips and fine things he gave her, his devotion should have been enough. She had so much but appreciated so little.

After the crash in Traverse City that took his life, she loved him, missed him, and would forever regret the way their marriage ended. If they were together today, he would probably be out in the driveway waxing his car, listening to Joe Cocker on the radio, and she would be at the kitchen table at her laptop working on the book she always planned to write. Her reference materials would be scattered all over the table with notebooks everywhere, and if she were still with him he probably wouldn't have cared. Their commitment to each other would have been enough. Hindsight is twenty-twenty.

Brian Parker Hall would be a father by now, probably with a bunch of kids and a dog or two. They would live in a country home where all the kids' friends would gather to play and stay for dinner if their parents let them. They would do homework after school and get good grades, understanding at an early age the value of an education, just like their dad. If the house was messy, Brian and his new wife would choose the joy of being a family over a need to make everything perfect. Brian was the perfect husband even though Miranda was so young and insecure. She never appreciated all he did for her, or how much the love and loyalty of a good man was worth. Yes, he was committed to building his practice, which, as a pediatrician kept him busy most of the time, but his devotion to keeping children healthy wasn't exactly a bad quality, was it?

The sky above the villa on the caldera was getting dark, and the sea had calmed itself. Miranda could hear Dominic slamming kitchen cabinets and swearing. Something fell and shattered. She got up to lock the guestroom door and shoved a heavy armchair in front of it. She did this spontaneously without any thought. It was part of her regular bedtime routine, like brushing and flossing.

Miranda recalled the nights when Brian Parker Hall came home exhausted, went to bed early, then got a call at midnight. It might be the parent of a toddler with an ear infection that couldn't wait till morning, or a mother whose baby was spiking a fever. Miranda often rode with him to the office, still in her pajamas. He'd stop for donuts on the way which she ate at his desk while he cared for the sick patient. Whether the parents could pay or not, Brian never turned anyone away. Had she stayed, had she slowed down and considered the foolishness of her choices, they would probably be sitting in a high school stadium right now, watching one of the kids play soccer... a boy or girl who would work hard and excel, just like their father.

Charlie Fine was another story, hardly worth a place in her Failed Relationship Hall of Fame. How many other girlfriends had he had since that fateful afternoon on the bow of his boat. How many times had he pressed his business card into someone's hand, or bought them a Chanel bag on a business trip where his wife was probably with him? The Classic Chanel Double Flap, in black quilted lambskin, was the same bag carried by Audrey Hepburn and Jackie Kennedy. It was part of the nation's cultural history. The Chanel sat alone behind the glass, its leather woven chain strap draped over a decorative chrome display stand to prevent it from touching the leather. She wondered if he and Maryanne were still married. She knew he was cheating so why would she stay? If she left him, as she darn well should, he would be alone for all his days... no kids, not even a dog to comfort him in his old age. Miranda was pleased with the way his futured looked and ended, especially if it were true! While it was pointless to dwell on these things, alone in D-Block she had nothing but time.

Linda Lewis

Shorty Pajamas

Miranda didn't need to wonder about Drew Becker. In her reality he was always there. When she started her day, she embraced the aroma of coffee and imaginary bacon frying with a sideways glance and a grin on her face. *Good morning, kitten,* he would say, wrapped in a worn-out bath towel and looking right at her. This always made her blush. She was thinking about that night at the boathouse. Not that she was shy or anything like that, but being with Drew was her first experience of knowing the right man and giving herself to him completely. If Miranda had it to do over again, she would have never left that day. Ever. Ever. Ever. The sound of a motorcycle in the distance, real or imaginary, interrupted her thoughts. She found herself winding down U.S. 31 between Petoskey and Charlevoix, holding on tight as Drew leaned into the corners. She nestled her face in his neck— he smelled like sunshine and happiness.

By now Drew probably had his grandfather's HackerCraft up and running. Miranda understood the rewards of restoring an old boat, having done it herself before she moved aboard the old Marinette that winter at the Boat Basin. Drew's determination to keep the restoration all original was admirable. She would expect nothing less. Someday when she returned to Michigan, sometime when her nightmare with Dominic was over, she would get to see the fruits of his labor and maybe even join him for a ride. To this day she had no idea what she did to make him angry with her. She refused to believe he was the kind of person who would sleep with a girl then never call, at least not with her. There were a lot of complications around the time she left Petoskey with Dominic. Had Drew called her or shown up at her little house, she was sure they could have worked things out. She couldn't imagine anything so bad that it could keep him away.

A tall, built-in lingerie chest with burlwood drawer fronts stood opposite the handbags and next to the window. The antique pulls were crafted from real crystal and were cold to the touch. She reached inside a drawer and pulled out some pajamas, a worn-out pair from Victoria's Secret that she had on her boat. When she was young, girls called these "shorty pajamas" because the bottoms were so short your underwear showed! They were faded and the pink drawstring was long gone. The top was shear and styled like a man's dress shirt with lace on the lapels. Miranda still secretly dressed for Drew in case he called and asked what she was wearing.

As far as she knew, he was probably having the time of his life at the old boathouse, clipboard in hand, phone in the other, calling all over the country searching for parts. From what she recalled of the old boat, the planks and stringers were in surprisingly good condition and could probably be repaired rather than replaced. Dry rot was limited to a few small areas, thanks to the fact that the boat spent more years out of the water than in it. The most tedious part of the job had to be replacing the deck's mahogany planks, then applying thickened white epoxy resin between each one. Miranda's aluminum boat just needed sandpaper and paint to look like new, and even then it was a mess!

The work on the Hacker would put Drew's skills as a craftsman to the test. The mahogany planks had to be carefully selected, then book matched one against the other. Once the job was underway there was no turning back, and an ill-suited board would be stuck on the bow forever. One of the tricks Drew learned from Hank Becker, master craftsman and Drew's beloved grandfather, was to use a good quality vinyl pinstripe tape to lay out the feature lines. Done correctly, the resulting stripes are what gives a HackerCraft its distinctive appearance. Miranda could smell the powerful caustics and acids in Drew's shop as he soaked and scrubbed fittings and fasteners, pistons and cylinder heads. He wouldn't know if the parts could be saved until they were clean enough to take a closer look. He was already seeing some rust. Miranda's eyes burned at the thought of it.

They both agreed there was no better woody on all the great lakes, and that's why people paid a fortune to restore them. Local shops used a dozen coats or more to seal and protect the completed deck, also adding the glassy shine that Hackers are famous for. Drew was such a perfectionist, Miranda was sure he would use sixteen or more, as did the premier boat shops in Hessel and Cedarville. If he finished the work by July, he could launch and test it locally, then run it up to Hessel for the annual Les Cheneaux Islands Antique Wooden Boat Show the second Saturday in August.

Drew never talked about old girlfriends, but she was certain he had a few. Maybe after she left with Dominic he reconnected with someone from his past or even met someone new. He was not the type to hook up with a girl he just met at a bar. Every year the Little Traverse Yacht Club in Harbor Springs attracts some of the best sailboat racers (and prettiest girls) for one the nation's best sailing traditions called, Ya'Gotta Regatta. It follows the second of the Mackinac Races. Friday night there's a big party at the Irish Boat Shop that draws hundreds of guests, and plenty of sexy girls in short shorts with long tan legs. Sometimes they're there with their boyfriends— sometimes not. Drew Becker would have had his choice.

Judging by the Waterford clock on her dresser, Dominic would be drunk and passed out in the living room by now, probably on the floor, and possibly sleeping in a puddle of urine if he peed his pants. She closed the blinds in her dressing room and turned up the chandelier. It cast a soft glow on her shoes, all lined up with no place to go. Not that her night at Castle Rouge in Detroit was anything to be proud of, but the memory of ruining a pair of pristine red bottoms still filled her with regret.

Miranda could have stayed in Petoskey, worked hard and supported herself. She could have gone on with her life, with or without a man. As for doing yardwork, she wasted an entire month going on thirty dates in thirty days with strangers, determined to find a new husband. She couldn't sort out how a slight problem changing the cartridge on a Weed Eater, could lead to a life of captivity in Greece. She could have mowed the grass herself instead of acting like she was too good to do yard work. She could have quit drinking, straightened up her act, and treated Drew Becker with more respect. He was very good to her— she sure knew how to take advantage. But instead, she secretly ignored all the things that were wrong about Dominic Manos. She felt no affection for him, just pity. She could tolerate his boring stories as long as she had his credit card and a huge stack of David Yurman on each arm. Yes, he manipulated her, flattered her, and painted a picture of a life that would never be as he promised. The cottage in Weque never materialized. For all she knew, it was never even for sale.

In the quiet of her mind, a place of desperation and regret, Miranda began to see her part in it. She flattered him, laughed at his jokes, acted interested when she was really thinking of Drew. She hated marijuana but smoked a joint with him anyway just to further gain his favor and a prized financial position in his twisted world. She didn't want to be his girlfriend or his wife, but she accepted his ring and married him anyway. Miranda thought she might pray, but was she the kind of person God wanted to hear from? A girl who was just as big a liar and manipulator as the person who lied to her? She deserved Dominic's abuse, and for that matter, God's wrath. Her husband's foul language, accusations, and threats made her afraid, but she abelieved she had it coming. What was she supposed to do now with a charmed life that was built on deceit, and a future that held nothing but regrets of the past? She was too ashamed to go running to God for help. Miranda's suffering was her own doing— she was truly on her own.

Shoes for an Imaginary Life

Linda Lewis

Navy Blue Blazer

Following a predictable blur of meetings with the caldera staff, confirmation of mail forwarding, and packing all their personal things, a jet departed Santorini and landed at Kendall-Tamiami Executive Airport where a driver was waiting. Dominic and Miranda settled into the Miami Beach mansion, which Dominic affectionately called his Winter Palace. *Neptune's Hammer* and the crew were anticipating his arrival, all except for Hanna. Upon learning that she would not have a job when Dominic returned to the States, she swallowed a bottle of pills and killed herself.

Dominic wasn't the same after Hanna's death. He drank more and was quick to anger, not just with Miranda, but with the crew, the maids, the laundress, and pool boys. On the phone he was demeaning and loud, cursing in Greek when he spoke with business associates who didn't deserve his wrath. It wasn't his way to accept responsibility for anything but his own successes in life, but deep in his soul, Dominic knew he was to blame for Hanna's suicide. As much as he could love anyone, Dominic loved Hanna.

Between her classic beauty and keen intellect, Hanna made a stellar impression on his behalf. Even though she was badly damaged from her years of serving him and enduring much abuse, she showed him kindness. He appreciated all she did for him, but never told her so—and now it was too late. Most importantly though, Hanna was Dominic's beard. No one would ever suspect he was gay so long as he had a beautiful, classy woman on his arm, and in his bed at night. It was important for the world to perceive Dominic Manos as the man he pretended to be, and having Hanna made that possible. It was for those same reasons that Dominic chose Miranda.

She felt compassion for her husband's loss, even though she never fully understood the feelings Dominic had for Hanna, or the complexities of their odd relationship. It was late one night. Dominic had been out most of the day giving orders to the technicians who were servicing his boat. Miranda had picked up groceries while she was out. Even though she didn't exactly cook, she offered to put together something for dinner so they wouldn't have to get dressed to go out. She bought two frozen Lean Cuisine Shrimp Alfredo dinners (which she considered her specialty), plus dark leafy greens, some red peppers, scallions, and tomatoes which she cut up and placed in a crystal salad bowl, garnished with a pretty sprig of parsley. It was her best effort and knew it would please him, as long as he didn't see the two empty boxes on the counter.

Dominic excused himself to use the restroom and wash up before dinner, while Miranda set a pretty table. She carefully folded white starched napkins in the shape of little fans, the way they did in fancy restaurants. There was merlot on the table, his glass already poured. She lit the long-tapered candles, one at each end of the long dining table.

When Dominic returned, he stood over her, red faced with fire in his eyes. He spoke deliberately through a tense jaw, carefully spitting out each word. "How dare you insult me?!! Do you know who I am?!" Miranda felt her heart start to race. Her mouth went dry. It was best to stay calm, to act like things were okay until he calmed down. She stood perfectly still, a salad in each hand, careful not to meet his gaze which would only make things worse. Dominic picked up his glass and quickly drank the wine. "What a disappointment you turned out to be, Miranda! You're nothing but a @#$ #$%^ !@#$% &&*# #$%^." His words didn't reach her, as she had heard them a thousand times before, always in that exact order, spoken with the countenance of a demon. She lowered her head, averted her eyes. While he refilled his glass, Miranda quietly picked up the plates and moved toward the kitchen. She heard her name, a voice low and threatening. She turned and looked up. Standing still as a deer in headlights, a plate in each hand, she could not have anticipated what happened next. "@#$ #$%^ !@#$% &&*# #$%^. Leaning over with his head tucked down, he grunted and charged at her, head butting her in the face with such a force that she crashed into the counter and fell to the floor. The plates broke, salad was everywhere. Blood was rushing down her throat. Did she break a tooth? Her nose? Bite her tongue? Miranda wiped her face with her sleeve— there was just so much blood! She didn't look up. For all she knew, Dominic was still standing there. From somewhere outside herself she could hear her heart pounding. She spit blood out of her mouth and tried to breathe. Her nose was broken, she was sure of it.

The house fell silent. Miranda knew better than to let her guard down. The distinct smell of sulfur told her that Dominic had blown out the candles. How strange that he could be insane one minute, and thinking about fire safety the next. Looking out past the dining room, she saw light under the closed master bedroom door. He was done for the night. Miranda grabbed onto the counter and eased herself off the floor. A quick inventory of the damages revealed deep pain in her back, probably where she hit the counter. She couldn't put weight on her right ankle, either... maybe a sprain but not broken. She would ice it as soon as she put on her pajamas and check it in the morning. While she couldn't remember exactly how she landed, she must have fallen on her wrist which was already starting to swell. A closer look showed fingernails that were splintered and pulling away from the nail beds, still hanging from her fingertips, barely attached. The exposed skin and cuticles hurt more than the rest of her injuries combined. Motrin would help with the swelling, Vicodin for the pain, and

Flexeril to ease the muscles that would be very sore in the morning. This was a process she had completed many times before, and Miranda felt a sense of accomplishment in her ability to triage her injuries quickly and without emotion. It was far better to manage this herself than to get other people involved. Going to the emergency room would only make things worse.

Miranda wiped her face and hands on a kitchen towel and stood calmly by the window, trying to take deep breaths while weighing her options. The towel was quickly soaked with blood and she grabbed another. There was a phone book in one of the kitchen drawers. It took both hands to pick it up and carry it into a nearby bathroom. The door handle locked with a click that sounded loud enough to wake the whole neighborhood. Domestic violence never stops telling you how crazy you are. Opening first to the yellow pages, she started with the letter 'A.' Her finger moved down the margin of the page, leaving a wet stain, her hand becoming more bloody each time she wiped her nose. There were dozens of addiction centers, addiction hotlines, addiction counseling programs, and addiction specialists. If she made a call Dominic would know. Her cell phone bill was scrutinized each month by his local accountant, who was the Miami version of Neil Lipman. There would be consequences, but from the pain and trauma of what had just happened, what did she have to lose? She had dissociated the bruised and bloodied girl crying on the bathroom floor, from her smarter self who was about to make a phone call. Dominic would hit her again anyway, but Bruised-Bloody-Miranda was used to it and could handle another beating. Smart-Miranda opened her phone and dialed the number for Alcoholics Anonymous.

A man picked up right away. It sounded like he was eating something, and a television was playing loudly in the background. "Hhhnnyellow... Alcohawlics Anonymous." He had a raspy voice and was shouting over the TV. Miranda hung up the phone. That was a close call... Dominic would kill her. She went to the refrigerator and got some ice out of the door, dropping each individual cube into a Ziplock Bag, careful not to make a sound. Her nose was swollen. The sensation of not being able to breathe made her anxiety worse. Smart-Miranda needed to take control of the situation before she missed her chance. She sat at the kitchen island, trembling and tired, and held the ice against her face. Bruised-Bloody-Miranda started hyperventilating when she saw that she was surrounded by blood-soaked towels and handprints! Just as she was about to scream, Smart-Miranda covered the girl's mouth with a firm grip, picked up the phone, and dialed again.

"Alcohawlics Anonymous. What can I do fuh you?" It was the same man. Crap. She waited. "Can I help ya find a meet-n? We got meet-ns all over the place. What city ah you in?" He had a New York accent. Bruised-Bloody-Miranda admonished her to hang up the phone.

"Actually, I think I need to find a meeting for my... for my husband." She paused and swallowed a taste of

63

blood— a reminder that she was doing the right thing. Dominic needed help.

"So ya husband is an alcohawlic? What makes ya say that?"

Smart-Miranda had to remain calm. She cleared her throat and told the man what happened. Her voice was surprisingly clear. "It's not that he *always* hits me when he drinks. Sometimes he passes out and in the morning he's fine."

"Uh huh." The man didn't seem shocked at all.

"I'm really not even sure he's a *real* alcoholic. He never drinks before five and he only drinks expensive red wine. Have you heard of Chateau Lafite Rothschild? Well if you have you know it's $1300 a bottle and on our first date he ordered *two*!"

"Very impressive, sounds like a winner."

"And you should see his wine collection right here at the house! And also, he's rich... very handsome, always beautifully dressed. You'd never see him in public without a navy blue blazer! Come to think of it, he's actually more of a social drinker that drinks too much when we're out, and also drinks at home. Does that make sense?"

"I'm listening, go on..."

"I think if I can get him to a meeting he'll be okay. Usually he handles his liquor just fine... never even gets a hangover. You wouldn't believe how much wine he can drink at night and wake up feeling just fine..."

"You'd be surprised."

"He doesn't mean to hit me, you know... he just gets mad sometimes. If I wouldn't have made Lean Cuisine this would have never happened. We haven't been married very long... we're still figuring things out, y'know?"

"Marriage is tough."

"I'm not exactly the perfect wife... never even pretended I knew how to cook, but that seems like a huge overreaction, don't you think? I bet he won't even remember what happened in the morning."

"So. You're in what town?" Miranda could hear him flipping through some papers.

"Key Biscayne," she lied. She knew Dominic would only go to a meeting someplace where he didn't know anyone. He had his reputation to consider. As far as she could tell, this was perfect.

"Good. Let's see. We got AA meet-ns every day in Key Biscayne... good people, some long-term sobriety. But ya wanna know my personal opinion?"

He was still crunching away, eating his snacks.

"You need. To go. To Al-anon. Do. You. Know. What. That. Is?"

Miranda knew from her days in AA that a lot of wives of alcoholics went to Al-anon to get help for themselves. But she didn't need that— she was fine! She just wanted Dominic to stop drinking, that's all. She drained the water from the Ziplock bag, added more ice, and wrapped it in a clean towel. She was feeling much better and wondered if she was overreacting. Maybe she should thank the man on the phone and hang up.

"Listen miss. What's your name?"

She paused.

"Lola." *Lola? What a stupid name! Why in the world did I say that?!*

"Listen Lola... I'm an old man, I been around a long time. I seen alcohawlics get sobah and live happy lives. I also seen alcohawlics get sobah, then go back out drinking again. Sometimes they die. Sometimes they go ta jail. Sometimes it kills the people they're with."

Miranda thought about Hanna. *Oh my God, is that what really happened,* almost speaking the words out loud.

He gave her the name of a church and an address on Key Biscayne Boulevard. "The meet-ns at 10:00am. Get there early, ask for Lucille— she'll be waiting. And good luck to you."

Shoes for an Imaginary Life

Lola

Lucille was a big Italian woman with big red hair and a ring on every finger. Dressed in a traditional African caftan, she cast a commanding presence, smoking cigarettes and pacing the sidewalk along a row of ancient palms in front of Fellowship Hall. Swirls of lightweight couture in shades of midnight, royal, and gold fell from her shoulders and nearly touched the ground. It reminded Miranda of Charlie Fine's antique marbles, especially the blue swirls and carnelians she so admired. Lucille looked at her watch, glanced out to the parking lot, and spotted Miranda hiding behind a poorly maintained hedgerow. She pointed a thick finger and made a gesture that Miranda should come to her at once.

Miranda had great respect for women who knew how to accessorize, and Lucille was no exception. Around her crinkled neck there were layers of necklaces that settled on her large breasts and down her freckled décolleté. The most prominent was a long tribal piece, crafted with carved bone medallions and shimmering black stones. It was strung with bright red beads and chunks of uncut amethyst. Another necklace had a large turquoise cross hanging from a leather cord. It's beauty was in its simplicity. A string of facetted jade was long enough to wrap around twice, but nearly disappeared among the stronger pieces. Lucille's necklaces wove a tapestry of places she'd seen and the memories she carried. Miranda didn't realize she was about to become part of that journey.

"Hurry up, hurry up an come oh-va hee-ah, already... ya late!" It was ten till the hour, but who was Miranda to argue? Lucille's New York accent was as strong as the man she spoke with on the phone the night before.

"Ah you okay? Ah you safe? Does he know where you ah?"

Dominic was asleep in his room when Miranda peeked in to check on him that morning. She left a note that she went to the mall and out to lunch with some friends, but hoped he would still be asleep when she got home. He always told her never to wake him, which gave her some much-needed flexibility in the morning.

"I'm okay"

"Well ya look like hell... pretty young lady like ya-self getting the crap beat outta ya by a drunk."

"But he didn't really mean to...

"Save it honey. Lola."

Miranda was bruised and bewildered. And she was starting off this important friendship with a name like Lola. Why was it so easy to lie when the truth would have worked just fine?

"So if I'm gonna help ya... and I've helped lotsa women in Al-anon... we can staht with introductions. I'm Lucille M., and your *real* name is...?"

"Not Lola... I lied. My real name is Miranda. But if my husband finds out I'm here he'll kill me. I swear he will."

"We've all lied, Miranda. We've lied ta protect ahselves, we've lied ta survive. It's one of the 'isms.' It'll be okay."

Lucille tossed her head for effect, red hair flying, with long strands escaping the bobby pins of her top knot. Glancing toward the door of the white stucco building, she put her hand on Miranda's shoulder and said, "Let's go."

The ladies in the room were pouring coffee into Styrofoam cups and choosing from several boxes of pastries. They were laughing and hugging each other like sisters at a family reunion, each one sharing the burden of the other's secret life. Miranda was puzzled. With her nose still swollen and Gucci sunglasses hiding a black eye, she knew these women could not possibly understand. Ladies from all walks of life— rich ladies wearing David Yurman and Donald Pliner, health care workers in scrubs, and younger women with too many piercings and tattoos— all of them gathered together, but for what?

Miranda just wanted the playbook, the owner's manual for fixing a broken alcoholic. The ladies extended their hands, introduced themselves, and said *welcome*. A card table with Sharpie markers and paper nametags was set up by the door. There had to be forty women, with more still coming in, filling the seats against the walls along the room's perimeter. Lucille wrote her name in big block letters on a nametag, then doodled hearts, smiley faces, and flowers all around it. She scribbled a leafy vine, artfully connecting the little pictures. Miranda wrote her name in tiny letters, plain and discrete. If she decided to disappear, her nametag would disappear with her.

Miranda poured a cup of Kona Hawaiian and put a glazed donut on a paper plate. Had she been more confident, she would have chosen the chocolate éclair, covered in thick frosting with a big blob of goo in the middle. But her hands were unsteady. If she dropped a crumb or got frosting on her face, she would never be accepted by these perfect women who managed their donuts so beautifully. She didn't want to be judged, didn't want to be married to an alcoholic, and didn't want to go to meetings to get help. Miranda thought about getting up and going to the mall; perhaps a fresh tube of Nars Jungle Red would comfort her, but it was too late. The chairperson rang a tiny bell and began. "My name is Sylvia, and I'm a grateful, recovering member of Al-anon." Sylvia was smiling, but her eyes looked sad.

"Hi Sylvia," replied the room.

"I've asked a friend to read the Welcome."

A middle-aged woman in blue scrubs had her lunch unwrapped on the table in front of her. Her hair was pinned back in barrettes and her roots were gray. She seemed overwhelmed. She picked up a laminated sheet from the table and began. "Hi everybody, my name is Pam. We welcome you to this Al-anon Family Group meeting and hope you will find in this fellowship the hope and friendship we have been privileged to enjoy. We who live, or have lived, with the problem of alcoholism understand as perhaps few others can. We, too, were lonely and frustrated but in Al-anon we discover that no situation is really hopeless and that it is possible for us to find contentment and even happiness whether the alcoholic is still drinking or not." *

Lucille squeezed Miranda's hand under the table. "Now see? Isn't that just like I told ya?"

The other ladies followed suit, each one saying her name, while nodding and glancing around the room as if they were all in on the same secret. When it was Lucille's turn she introduced herself with the enthusiasm of a coach who was ready to lead the team onto the field and beat their biggest rival.

"Good morning, good morning my wonderful teachers, sisters, and friends! I am Lucile M., and I've had a wonderful week thanks to God, you people, and the tools of this program."

"Hi Lucille," they all said in unison.

Lucille smiled and nodded as if acknowledging applause from a crowd, then glanced at Miranda.

Miranda looked down at her hands. "I'm Miranda. I need my husband to stop drinking." That was more than she intended to say, but the ladies made it so easy to share, and listened with compassion. They looked into her thin face and studied the girl with the swollen nose and whatever she was hiding behind her sunglasses. They let her speak; many had lived her story. When Miranda finished explaining about the Lean Cuisine Shrimp Alfredo, the pretty place settings, and Dominic's unexpected rage, they simply nodded. No answers, no advice, no judgment.

Lucille put her hand on Miranda's shoulder. In one voice the room said, "Keep coming back."

There were stories shared. The mothers were broken hearted; the wives were outraged. They were living in Miranda's world, scared and alone— except they had each other. The ones who were doing well and managing their lives in a healthy way made comments about what worked for them and offered encouragement. Others cussed and cried. Pam in the blue scrubs got up and ran from the room in tears. A polished older woman in a fancy hat said her son had just died. She wasn't sure if it was an accidental overdose or suicide. In a matter-of-fact tone she said she was waiting for the coroner's report. It was as though she had been on this journey a very long time, and was as much exhausted as sad. The lady seated beside her gave her a hug and passed a box of Kleenex. The room sat silent while she wept.

"We're glad you're here," said the lady wearing Yurman.

"Keep coming back," said a few more in a whisper.

Sylvia rang the bell and addressed the room. "It is now ten minutes till the hour. Does anyone who didn't get a chance to speak have a burning desire to share?" The room paused, patiently waiting.

"Please pray for my daughter. Her husband is in jail," said an older woman who spoke very softly.

"Please pray for my boyfriend," said another. "He got fired from his job and he spent all our money on drugs. I'm not sure how we're going to feed our baby."

The members of Al-anon wrote the requests in small notebooks. They would lift up their friends in prayer over the coming week.

"I have my last chemo treatment on Monday," said a woman with dark circles under her eyes and wearing a cloche. "I get so sick afterwards and my husband blames me for it. I really don't have anyone, y'know?"

Another member commented, "I'm still thinking about leaving. I have my safety bag packed and some money put away he doesn't know about." Please pray for me. Miranda recognized fear on the woman's face. It was the same expression she saw when she looked in the mirror.

Sylvia glanced around the room. "Would all who care to join me in the Lord's Prayer." They stood, reached out for one another's hands, heads bowed.

"Our Father, who art in Heaven, hallowed be thy name. Thy kingdom come, thy will be done, on earth as it is in Heaven. Give us this day our daily bread, and forgive us our trespasses as we forgive those who trespass against us. And lead us not into temptation, but deliver us from evil. For thine is the kingdom, the power, and the glory, forever and ever, Amen."

Miranda was exhausted. The brief glimpse of serenity she felt as the women held hands and prayed was replaced by the realization that Dominic was probably awake by now and waiting for her. Her heart raced and her mouth got dry. She had to go. Lucille was busy hugging people. It was the perfect time to escape.

"So you'll join us at Deeny's?" It was Sylvia, the chairperson. *Why did she single me out?* "Everyone is invited. It gives us a chance to get to know each other a little better outside the rooms. It's the meeting *after* the meeting!" Sylvia turned to hug someone. It was the lady whose son had died. Miranda politely declined the invitation and explained that her husband would kill her if she was gone too long. Sylvia wrote the address on a page in her notebook, tore it off, and pressed it into Miranda's hand. "It's just two blocks down Key Biscayne Boulevard on the right." She added that parking was around back; very discreet.

Al-anon practiced the same principles of anonymity as Alcoholics Anonymous. The other women wouldn't give her away, and neither would her car parked behind a random lunch spot on the causeway. It was much easier to be discreet in a huge city like Miami than a small Greek island. She considered the kind offer but declined. She really needed to get back.

The cars pulled out of the church parking lot and drove toward the restaurant. The cars turned right, one by one, at a painted sign that said, *Deeny's Café, then* followed a winding path around back to a gravel parking lot, nestled between two stucco office buildings and clumps of trees. Miranda turned right and followed them. She was feeling stronger and pulled into a parking space. She wanted to talk to Lucille. If she was so happy, why was she going to meetings? Miranda got out of her car, got back in her car, and drove away. Maybe next time. She decided to keep coming back.

*Al-anon Family Group Headquarters, I. (1964). Welcome/Opening Statement. New York: Al-anon Family Groups.

Shoes for an Imaginary Life

Lucille

Three-time spelling bee champion Lucille Carbone didn't mean to get pregnant in high school. She knew she had gained some weight since she started working part-time at Eddies Sweet Shop where Mr. Morelli, the owner, said she could eat as much as she wanted as long as she took care of the customers. Joey "The Pig" Morelli earned his nickname not by eating too much of his own ice cream, but by winning every hotdog eating contest he ever entered, including the Annual Feast in Honor of Santa Rosalia, Patron Saint of Palermo. Every year Joey easily won the preliminaries and moved on to the final competition against nine other men, striving to beat his own record. Customers at the shop sometimes asked to see his "hollow leg," and after so many wins, the prize committee presented him with a sawed-off mannequin limb he could show his guests. Ironically, Joey was so tall and thin that his apron strings wrapped around him twice.

Then there was Joey's wife, Fernanda, who weighed more than three hundred pounds and ate everything in sight. She was the love of his life. As a girl growing up in

Bushwick, Fernanda was already chubby in grade school, and was squeezed into too-small dresses that her mother said were slimming. As she moved from grade to grade then onto high school, she was teased mercilessly by boys and girls alike who told her she'd never have a boyfriend. Fernanda started driving her sophomore year and liked running errands for her parents. Eddie's Sweet Shop in Queens quickly became her favorite destination. The owner's son, Little Joey, loved her bawdy sense of humor and unrestrained laughter whenever he told a joke. Her rich chestnut hair was styled in neat curls, with her eyebrows drawn on like a movie star. She was Gloria Swanson in a much bigger body. With Fernanda's pale rolls of fat tumbling one upon the other down past her invisible waistline, she was the most beautiful woman he had ever seen. While she sat at the bar sipping an egg cream, Little Eddie imagined how it would feel to be next to her doughy softness and girth on a front porch swing or beside her in bed. At that time, there weren't many overweight girls, and Fernanda was a rare treasure.

In the post war era, American women began to gain weight. Coming out of the Great Depression, families were grateful to have food again, and parents could be heard admonishing their children to *eat all your food*, and *clean your plate whether you're hungry or not*. As a result of an entire decade of mandatory family meals and good eating, medical sociology reports that an increase in stigmatization of fatness occurred. Suddenly being fat made women depressed! Advertising and marketing firms came to the rescue, flooding magazines and televisions with ads for a new pill that cured depression. And since it was fatness that was making women depressed, both conditions were classified as a mental illness.

Retrospective epidemiology reports obesity as the epidemic of the 1950s. The American Medical Association called it the greatest epidemic in preventive medicine, and the March 1954 issue of Life Magazine featured an article called, *The Plague of Overweight*. Benzadrine 10mg was the initial treatment of choice, followed by Dexadrine dextroamphetamine 1.5 tabs. New generations of the weight loss drug followed, and before long the consumption rate was sufficient to supply ½ million Americans with two tablets daily, the standard dose for depression and weight loss.

Joey-the-Pig and Fernanda fell in love and got married, and ran the ice cream shop together. Joey kept winning his hotdog eating contests, and Fernanda never stopped eating. Her passion for consuming food was tremendous, and the bigger she got, the more her husband adored her. She spent her days managing the inventory, keeping the books, and sipping milkshakes. The neighborhood kids who came by after school always got special treats, and for the ones who had trouble with their studies, she was happy to help with their homework. The little ones started calling her "Nana," and the nickname just stuck. It suited her to a T.

Joey and Nana had one son, a boy named Carmine, who got himself into a lot of trouble in high school. Miraculously, he graduated from Richland Hills in Elmhurst and began working for his parents full-time. He had no aspirations to follow in his father's footsteps. As he saw it, he would do well as a professional athlete (and since he had a good arm and played quarterback in high school there was a good chance that might happen). His other option would be to have a big successful company and he would be the president. He considered himself a good leader with good ideas. Unfortunately for Carmine, he had a disability where words and numbers got mixed up on the page, and didn't make sense when he tried to read. At restaurants he always ordered a cheeseburger and fries or whatever his friends were having, to avoid embarrassment. Lucky for Carmine, he was the most handsome boy in school, the best athlete, and wildly sought after by all the pretty girls, most of whom he eventually slept with. He learned how to work around his dyslexia, and didn't see it as a problem— but that was about to change.

The 1950s were a time of conformity and self-restraint. Women had dieted themselves down to a 25-inch waist so they could fit into a size 10 dress. In Bensonhurst, compliance with moral laws was even stricter, given the role of the Catholic Church in the predominantly Italian community. Religious doctrine governed society, and priests were revered above everyone else. Lucille had little interest in either. She was ambitious. Keeping a nice house and looking pretty for her husband had little appeal. Hardly anyone at Bay Ridge High School would go on to college. Most would get married and have kids; the less pretty ones would work at a shop or the glove factory. But that future was not for her.

Lucille welcomed competition at every level. Bay Ridge was an all-girls school where her classmates were more interested in gossip than math. The debate team was a place where the brightest students could practice rigorous discipline and gain confidence across a broad academic field. Sadly, the girls on the team could hardly keep up, and her starving intellect went unmatched. She lettered in basketball and field hockey, and would have played more sports if her studies allowed. She wanted to go head-to-head with the students at New Utrecht's, the boy's high school nearby.

Eddie's Sweet Shop and Ice Cream had been at the corner of Metropolitan and 72nd in Queens since Woodrow Wilson was president. Lucille believed it was her good grades and recommendations from her teachers that won her the interview. Being chosen to work the ice cream counter with Mrs. Morelli was considered an honor. Socially, it ranked far higher than winning the Bensonhurst Spelling Bee three years in a row, which had never been done before in the history of Brooklyn Schools. While Lucille only entered the contest because her parents forced her, there was an important detail about winning that paved the way for a more interesting high school experience.

For the contest, Lucille stood at the front of the stage of the Bay Ridge High School gym, straight and tall before the microphone. The head judge at the table beneath her gave the word, "Eczema."

Little Mary Boleski, whose family was the wealthiest in town, took a deep breath and paused. "*Eczema.*" She was biting her lip. She didn't know it! "E-X," Mary paused. Little Mary looked out at the crowd as if to apologize to her parents and all the relatives who helped her study and train all those months. "E-X-E-M-A. Eczema."

"That is *incorrect*," said the judge.

"Lucille, the word is 'Eczema.'"

She didn't need to hear it in a sentence; it was an easy word. "*Eczema.* E-C-Z-E-M-A. Eczema."

"That is correct! Lucille Carbone is the winner!

The crowd clapped and cheered while the teacher in charge climbed the steps at the side of the stage, trophy in hand, and something else in an envelope. Having won twice before, she knew what was inside. Lucille extended the trophy over her head, nodding at the crowd as she discreetly shoved the envelope in her dress pocket. A cash prize of $10 was a small fortune, and just like the other times she won, it would remain a secret.

(Note: In 1955, $10 had the buying power of $96 in 2020. Tuition at The Ohio State University was $96.24 per semester, a subway ride was 10-cents, and a decent used car could be bought for $50.)

Linda Lewis

Long Hair Goat Trans-Siberian

Since that night at the house, the night that Dominic Manos head-butted Miranda in the kitchen, her husband had been on his best behavior. Dominic always had a reason: *There's a problem at the factory in Flint because someone is stealing parts and the manager is a moron.* Or, *that damn navigation system on the boat is acting up again... I knew the technician who installed it was an idiot.* He would swear, and pace, and mumble to himself. But his most likely grievance was always about Miranda. *You forgot to pick up my shirts again... You were out past 5:00 without permission... You wore the wrong shoes to dinner and ruined the evening... and you look fat!* They never spoke of Miranda's injuries, even though the bruises and scabs were vivid against her tanned and otherwise perfect skin. Rather than dwell on the damage her husband had done, she looked forward to her next Al-anon meeting. She wondered if Lucille would be there. Miranda was distracted by a package that had arrived from Saks Fifth Avenue earlier that day— it was right on schedule.

Every year once they were settled in Miami, Miranda made an appointment at Saks to see Claire. She put on swanky clothes and boots by Jimmy Choo, and made sure her nails were perfect. The dress was Tom Ford in black crepe, a body conscious design with a wide calfskin belt that dipped low on one side. It was flattering. On sale at Neiman Marcus last winter, it cost more than her first car. There was one long sleeve that brushed the top of her hand, and on the opposite side, a bare shoulder with no sleeve at all. She bought it because she knew Harry would love it. Miranda's imaginary relationship with her late ex-husband was warm and jovial, even better than it had been when they were married. Miranda was more mature now, and was able to look past the issues that once came between them. It was easier now that he was dead.

Louis Vuitton was Miranda's choice of handbag. So many women who shopped at Saks carried Chanel that in Miranda's opinion, it was no longer special or rare. From the Fall/Winter collection, Miranda's bag paid homage to traditional Louis Vuitton golden vachetta, styled in a dramatic and transformative way. It was an east/west satchel, roughly the size of a Speedy 30. The bag was crafted in Italy from dip-dyed long-hair goat fur, inspired by the Trans-Siberian Railway that connects Moscow to the Russian Far East and the Sea of Japan. The Louis Vuitton Long Hair Goat Trans-Siberian made Miranda feel as if her life was connected to something bigger! While it didn't have any telltale monogram canvas like most of her LV's, the true snob appeal was in its history and purpose. Extremely rare, only seven were made.

A black and white striped canopy extended from the main entrance to the circular drive. It was important to know the correct procedure when choosing valet parking, so you don't look like a dazed Walmart shopper pulling up to the wrong address.

You put on your game face— wet your lips and lock on a rehearsed smile. Head tilted slightly; you reach the stand.

"You look lovely this afternoon, Mrs. Manos. Welcome back! Are you excited about the season?" Ethan, the valet, was following in his father's footsteps attending the University of Miami in Coral Gables. With an SAT score of 1350 and a high school GPA of 4.2, Ethan had his choice of schools. A double major in finance and accounting would prepare him for the job already waiting at his father's investment firm. While his parents could easily afford his tuition, his dad said working part time at Saks would build character.

Ethan opened the car door and reached for Miranda's hand, her four carat, near-flawless diamond blazing in the sunlight. The stone was ten millimeters at the crown— it was hard to miss.

After the greeting, the process continues. Exiting the car should be performed in one fluid movement, even though it's more complicated than that. Place both feet square on the ground, one slightly ahead of the other. Lift without leaning forward... head level, shoulders back... like when Cinderella stepped out of the carriage. Though Ethan was there to steady her, this was a courtesy, not a physical assist.

"Would you like a cold bottle of water to enjoy while you shop?" She hands him the keys, he looks into her eyes. With his chiseled features, dark hair, and a dimple in his chin, Miranda decided he's probably sleeping with half the women who shop there.

Body language experts agree that carrying one's handbag in "the crook" indicates a priority on status and position. It tells the world you don't need to use both arms to move about, and if you have too much to carry, assistance is expected and welcome. Queen Elizabeth carries her Launer Traviata in this manner, and actually uses her bag to send coded messages to her staff. If the bag moves from her left arm (where she usually carries it) to her right while she's talking with someone, it signals her handlers to wrap it up— James Bond in a crown and pretty blue dress.

Miranda took a deep breath, removed her sunglasses, and placed her handbag in the crook of her arm, angling it to show off brand specific details and monogram canvas that fashionable women always recognize. Then it dawned on her— the Louis Vuitton Long Hair Goat Trans-Siberian Satchel had none.

Shoes for an Imaginary Life

Ball and Chain

Claire was an attractive girl Miranda's age, and managed the David Yurman counter. Dressed all in black, she was friendly and refined, but pushy enough to get the job done. Her fingers were always stained with a hint of tarnish from polishing the jewelry to a bright, expensive shine. The Yurman showcase was the piece de resistance of the jewelry department, and everything had to be perfect.

"Oh my gawd, Miranda, you look wonderful... so skinny and so blond!" Kiss, kiss, "and right on time!" Claire was a stickler for punctuality, as Miranda found out the one time she was late. Born and raised in North Jersey, Miranda envisioned her as a character from The Sopranos. While she was beautifully turned out for her prestigious role at Saks, Miranda imagined her in a spandex dress from Cache and plastic hoop earrings, with her smooth black hair styled with a tacky bump— the kind of girl who chewed gum when no one was looking. Claire was taking classes at FAU, hoping to get out of retail someday. Aside from envying her confidence and fearing her panache, Miranda liked her.

"Hi Claire." Miranda always felt self-conscious at the jewelry counter, embarrassed by the charade that brought them together each year.

"I tawked to Mr. Manos last week... such a wonderful man, and so thoughtful!" Claire spoke as if reading from a script. Miranda wondered if Claire knew... if other happy couples had the same arrangement.

"Yes, he really is. And he's very good to me, as you know... very generous." Miranda smiled a fake smile and tucked her hair behind one ear. Other ladies passing through the jewelry department were watching her, probably because of her handbag.

"So. You got the catalogs I sent you? Very pretty pieces, right? Claire's voice was like a song as she pulled a black leather tray from under the counter. She was caressing the jewelry as if flirting with a date. Each client had their own notebook with photos and prices of pieces that had been purchased in the past, which allowed Claire to prepare for their meeting. Miranda was focused mostly on her own survival these days, and didn't really care about the jewelry that would be delivered to the house throughout the winter.

"Pendants are an important trend this season, and since you have *so much Yurman already*, you'll be able to mix and match! Isn't that exciting?" Claire was good at her job and probably made a ton of money catering to men like Dominic who never even had to show up at the store. It was Miranda's goal to make this easy for everyone.

"Oh, gosh... I *love* the sterling heart pendant with pave diamonds," cooed Miranda.

"Oh my gosh, yes! It has thirty points of beautiful diamonds on the heart. Nobody does pave like Yurman." Claire's affection for the jewelry was authentic, and with good reason. The collection was stunning, but Miranda was just feigning an interest to be polite.

Her eyes landed on a piece she had never seen before, not even in the catalog. Was that a huge trefoil disco ball on a 36-inch figaro chain... with diamond pave throughout and long box-link tassels? She held it against her cheek; the fringe was silky and cool to the touch. Claire reminded her to exhale and set it aside with the others. In that moment, Miranda no longer cared about Dominic's abuse and why he sent her such expensive gifts. She. Wanted. The Necklace.

The 10-carat Blue Topaz Albion ring with diamonds was stunning, and so were the matching dangle earrings. The collection was featured on the cover of David Yurman's recent catalog, modelled by Kate Moss. Miranda recalled the earrings alone were $1350. "These are so pretty!"

"Perfect to wear out, or for everyday with a tee shirt and jeans! My customers who are wearing these get nothing but compliments... the perfect earring for every lifestyle, simply divine!" Miranda was aware she would eventually get everything Claire picked out for her before the season was over. With that in mind, she gave a nod of approval for the entire tray and thanked Claire for making such nice choices.

It was ironic that Miranda's next Al-anon meeting was about gratitude. While she always acted surprised and said thank you when the packages came, something still didn't feel right.

Listen and Learn

Seated at the head table in the crowded fellowship hall, Lucille was preparing to start the meeting. The laminated readings had been passed around, and the little bell was positioned for the hour to begin. Lucille winked at Miranda and rang the bell. "Hello, hello my wonderful friends and Al-anon family! I am Lucille M., and I am a grateful, recovering member of Al-anon. What a joy it is to be here with all of you on this glorious winter's day. I am extremely grateful to be here, and glad you are all here, too."

"Hi Lucille," replied the room. For members who were well along in their recovery, Lucille's enthusiasm was contagious. For anyone still suffering— women like Miranda— it seemed like overkill. She had to be faking it.

"I've asked a friend to read the Welcome."

Lucille glanced toward the lady whose son had overdosed a week ago. *Why in the world would she put this poor woman on the spot?* "Hello everyone. My name is Evelyn, and I am a grateful recovering member of Al-anon." She cleared her throat and picked up a laminated sheet from the table.

"We welcome you to this Al-anon Family Group meeting and hope you will find in this fellowship the hope and friendship we have been privileged to enjoy." The readings continued, including the Twelve Steps, and then the introductions around the table. "My name's Miranda, I'm happy to be here." It was a giant step.

"Thank you, my dear, dear friends. It makes my heart smile to see you all here today, where we can share our experience, strength, and hope. The topic I've chosen for today... is... GRATITUDE!! An exaggerated smile crossed her face, her eyebrows raised in anticipation. The group roared. "What a surprise, right?" What Miranda didn't know was that Lucille *always* chose gratitude. Someday Miranda would find out why. "And now, a reading from *How Al-anon Works*." Lucille opened a small book and read aloud.

"Actively practicing gratitude is one way we can *Promote Attitude Adjustment, according to the book.* Instead of taking for granted the many blessings in our lives, we make a point to *mentally acknowledge them* until doing so becomes a habit." *

Miranda felt a surge of disappointment. Clearly gratitude had nothing to do with alcoholism, and for that matter, her attitude was fine. She felt a sense of betrayal; first by the old man she spoke with on the phone that night, and now Lucille. Had she not been sitting so far away from the door she might have walked out. "We will now go around the room and share one thing for which we are grateful." Lucille looked toward the girl on her right.

"Hi. I'm Amy. I'm in a bad place right now. My alcoholic picked-up again. I'm happy to be here. I think I'll just listen."

"Thanks, Amy. Glad you're here, keep coming back." There were no judgmental glances toward the girl who didn't speak. Miranda made a note.

"Hello everyone, I'm Es-tah." Miranda guessed she was from New York.

"Hi Esther."

"Even though I am a very old woman, I am grateful for my husband whose drinking gave me a reason to join this program 35 years ago. I am still growing and learning. When my husband died last year at the age of 83, I was grateful for the 19 years he was sober, and for the love that we shared. I'll pass."

"Thank you, Esther." One lady was crying; Lucille passed down a box of Kleenex.

One by one, the ladies made their comments. Some were grateful for simple things, like *you people,* and *sunshine.* Others were dramatic and heart wrenching. It was painful to listen to their stories, but for some reason Miranda was glad she stayed.

When all the members had spoken, it was Lucille's turn to share.

* I. (1995) How Al-anon Works. New York: Al-anon Family Groups.

Shoes for an Imaginary Life

Bensonhurst

"Many of you have heard my story, some of you have not." Lucille took a sip of coffee and cleared her throat. "Let me start by saying that I am grateful for everything I'm about to tell you."

"I am not *proud* of the fact that I got pregnant in high school. The guy was such a loser, a couple years older than me, but boy was he good looking." She chuckled. "I had an after-school job at an ice cream parlor... Eddie's Sweet Shop in Queens, which is still there to this day. My parents were fairly strict, but Mr. and Mrs. Morelli had a good reputation. He always won the hot dog eating contests, and in my neighborhood that meant something. Pa knew they'd keep an eye on me. I should mention that I had a secret stash of money and a decent job which gave me more flexibility than most girls my age. I could take the subway to work for 10-cents a ride, and buy decent make-up which I applied along the way. So. There I was, age 17, at work in my school uniform and knee socks, with my big red ponytail, a chiffon scarf, and a face full of Maybelline." She paused for effect and nodded knowingly. "And yes, red is my natural color."

The lady seated next to Miranda got out her knitting and put her feet on a chair; another woman was passing around popcorn. "By the time I got home from work at night, my father was drunk and Ma was locked in the bathroom crying. They'd have killed me if they saw me all dolled up, but I never got caught." Some of the women knew the story of Lucille's baby brother who was stillborn. It was her parent's final attempt to have a son, after raising a house full of girls. Her mother never recovered emotionally and rarely came out of the bedroom. Her father, Antonio Francis Carbone, became an alcoholic and blamed his wife for making him drink. The baby was to be his namesake.

"Carmine Morelli. He was the bosses' son. We worked the ice cream counter together. Correction— *I worked.* Carmine hung out with his friends and smoked. He used to make a sundae called *the Donovan,* which wasn't on the menu. Vanilla chip ice cream, a shot of espresso, a swirl of hot fudge... then filled to the top with rum that Mr. Morelli kept locked behind the counter. The night he made one for me after closing was the first time I got drunk. So. I mentioned he was handsome, right? By the time he kissed me I couldn't resist. Ladies, I don't have to explain to you where babies come from, but that's the night I found out." Miranda was listening intently, eating popcorn and hanging on every word.

"I got pregnant; Carmine signed up for the army. Since he couldn't read or write he only scored high enough for kitchen duty... a *Food Service Specialist,* they called it! When his Ma found out she told him if he did a good job he might get promoted to assistant manager like his cousin Angie at Frisch's Big Boy. He would have a crap job, a small paycheck, and no future to speak of. "How could I resist? *I married him!*"

Lucille grinned and nodded, working the crowd as though she had told her story dozens of times, which was exactly the case. Her sense of timing and sardonic wit made her a hit at Al-anon meetings throughout the state. She took a sip of coffee and continued.

"Now Fort Jackson was not a place I would choose to call home, but that's where we were headed. We got married at the courthouse a week before the Annual Feast in Honor of Santa Rosalia. I was hoping to see some extended family before we left, and before I was showing. We decided that when it was time for the baby to come, we would name him Antonio Francis to honor my Pa and baby brother if it was a boy, and I was pretty sure it would be.

"I knew Uncle Baldassario, Pa's oldest brother, would not be able to attend. I forget who he was named after, but what a moniker, right? To me he was always Uncle *Castoro*, which means *big white teeth*. Pa always said it was his movie star looks that got him the teller's job at the bank. After that, he was elected Comptroller, which put him in charge of the city's payroll, accounts payable and receivable, and also income statements and reporting. When he got promoted to Vice President of the West End National Bank, it was his job to run audits on all the activity of the City Comptroller, which also happened to be him. Let that sink in.

"So. He did his time at Leavenworth with all the big shooters... George 'Machine Gun' Kelly, Benny Binion who got sent up for gambling and bootlegging... and a couple of rum runners, Hank Becker and his partner. They got four years for transportation under the Volstead Act; the Feds never found the money. As for Uncle Castoro, he died in prison, God rest his soul." Miranda choked on some popcorn, swallowed a kernel, and couldn't stop coughing.

Wait. Did she just say Hank Becker. HANK BECKER?! It was probably a common name back in those days. Lucille had to be talking about somebody else!! Besides, Bensonhurst is a million miles from Lake Michigan. She thought about Drew and their plans to take his grandfather's old Hacker up to Hessel someday. Hank Becker was a good man. Miranda put her face in her hands and cried. Someone passed the Kleenex; Al-anon doesn't stop for tears.

"Next is Uncle Benito, Uncle Benny for short. He wasn't exactly bright and never finished high school, so he went to work as Castoro's runner. Benny got to meet some very important businessmen, going around town to pick up rent money, and also the special payments to keep the tenants safe. It was unfortunate when Jie Li Laundry burned down, but everyone knew the rules. When Castoro got sent up for embezzlement, Benny heard of a job in Cleveland that paid $3.25 an hour which was a lot more than he ever got from his brother. He left Bensonhurst, moved to the YMCA at Franklin and West 32nd, and became a skip operator at Republic Steel.

Benny never got married, and never came home. Go figure."

A few members quietly excused themselves; others got up to stretch or use the ladies room. Miranda got more coffee and hurried back to her spot at the table. Lucille cleared her throat; it was time to continue.

Shoes for an Imaginary Life

Linda Lewis

Red Sails in the Sunset

"So. As Paul Harvey would say, are you ready to hear the rest of the story?" Lucille raised her eyebrows in an exaggerated fashion to pique their interest.

"My Aunt Elena came along after her three brothers were nearly grown, and my grandparents were too old and tired to chase after another kid. I'm sorry to say she is now in a nursing home in Detroit. I will tell you that in her younger days, she was quite the looker, and had *three marriage proposals* before she even graduated high school. Who knows how many after that. Her story begins with the completion of the Girl Scout Sewing Badge and a troop leader named Miss Vivian.

"Now mind you, Aunt Elena came up during the Depression, and her parents didn't keep a close eye on her... maybe because they figured a girl couldn't get in as much trouble as her brothers. The Girl Scouts met every Wednesday, and while other girls were working toward their badges for *Home Nurse* and *Garden Flower Finder*, Elena had already completed the little apron with a pocket and rick rack trim. She did all the sewing cards, learned to embroider, and crocheted a potholder with a loop so you could hang it in the kitchen. Since people didn't have money to buy clothes in those days, girls had to wear dresses made from feed sacks, the big burlap bags that potatoes and animal food came in, the ones that had Pillsbury and Purina stamped on in big letters. The material was free, and the clothing was sturdy enough to pass down to the next daughter in line. Elena shunned the scratchy fabrics and shapeless fit, and wanted to wear dresses that made her feel pretty.

"Miss Vivian lived in the brownstone halfway down the next block. Her husband was the custodian at PS 48 Mapleton Elementary, and she worked mornings at the Horn & Hardart automat on 86th Street, slicing meat and making sandwiches for the machines. She was always home in time to meet her boys, Tommy and Peter, who both attended New Utrecht. Soon Elena was at the brownstone every day after school, learning to alter trousers, mend pockets, and replace broken zippers. The men gladly paid Miss Vivian for her services, and always seemed happy to see her. Between jobs Vivian brought down old dresses and nightgowns from her closet that Elena could restyle and practice on, learning about various fabrics and perfecting new stitches. It wasn't long before she was wearing her designs to school. Elena favored biased cut dresses with a slim silhouette that she copied from ads in the magazines. They were feminine and flattering, with darts added to create a fitted bodice and show off a narrow waist.

"Even as a teenager Elena went around looking like the cover of Vogue, and it was no surprise that men started to notice. She tweezed off all her eyebrows and painted them on with kohl every morning... thin perfect lines, applied high on the brow bone, inspired by film stars like Greta Garbo and Marlene Dietrich. On her pale skin she wore only a touch of make-up, accented by deep ruby lips. Her appearance was sensual and inviting.

"Elena quickly became Miss Vivian's apprentice, and eventually her partner. Because food was scarce and many people were malnourished, it was a time when a skilled seamstress was in high demand, and there was plenty of work for them both. Sometimes she skipped school when the shop was busy, which in her mind was okay because she was at a job making money, an opportunity many people did not have. Letters sent home from her teachers landed in the waste basket before they left the building, and her parents were never the wiser.

"Elena Carbone became the daughter Vivian Finello never had. They dreamed of fashion and Hollywood... patterns and accessories they could copy from movie stars and create with little cost. The night Miss Vivian invited Elena to go with her to a speakeasy, she brought down a pair of two-tone oxfords, a signature style from U.S. Shoe, and asked Elena to try them. The tall Cuban heels were made from fine layers of stacked wood, common in those days, with a straight breast and curved backside. Cut-outs followed decorative swirling lines down one side and across the rounded toe. Where the tongue would normally cover the top of the foot, there was only a wide satin lace. They showed far more skin than appropriate for a girl her age, but the moment Elena slipped them on she felt a surge of power, a carnal greatness. They would become the shoes for her imaginary life.

"It was clear that Miss Vivian had been to Club 21 before. They walked together down the street toward a decaying office building with a row of vacant storefronts. Elena reached in her bag for a tissue to blot her lipstick, Revlon *Cherries in the Snow*... a soft cheerful red with blue undertones. She was carrying a Louis Vuitton Speedy 25 on loan from Miss Vivian's collection. The tiny satchel had a zip top, two honey toned handles, and a small brass lock. Vivian carried the Petit Noe, a new bag created by Gaston-Louis Vuitton for a Champagne producer to discretely transport bubbly. Four bottles could be carried upright, with a fifth turned upside down in the center. A leather drawstring closure completely obscured the contents. Elena blotted her lips, powdered her nose, and was about to close the bag when she felt something strange inside. She reached to the bottom and felt glass... three small orbs, smooth and cool to the touch. She nearly laughed out loud and thought to herself, *I suppose anything is possible, but I just can't see Vivian playing with marbles!*

"They walked another block, turned down an alley, and passed silently through an unmarked door where they waited for their eyes to adjust to the dark. They stood in a damp vestibule no bigger than a broom closet. Vivian held her index finger to her lips indicating they must stay quiet. Elena could hear faint sounds of jazz music and laughter somewhere far away. Vivian knocked a secret knock on an interior door that was painted to match the walls. You would never see it if you didn't know it was there. A tiny door opened; a man's squinting eyes peeked out and he nodded. They made it through the first checkpoint and were allowed to proceed.

"Vivian took Elena's hand and whispered, *Watch your head,* as they moved swiftly down a narrow passage, their heels click-clicking with anticipation as they neared their next destination. Between her inexperience running in fancy shoes and the thick smell of cigar smoke and mold, Elena kept telling herself she could make it. When they reached the end of the tunnel a man whispered, *Password?* Vivian responded, *Red sails in the sunset.* The man accompanied them to a huge walk-in freezer with a heavy door on large hinges. He pulled it open and they stepped inside.

"Down, down, down a rickety flight of steps they ran, following a dim light and watching it get closer. They landed breathless and sweaty beneath a brick archway. Vivian brushed herself off and waved at someone in the crowd. Elena was teetering on top of her shoes, trying to regain her balance without letting on that she was new at this. There were people packed into upholstered banquettes and round tables in the center of the room, while more people danced their way through the crowd and up to the bar for drinks. Elena hadn't seen adults having fun before, unless you counted her parents falling asleep over a game of pinochle on a Saturday night. These people looked more like actors in a movie having the time of their lives! Men and women were three deep at the bar, there arms around each other, some with a drink in both hands! A sign said, IN COMPLIANCE WITH THE 18TH AMENDMENT, NO INTOXICATING LIQUOR ALLOWED ON THE PREMISES! Whether it was hanging behind the bar out of respect for the law or to make fun of it, Elena couldn't be sure, but she would have a grand time figuring it out.

"The barkeep shouted Vivian's name with a familiar grin and leaned across the bar for a kiss. She ordered an Old Fashioned, and a Bee's Knees for Elena. *Light on the gin, heavy on the honey, hunny... Elena's new here.* Mixed drinks were specially made for the ladies using sweet mixers and fruit to cover the acrid taste of bootleg whiskey. The drinks were, however, just as lethal. The bartender placed the cocktails on the bar, but when Vivian reached for her wallet to pay the man, he waved his hands and said, *Your money's no good here, doll!* She smiled and kissed him on the cheek, and people cheered. Elena looked puzzled. Vivian took a sip of her Old Fashioned, squeezed her eyes tight as she swallowed, then let out a dramatic, *Ahhh...*

"People were noticing Vivian's new friend, possibly because she was beautiful and vivacious, not at all darkened by the sadness of the times. But more than likely it was because Elena was very young to be in a speakeasy dressed like an adult woman and consuming alcohol. No matter how it was mixed, bootleg could really hurt someone who wasn't used to drinking. Before prohibition people drank a beer or two, or a glass of wine with a nice meal. But with the passage of the 18th Amendment, people wanted more of what they couldn't have, and the practice of binge drinking was born! There was no reason to moderate when liquor was readily available, and after the first drink the taste of bootleg whiskey was notably better.

"Bankers and businessmen in fine suits were drinking with men in work clothes. Ordinary housewives were sipping Champagne and dancing with wispy flapper girls, their bare arms pale and long, their knees rouged and stockings rolled down. Elena never had much of a social life and missed a lot of school. Initially, being in a crowd full of strangers was unfamiliar. Lucky for her, she was just a few sips away from becoming fearless. Someone was trying to get to the bar, passed behind her, and bumped her hat. As he apologized and kissed her hand, a long curl fell from her feathered cloche, then another, and another. Before she could take back her hand and position her hat the right way, another curl fell across her face. Aware that people were watching her, Elena pulled off her hat and her long red locks tumbled down onto her shoulders. In her imagination she waved and took a bow. She was as beautiful as the star she pretended to be.

"At first is seemed strange that Miss Vivian had so many nice things. Given her husband's small salary as a custodian, coupled with the cost of raising two boys in a desperate economy, Vivian *always* had money. When her husband was home, he was either at the kitchen table building a scaled replica of the Santa Maria (which would fit inside a glass bottle someday), or asleep on the sofa with his shoes on. Sam was a lot older than his wife, and Elena wondered what she saw in him. On the other hand, the men at the club showered her with attention. Some of them were her customers at the alterations shop and brought flowers and other gifts when they dropped off clothes. Elena recognized them but said nothing. Some of the men left only an envelope, and if Vivian was out, they left it with her son, Peter, who took care of the books. The money inside was often enough to buy a whole new wardrobe.

"As she spent more time with Vivian, Elena drew two conclusions: One, the men at Club 21 were more than casual acquaintances. And two, the money for alterations involved far more than just fixing pants. Human behavior was interesting. She was getting a much better education than she would have ever gotten taking home ec classes at Bay Ridge. Besides, those skills would have only gone to waste since Elena didn't plan on ever cleaning her own house or doing laundry. She would pay people for that. Now a student of how things worked in the real world, she studied the men and their dates whenever she went out drinking.

"Gone were the days of sipping watered down cocktails with too much honey. Liquor still needed to be cut with mixers, of course, because the taste was horrible. Some preferred a chaser of Pickleback to cleanse the pallet and ease the burn, but the taste of

111

pickle brine was even worse than bathtub gin! Regardless, there was always a way to make liquor palatable. Elena drank Gin Rickeys when she wanted a quick mood brightener, and a French 75 if she was helping friends celebrate. The right balance of gin, Champagne, lemon juice, and sugar was festive and had just the right amount of kick. A retired soldier at the bar said it was named after a World War One artillery piece, but someone else said it had to do with sex. Elena had no interest in being involved with men that way. It was her senior year and she had no plans of building her future with a baby on board.

"The dynamics between men and women were often subtle and unspoken. By watching the other girls, she quickly learned to manipulate situations to work in her favor. Elena flirted with rich men, drank with unemployed factory workers, and giggled over Sidecars with decadent girls who embodied the spirit of the jazz age. Had Club 21 been a classroom, Elena would have been a straight 'A' student and would eventually end up teaching the class. While there was high value in being beautiful, and she was, it was far more important to be curious and engaging... to listen intently and ask a man about himself. Direct the conversation back to his strengths and achievements, and say things like, *that must have been very exciting,* and *how did you learn to do all that?* If it's funny, laugh... and if it's not, roll your eyes in a silly way, shake your head, and grin.

"Don't be solicitous and don't be coy... men see right through it. And if he mentions his money, a lot or a little, remain nonplussed. If it seems he's wealthy, even more so. And if *you're* broke, never let on. Accept gifts but never accept money. Once the Pandora's box of his money and yours is opened, the dynamic shifts and not in your favor, so don't even seem curious. If you're at a restaurant and someone walks by, don't look, not even a brief glance. You've just made yourself more valuable by showing him he's more important than anyone else in the room. It's called respect and men like it. When he is overcome with the realization that he likes himself best when he's with you, he will call it love, and he'll be yours for the taking.

"Vivian could make in an evening what ordinary girls earned in a week. Elena had known for some time that the part time job at the automat was a ruse. Vivian was not put on this earth to make sandwiches. Instead, she used her mornings for shopping and hair appointments. She got her nails done every Thursday at an exclusive salon, and spent hours wondering around Frederick Loeser's at Fulton and Bond, trying on eyeshadow and drawing lipstick shades on the back of her hand. There were fragrant body lotions to sample with perfume to match, and soaps that smelled like lavender. But Vivian's power was not in the way she smelled or styled her hair, and Elena knew that.

"Vivian's oldest son Tommy was as big as he was dumb. He breezed in and out of the house after school with a bologna sandwich stuffed in his mouth and one in his pocket for later. Other than loudly grunting hello with his mouth full, he and Elena rarely spoke. Peter, on the other hand, was a treasure, and not just because he did Elena's homework. Peter was a diminutive boy, quiet and pale, as if he had never fully recovered from having mumps as a child. Even as a senior in high school he appeared tired and malnourished, although he ate his share at dinner and was always snacking. He was the brother Elena never had, and the feeling was mutual. The bantering between them never stopped, and they spent many companionable afternoons at the shop, with Elena stitching and Peter reading the evening paper as the sewing machine hummed. Although Elena wasn't near the student he was, she was just as smart and he respected her for that. Peter was aware of his mother's added happiness since Elena had become an unofficial member of the household, and her work at the sewing table increased profits measurably. He knew this because he was his mother's bookkeeper.

Peter was attracted to numbers the same way other boys liked football. Numbers came to him in waves, always moving. Whether they were fast or uncharacteristically still, and regardless of their color, it was that motion that allowed him to perform astronomical calculations in his head. He sensed emotion in mathematics, and used it to work with the various shapes... the bouncing curves of the numeral 8, and the angry lines of number 4. Peter's brain had a bond with math problems that no one but Peter could conceive.

Various algorithms were sensitive and cared about Peter, protecting his brain from information overload and steadying his thoughts as he performed. Individual numbers, each with their unique form, moved like puzzle pieces until they connected, filling in the gaps, and creating a new image which displayed the final answer. His classmates would have teased him if they knew about his gift, and other than doing Elena's homework, he wasn't interested in manufacturing good grades for the other kids at school. If they could perform the basic functions it would be enough to land a job that suited them. Managing money was Peter's forte, and as gifts of cash came into the shop, he assured his mother he would take good care of it. Everything was entered neatly on a daily ledger; it wasn't his job to ask questions. And besides, the IRS had better things to do than check the tax filings of a small-town boy and his mother.

If Peter was a bit of a mama's boy, it's because Vivian made him that way. Because of his childhood illness, she doted on him and worried over a runny nose or a cough, rushing to pick him up at the nurse's office. It was assumed that he would always live at home and never venture out beyond his mother's comfort zone. There was no question he had the potential and innate intelligence to do much more, but Bensonhurst was no longer a place where a young man could get ahead. Many of the jobs that were lost during the Depression would likely never come back, and Peter's identity as a pale, sickly child would remain with him as long as he stayed. Although Peter was now a grown man with a clean bill of health, Vivian would never have peace if her son was away from her tender loving care and truly on his own. She hoped he would meet someone nice to look after him the way she had. Peter would need a wife who was caring and strong to assume that role. Sadly, one of the lasting effects of the mumps in boys was a condition called orchitis, also known as testicular atrophy. Whoever Peter married would have to accept that she would never have children."

Shoes for an Imaginary Life

Linda Lewis

The New Deal

"Post-Depression America was filled with hope. The Works Projects Administration promised nationwide employment and relief for the millions of families living with years of extraordinary hardship. Franklin D. Roosevelt's New Deal would implement novel strategies to reform and fuel recovery from the worst economic downturn in the history of the industrialized world. Bold, experimental plans included nationwide employment based on work relief rather than welfare. The Civilian Conservation Corps. created nationwide work camps where young men could earn a wage for planting trees, maintaining national forests, and creating fish and game sanctuaries. Other programs would employ men to build major infrastructure. Airports, bridges, roads, and schools would be needed for America to move forward, while nearly eliminating unemployment. The fathers and husbands with ashen faces and grim expressions finally found a sense of hope.

"No one was more excited about the New Deal than 18-year-old Peter Finello, who knew there was no limit to what he could achieve. The only thing that made him happier than the prospect of having a job, was the opportunity to finally get away from his mother! Peter resented all the years she smothered him and restricted him from participating in the normal things boys enjoy. Of course, playing sports was out of the question; even staying after school for chess club meant being exposed to unnecessary germs. There were no movies, no dances, no dates. He understood his mother was protecting him from the disappointment of rejection, but it didn't change the facts— Elena was his only friend. Students at New Utrecht and Bay Ridge got together every year for prom and homecoming, which was a rare opportunity to socialize with the opposite sex. If he didn't get out from under his mother's wing now, he wasn't sure he'd get another chance. Being small didn't make him less human, and an illness as a child didn't mean he was still sick today.

"As his mother's office manager, Peter was far more perspicacious than he ever let on. Just as Vivian had her discrete sources of income, so did he. Even as a teenager he understood the value in keeping two sets of books. There was Vivian's money, the shop's money, and money to cover the administrative fees for his services each month. That amount never got written down, and never got discussed. There was a pawn shop in Flatbush that Peter used to liquidate various gifts and chachkis that Vivian would never miss. And because he gave all his business to one broker, the owner treated him right. It was an easy ride on his bike. The proceeds went directly into his makeshift savings account. Peter was always such a good boy that his mother never looked in the back of his underwear drawer.

"Peter didn't know how to tell Vivian he was going to Detroit. And he had no idea how she would react when he told her that Elena was coming with him. There was no denying they made a good team; both had become skilled grifters under the tutelage of Peter's mother, and both had dreams to fulfill. With millions of jobs being created, thousands at the Ford River Rouge plant, Peter was ready. Regarding Elena, he couldn't exactly say what love *is*, but he knew it wasn't what he saw growing up, with his parents rarely in the same room, never a kind word or conversation. In the old country they called it a marriage of convenience. Historically it could mean an alliance between two families, or in the case of concealing someone's sexual orientation, it gave the appearance of propriety.

"Elena was working on a new dress and Peter was reading the evening paper. The was a length of dotted swiss left over from another project and she was making something pretty for summer. She cut the threads, turned it right-side-out, then slipped out of her work clothes. She pulled it over her head and reminded Peter to watch out for the pins as he zipped her. This was as close to an intimate moment that their marriage would ever know.

"I'm going to Detroit to work for Henry Ford, and I want you to come with me."

"Two weeks later with his mother's blessing, Peter Finello and Elena Carbone were married in a small church wedding, attended only by close relatives, Vivian, and Elena's siblings currently not in jail. As a gift, Vivian gave them train passes for the 24-hour trip to Detroit, a key to a home in Grosse Pointe Woods, and the Louis Vuitton Speedy 25. She said the marbles inside were for good luck."

"What a story… am I right?"

Linda Lewis

The $64,000 Question

Lucille grew uncharacteristically quiet and paused. Looking past the smiles of her friends, lips pursed, she collected her thoughts and continued.

"Domestic violence was not something we talked about in the 1950s. Women had very little power. Husbands had all the authority, and the wives never questioned it. When I went with Carmine to Fort Jackson, I didn't expect we would have a perfect life, but I thought the three of us could at least be a family. What I saw growing up with Pa's drinking and Ma crying all the time taught me one thing. Yes, the Carbone family was full of drama and secrets, and I was not about to watch history repeat itself with me and Carmine.

"I might have mentioned that Carmine started drinking in high school, back when we were working the ice cream counter together; maybe even sooner. People didn't talk about things like alcoholism, and a wife would have been looking for trouble to even say anything, especially when he came home drunk! I thought once we got away from Bensonhurst and away from his old friends, things would be different.

"At first Carmine liked working in the mess hall. I think the structure was good for him, and he got along fine with the other men. After four years as high school quarterback he had an ego the size of you know what, and I was just glad he wasn't starting fights and getting in trouble. Now I never cared that after they cleaned up at night, Carmine and some of his buddies stayed after to drink beer and play cards. I was pregnant, fat, and miserable, and it was always hot as you know what in South Carolina. I was happier alone.

"Is it good to have friends? Yes. Is it good to come home drunk every night? No-sir-ee, it was not. The first time Carmine came after me it was a typical night with him being drunk and me being in bed asleep. He always got a ride back to our little apartment, and I usually heard the car door slam, but this time I heard nothing. Now I don't know what happened that night at the mess hall— remember, I wasn't allowed to ask questions— but in comes Carmine, swearing a blue streak, calling me all sorts of horrible names and wanting to know, *Where's my dinner?!* Well, given that he was an army cook, you'd think he'd have the sense to eat dinner at work, right? Where there was already plenty of food already made? So he comes in the bedroom shouting, *Get your fat ass out of bed, you lazy bitch... if you can't cook a meal for your husband now and then, what good are you? Maybe you and the baby should find another place to live!*

"I hoisted myself out of bed to heat up some leftovers. My back always hurt due to the baby, and it took me a minute. I was still half asleep, still hot and miserable, when he grabbed me by the shoulders and slammed me against the doorjamb which hit right in the center of my back. It knocked the wind out of me and I must have lost my balance because I fell down the stairs. When I woke up at the clinic the medic told me I had a broken wrist, a concussion, and I lost the baby. He said it so matter of fact that it didn't really sink in. I think they had me doped up because of the pain.

"Well, I knew what happened when a wife didn't give her husband a healthy baby. We found out it was a boy; little Antonio Francis. It would have made Ma happy. After that night we never discussed it. Carmine was nice for a while, but I worried he'd come after me again. The bones in my wrist ached, and there was sickness caused by the concussion. They say you don't really know someone until you live with them and this was definitely true.

"Just when I started to feel better, just when I let my guard down, I was in the kitchen making spaghetti with my homemade meat sauce. There was garlic bread in the oven and our little apartment smelled wonderful. It was his day off and I was looking forward to a nice meal together. I tried not to be bitter, tried not to think about the baby, because that only would have made things worse. I was grieving badly, but I was also relieved that I wouldn't be bringing a baby into a home with a horrible man for a father. There we were on a base with thousands of men and their wives, yet I was completely isolated. So about the spaghetti. I was stirring the sauce like I always do, the noodles were boiling, and I heard a smacking sound. Smack. Smack. Smack. I turned around to look, and there's Carmine standing right behind me, punching his hand with his fist. I didn't say a word, didn't want to set him off. I picked up the pot with the noodles, carried it to the strainer in the sink, and he punched me right in the jaw. He had been drinking beer all day, watching his shows on the television we bought with our wedding present money.

"Boiling water spilled all down the front of me and onto my legs which gave me severe burns. I still have the scars today. Once again we never discussed it and life went on as usual. Now some of you may think that I'm a pretty smart cookie, but when all this was going on, I was so nervous all the time that my memory started to go. I would hide my headache medicine so he wouldn't steal it, and five minutes later I had no idea where it was. I was two years out of high school and I was losing my mind. Even though Carmine was gone all day, I never left the house and I never turned on the TV. He told me, *Don't let me catch you with that TV on. I don't want you to get any big ideas from those game shows. Trust me when I tell you you're not even smart enough to play along standing behind your ironing board.* Truth is, I was pretty good and knew a lot of the answers. I imagined myself winning the "$64,000 Question" and leaving Fort Jackson for good.

"Shortly after the incident with the boiling water, I was doing Carmine's laundry and I heard a lot of noise out front. A group of women were getting out of a car, laughing and hugging each other. I opened the door to look out and my neighbor Fran said, Why don't you come over for some lemonade. Carmine won't be home till late and he'll never know. I was in my housecoat and hadn't showered. I looked like crap; she looked so pretty. Why I said yes to those ladies I'll never know, but looking back, I think it was God trying to tell me something.

"I wasn't sure why they invited me in. They were all ages, some looked great, some were a wreck like me. A lady in the group was going to tell us her story... what it was like before, what happened, and what it was like today. Week after week I listened to stories very much like mine... the alcohol, the abuse, and the fear. The difference was, these women had faith in God, and I had no one. Did I learn to find happiness whether Carmine stopped drinking or not? Yes, but only through the help of this program, and the help of my Higher Power, whom I choose to call God." Lucille paused to let that sink in.

"I was practicing the program and working the steps with Fran, who became my sponsor. I was using the tools of the program and working on myself. After all, I'm the only one who can change me. Am I right? I had shortcomings galore, but Fran told me God would help me with all that, I just had to ask him. I didn't think much of the Catholic church as a kid growing up in

Bensonhurst, but the God I was talking to now was different. *I liked him!* Our long talks gave me peace and gave me hope. When Carmine came home drunk and passed out on the floor, I put a pillow under his head, kissed his cheek and went to bed, just as my sponsor suggested. What I couldn't do by my own will, I did to honor God. I grew to be happy, and I keep coming back. Today I am married to my wonderful husband Bob, who puts up with a lot, believe you me. I'm a nana to our nine grandchildren, five girls and four boys, and today I am celebrating forty years as a grateful recovering member of Al-anon."

There was a round of applause and an announcement that everyone was meeting at Deeny's for cake and fellowship.

Lucille paused and looked at the floor. "In spite of what I learned in those early years of Al-anon, I never got over the loss of my son at Carmine's hand. I had moments of rage where I hated my husband and wished him dead.

"One night I was watching my show and there was a knock at the door. It was an officer who said something happened to Carmine. I figured he was drunk and I had to go get him, but it was more than that. The way he explained it, was that one of the KP's brought a football to the mess hall that day, and when they were all supposed to be cleaning, they were drinking and playing football instead. Carmine, being the big man on campus, told his team to go out for a pass. He was running backwards watching for someone to get open when he bumped into the stove and knocked off a pot of hot grease. But that isn't what killed him. One of the KP's was on a ladder restocking shelves. When Carmine hit the floor and started screaming it startled the man on the ladder who lost his footing and dropped a huge can of creamed corn right on Carmine's head... killed him just like that, face down in a pool of his own blood."

"And now ladies, who wants cake?!"

Linda Lewis

Lunch at Deeny's

You better believe Miranda went to Deeny's with the ladies that day. She didn't care where she parked or if she got caught— she just had to know the rest of the story about Lucille, who was hugging people when she came in. Deeny's was the kind of place where you walked up to one window to order your food, then another window where you picked it up, much like the Dairy Queen in Petoskey. When Miranda stepped to the front of the line, she recognized the man behind the counter.

"Well, well, well... would ya look at what the cat dragged in." Sure enough, it was Deen Jr. of Deeny's Hideaway, a dive bar just outside Traverse City, close to where Harry got killed that night. She felt uneasy. Miranda had too many secrets lingering from the time she lived on her boat. Unfortunately, Deen knew about most of them.

"Fancy meeting you here, Deen Jr. Last time I stopped by your place up north there was a sign on the door... something about you being in trouble. I figured you'd be in jail by now, but here you are in south Florida! What a lovely coincidence!" Miranda was just messing with him. As a rule, they got along fine— she just didn't trust him.

"Well, you're half right. I left the Hideaway before the law caught up with me and came down here to *hide*— get it?" It was a play on words. He was so clever. "I got a pool table and everything... I was savin' a place for ya!"

Miranda turned and saw her Al-anon friends seated at two long tables, a big cake, a stack of paper plates and plastic forks at one end, a pool table at the other. *Oh my God, oh my God, oh my God... what am I gonna do now?*

"You know, Charlie Fine stopped in for a drink just before I left town. He had a real pretty girl with him." Miranda really didn't need to hear about Charlie and his dates. Deen Jr. chuckled. "I remember he got her good and drunk and the next thing ya know she was doing belly shots on the pool table with a coupl'a half-naked hookers, just like the old days. Quite a guy, that Charlie Fine. Even though I'm in Florida now, we keep in touch." Miranda cringed. That situation with the pool table happened one time and she wasn't exactly proud of it. Deen had a great memory for details. "Not that it matters now with you being married to that old, rich Greek fella and all," Deen whispered, "but Charlie always said he could never replace you... ya broke his heart when you dumped him." Then he added, "The girl on his arm that night... she was just the flavour du jour. That's French, ya know."

"Don't be an idiot, Deen. I didn't just fall out of a banana tree." Miranda was trying to be a better person these days and wasn't in the mood to dwell on the past.

"Heard all about you and Jim Tiller. *And Drew. And The Dominic...* heh heh." He was getting loud and one of the Al-anon ladies turned around to look. "Miranda, are you down here hiding, too? You and me, partners in crime, just like the old days!!" He threw his head back in laughter that was exaggerated for effect.

Tiller? He must have heard she got fired, or something. There weren't any stories worth telling about her old job, although she missed it terribly. Miranda's eyes were burning, trying to fight off tears.

"So what can I get ya?"

Miranda fled the sandwich shop without a hug from Lucille, and without a piece of cake.

Linda Lewis

Drew Becker

Meanwhile, winter was closing in on Northern Michigan and Charlevoix had become a ghost town, except for the 2000 or so locals who couldn't afford to leave, and the few brave souls living aboard their boats at the Boat Basin. Though you'd never know it during the season, more than half the year-round residents lived below the poverty line. They were the housekeepers, cashiers, and shift workers at McDonald's. They ran the ferry to Beaver Island and manned the factories in Petoskey— laborers who spent the nicest months working long hours indoors, and were nearly broke by the time spring arrived and the process started all over again. Sadly, the wealthy summer crowd who needed their services went away in September, and so did most of the jobs.

Drew Becker loved the winter. The seasons marked the time and reminded him of the people and places that brought him joy, and also some that did not. It was an important learning experience either way. His ice fishing gear was carefully laid out in the gravel lot behind the boathouse. Putting things in order was a ritual that calmed him, something he learned from his grandfather. His old clam tent could make it one more season. No reason to spend money on things that didn't need to be replaced yet. He set out his new power auger, an expensive upgrade from his old one that was beyond repair. A set of new blades sat beside it. Rods and reels from last winter were clean and in good order. He put those back in the case. A tackle box of hooks and bobbers was also ready to go. Drew kept a variety of fishing line on hand for colder temperatures— clear blue, smoke, green line, and a variety of braided and monofilament. These were things that should be well organized before heading out to the ice shanty and realizing you're not prepared. Some of the tack was too old to use, but memories of ice fishing with old Hank Becker made him smile. He would keep that old fishing gear forever.

Drew reached into an old white paint bucket and found three pairs of ice cleats- a pair of heavy stabilizers that were his favorites (and by far the safest), his chain Treckers, and a small pair of slip-ons. Drew turned the bucket upside down and took a seat, staring out at Lake Charlevoix. It was nearly frozen. Among the things Miranda kept when she sold her boat, were her treasured ice cleats. They were just an inexpensive pair from L.L. Bean, but he urged her to hang onto them so they could go ice fishing together. In those days he believed they might have a future. It was getting dark so early now. He stood up, kicked over the bucket, and gathered his fishing gear. On the way inside he dropped Miranda's ice cleats in the trash. While Drew Becker was no stranger to loss, he had to admit, he was bitter.

The night Daniel Bering showed up at the boathouse and told him to stay away from Miranda, Drew couldn't believe what he was hearing. He obsessed over that night more than he cared to admit. He was stronger than that but just couldn't let this go. No matter what that overrated thug told him, he refused to accept that she was really interested in Dominic Manos, especially after that last night they spent together.

For a date or two, maybe. But she was using him... maybe for a nice dinner, even a new handbag or two, but certainly not for keeps! Rumor had it that Manos preferred men. Did Miranda somehow miss that? Manos was an alcoholic. If she was drinking, anything could have happened. Drew had this conversation with himself over and over but never reached a conclusion that satisfied.

When Bering said she had had an affair with Jim Tiller, that was the last straw. He knew Miranda adored her former boss. She was in awe of his talent, and enamored with his career as a Federal Agent. She used to talk at length about the pictures in his office and his courage while protecting the President. Drew met him once and really liked the man. Tiller had a commanding appearance that would appeal to Miranda, though he never considered it in a sexual way.

There were all those trips, he thought... *and there were times when she was gone for a few days, even a week, but that was about work. Or was it?! Of course, they were at job sites together, but I cannot accept that they were "together" together... not like that anyway.* His imagination was getting the best of him. *But what if it was true?* Drew and Miranda had their own lives, they lived in different towns. He liked his evenings alone and didn't mind when she was away. It just made their time together that much more special. Other than that awful incident at Castle Rouge, he never even considered that she might have been having sex with someone else. His thoughts repulsed him.

Drew climbed the stairs of the old boathouse, flopped down on the couch, and opened a beer. He was never one to obsess about money. The inheritance he got from his grandfather was certainly a welcome surprise. Since Miranda left he found safety deposit boxes in small banks all up and down Michigan's west coast. Some contained money banded neatly and in stacks. Others were stuffed with large bills, crumpled and shoved inside until no more would fit. Maybe someday he'd get over the shock of having all those millions of dollars. If Hank Becker were alive today, he would ask him where it all came from, why was the money hidden all over the place, and what should he do with it today? The irony of Miranda leaving him to marry a millionaire never escaped him. But of all people, why Dominic Manos? He shook his head and sighed.

He came to the conclusion that he really didn't know her at all. Miranda was skilled at showing only the parts of her life she wanted people to see. There was nothing about her family, nothing about her life or relationships before Harry. Who knows how many times she'd actually been married, and besides the money, what was she really after? It was loosely implied that she met Charlie Fine while she was still married to Harry. Drew always had bad feelings about the man. For all the times she supposedly broke up with him, Miranda continued to meet him for drinks and accept his expensive gifts. Drew always believed there was more to Charlie Fine than Miranda was telling him. What was the actual reason he made all those trips to Detroit? Did he really own a business, with real employees and a legitimate paycheck? Maybe he got his money in an unscrupulous, illegal way. Was he somehow tied to the mob? Maybe he worked for an organized crime family, and his so-called company was a front for money laundering and tax evasion! That sounded more like the Charlie Fine he knew— *or didn't know.* He had never actually met the man, but he was certain there was more to his imaginary business than meets the eye. Drew Becker hated him just enough that he may look into that someday.

The more he thought about Charlie Fine, the more Drew was certain that Miranda cheated on Harry, too. If she was the kind of person who could juggle two men at the same time, one of which was her husband, who she supposedly loved so much, she could certainly have had a romance with Tiller. She was discreet. She knew how to handle herself. Drew was consumed with thoughts of Miranda riding in Tiller's BMW, stopping for a leisurely lunch on the way to Ohio Stadium, and looking at him in an admiring way as they toured the legendary venue. She was in Columbus on that project for nearly a week. He pictured her in his arms, laughing. Drew had been a fool.

Looking back, he must have been dreaming. Drew replayed the imaginary tapes of their time together, searching for the one that ended happily. He recalled the day he learned she had married Manos. Word of their union was spread far and wide by the bartenders, charter captains, and local gossips who hated the man. He had nothing but time to think about what might have occurred in the weeks and months of their friendship that caused her to reject him. If Miranda chose to spend her time with Jim Tiller while they were a couple, then chose to leave him and run off with Dominic Manos, what did that say about him? If she didn't want to watch sports on TV, he'd buy another television! Maybe she was sick of pizza... and the fries at Jack's Steakhouse... or Oreos. If Drew was a disappointment in bed that night at the boathouse... No, that wasn't it, wasn't it at all.

He was open minded. He was accommodating. Why didn't she tell him what she wanted? Why didn't she stay?

Shoes for an Imaginary Life

Daniel Bering

While Miranda considered the mistakes of her past, Daniel Bering was doing the same in a hospital room in Petoskey. The fire that nearly took his life was admittedly his own fault, which made his suffering that much worse. The stately 1965 Burger Motoryacht had been impeccably maintained, and had a generous budget for additional projects and upgrades as Bering saw fit. The Wequetonsing couple that hired him to captain their new boat were eager to start the season on Little Traverse Bay, but not at the expense of anyone's safety. An old boat has systems that must be checked and maintained at regular intervals before she's given a clean bill of health. Most of the work aboard "*Good Shepherd*" had been completed before Bering took the helm and had already passed inspection. The Detroit Diesel 8V71's were pressure checked and the drive systems were confirmed in good working order. Plumbing problems were common on boats of that era and the heads were upgraded with modern systems. The wiring harness was still in working order, but a decision was made to replace it anyway— better safe than sorry, said the new owner, who spared no expense in the restoration.

Daniel Bering was as safety conscious as a captain could be. He systematically checked the work of the marine electricians, making sure the draw did not exceed the safe current load, and confirming that no more than three wires were attached to any termination point. He was satisfied that all connections were tight and secured. Bering noted that the old junction box had been replaced by a new waterproof model, and while he was in the engine room he made sure there were no sharp bends or pinch points in the power leads. In the galley there was a new full size Norcold stand up refrigerator. Hanna would have loved that. Convinced that *Good Shepherd* was ready to start the season, Daniel Bering opened a beer and sat at the helm admiring the polished brass gauges and fine mahogany. Electric bow thrusters had been retrofitted, and a joystick was installed on the dash. The controller looked like something from a kid's video game, and made docking so easy a trained chimp could do it.

But what about the stove in the galley? On early inspection there were no signs of trouble; no worn wires or loose connections, and no real urgency to replace it. Vintage boat enthusiasts were the nostalgic sort, and it wasn't uncommon to hang onto original amenities as long as they were in good working order. On their first night tied off at the Mackinac Island Marina, the owner took his wife to the Grand Hotel for dinner and some jazz. It was their wedding anniversary. *Good Shepherd* was tied up on the outside of the last pier, the only dock in the marina long enough to hold the 75-footer. It was early in the season and the adjacent docks were empty, thank God.

The owner and the misses turned to wave at their children as they boarded a horse drawn carriage from the sidewalk at the marina entrance. Trent, seven, was a precocious toe head and was already wearing his pajamas. He was witty and smart beyond his years, always taking apart his toys and rebuilding them. He was named after his dad; his parents' pride and joy. His little sister had been adopted from a Shanghai orphanage just before her first birthday. The family named her Micaela, which means *gift from God*. At four years, she was a mild, happy child, with shiny black pigtails wrapped in little bows. With Micaela, their family was complete.

It wasn't uncommon for the ship's Captain and crew to babysit the children while the parents were out. Daniel Bering had been piloting yachts for nearly four decades. In that time, he looked after dozens of children and had complete confidence in doing so. During his career he took care of an elderly monkey named Garbo while the owner travelled downstate, and a few years before that he helped a family's golden retriever birth a litter of puppies. The mother and the little ones all survived, and he got the pick of the litter for his heroic efforts. Bering was responsible and qualified. There was no situation too big for him to handle.

But on that Friday night something went wrong. Bering heated up some mac and cheese for Trent and Micaela, boiled up two hot dogs, and arranged them in bite size pieces along the plates. He turned off the stove. Micaela was a fussy eater; Trent would eat anything. Once the children were in bed, Bering poured himself a rum and Coke, lit a cigarette, and went up to the deck to watch the sunset. The sound of horses clop-clopping down Main Street relaxed him. His back and hips always ached by the end of the day, and alcohol was no longer enough to manage the pain. He returned to the galley, hungry but not starving. There was half a hot dog left in the pan, and a nice piece of smallmouth bass in the refrigerator that would spoil if someone didn't eat it. Without Hanna by his side to scold him, he was free to make a nice dinner and also make a mess.

Daniel Bering rinsed the fish and seasoned it with salt and pepper. He poured oil in the pan, spilled some on the counter, and wiped it up with a kitchen towel. Hanna was such a fanatic about keeping things clean. It was a breath of fresh air to relax in the galley without being scowled at every damn time he turned around. Bering poured another drink and put out his cigarette in the sink. His pain medicine was below in the crew's quarters. A narrow winding staircase just forward of the galley led to two small staterooms with bunk beds, a full head, and enough locker space for clothing and shoes. Bering rummaged through a pile of jeans and tee shirts—some clean, some dirty. Hanna used to tell him that if he put his pills in the same place every time he would always know where to find them. They never did get along. That's a lie— *he really missed her.*

Bering emptied his pockets, found a receipt, some change, and a screw. The other side had the brown prescription bottle he was looking for. He rolled his eyes; it was in his pocket all along. Suddenly— a deafening, high pitched alarm was screaming at him from the galley— *Christ, the smoke detector.* Bering ran the stairs two by two, fighting the effects of the alcohol. He saw flames on the stove! The pan with the fish was on fire, and the towel was in flames! *Did I really leave it that close to the stove?* Bering reached under the sink and grabbed the fire extinguisher... pulled the pin, aimed, and got nothing. Hadn't he checked it? Wouldn't he have looked at the date? He squeezed the trigger again and again. Panic set in. There were children on board, probably awake by now. The Mackinac Island Fire Department would be useless even if he called them. The streets were full of horses and bicycles—they would never make it to the boat in time. It was a deadly place for a fire. Whatever the cost, he had to put out the flames and deal with the consequences later.

Bering lay silent at McLaren Northern Michigan Hospital's BICU unit. The sound of the machine that kept him alive was a constant reminder that he wasn't dead yet, which was unfortunate. The old, chronic pain in his back and joints was nothing compared to the agony of the burns on his face, head, and arms. The doctors still weren't sure if they could save his right hand, the one that reached through the flames to shut off the stove. Though he was conscious, he lost track of how long he had been there. The nurse said more than a month. Time was irrelevant in the burn ward; pain was the clock that kept ticking.

Daniel Bering was confined to a special hospital bed that distributed his weight in such a way to relieve pressure on the affected areas and help relieve pain, which was a lie. He had an IV that gave him morphine and anti-anxiety medication so he could rest while his body healed, which was also a lie. The inhalation injuries he sustained were not caused by the flames, but by the smoke he breathed in as he put out the fire. Thank goodness for the ventilator they jammed down his throat in the emergency room so he could breathe, an action that saved his life. Having had the experience of surviving this ordeal, death would have been the better option.

Nurses came to his room daily to remove dead tissue and apply dressings to prevent infection. Unfortunately, there wasn't enough morphine in the world to take the edge off that kind of pain. Somewhere nearby, he could hear his voice screaming. His doctor and a group of interns came every day to review his case and discuss his progress. They talked as if he were unconscious, but Bering heard his grim prognosis, every single word.

"Once again, we are treating this patient for third degree burns which were sustained in a kitchen fire aboard a boat. Who can tell me the basic anatomy of the body's largest organ? Dr. Ryckman?"

"Epidermis, dermis, hypodermis."

"Correct. Tell me about the epidermis, Dr. Chang."

"The epidermis is the outer layer of the skin, made up of stratified squamous epithelium with underlying basal lamina. It consists of Merkel cells, keratinocytes, melanocytes, and Langerhans cells. Should I continue with the additional strata?"

"You've impressed me enough for today, young man. Let's give Dr. Grey a chance... go!"

"Stratum corneum, stratum licidum, stratum granulosum, stratum spinosum, stratum basale."

"Correct. And an easy one for you, Dr. Fonzarelli. What do we know about the dermis?"

"It contains the papillary and reticular layers."

"And the function?"

"It's the layer of the skin where they inject the ink for my tattoos. I just got a new one if anyone would like to see it." Dr. Fonzarelli winks at Dr. Grey and reaches for the hem of his scrubs. She looks at him with disgust and turns away. If he didn't have a photographic memory, he would never have gotten into medical school.

"We can see that the patient's burns go beyond the epidermis, through to the dermis, and into a deeper layer of skin called the hypodermis." Bering listened between puffs of the ventilator and resented not being part of this discussion. "Dr. Sanchez, what is our biggest concern at this point? The worst possible complication?"

Sanchez was shy and hated being called on, but always knew the correct answer. "The worst complication would be a body-wide inflammatory response. It could actually make the patient's injuries worse. There could be damage to the heart, lungs, blood vessels, and other organs; also loss of fluid. If that caused him to go into shock, it could lead to edema. An immediate concern would be increased susceptibility to bacteria and a compromised immune system that could lead to pneumonia. He could actually die from any one of these conditions any day now."

The attending rubbed his temples and said, "A+ for a complete answer; C- for bedside manner. If the patient were conscious and listening to our conversation, you might have just scared him to death." The other interns chuckled. They all liked Sanchez but his communication skills were sometimes lacking.

"Obviously, we're looking at some skin grafts, which I'd like to get started on sooner rather than later. I will recommend creating a mesh from the tissue we take from his back and thighs, and in areas that don't respond we can get by with skin from a pig or cadaver. Of course, it's going to be a long road back for Mr... uh, Mr. Bering. We can talk about future surgeries and physical therapy to get his arms working again, but for now, let's just stay on course with burn therapy and see where it goes. Questions?"

"What about pain management? The intern who asked the question could see from his open wounds that the pain must be excruciating. "If he can't communicate, how do we know if the morphine we're giving him is enough? How would that be decided?"

"Dr. Grey." The young woman's mother had been a successful surgeon at the same hospital, and she was eager to follow in her footsteps. "Dr. Grey, in this hospital we follow protocol. Whatever the attending prescribes is what the patient receives. This man is in a medically induced coma and may never wake up. He can't feel pain or anything else at this point"

If Daniel Bering had the ability to speak, he would shout BULLSHIT!! He would scream that he was alive, that there was a living, breathing man inside this hideous body! *I need help! Please!* He opened his eyes just enough to see the group leaving his hospital room, wondering which one was Dr. Grey, and how he could ask her to help him.

Shoes for an Imaginary Life

Dutch Kavanaugh

It was only by the grace of God that Daniel Bering was able to put out the fire with baking soda and a lid he found in a cupboard. Beyond that, Bering remembered nothing. A pastor from a small Baptist church in Harbor Springs visited the hospital every day. There was a lady from his congregation who was recovering from a stroke, and he was kind enough to spend time with Bering, too.

"You need to start doing something for me, and I need you to start today." Dutch Kavanagh was pacing back and forth next to Bering's bed, a Bible in one hand, a can of Diet Coke in the other. As far as Bering could tell, the reverend was not a fanatic or some kind of holy roller. He seemed like a regular guy with a lot of stories to tell... what his life was like before, what happened, and what it's like today. Given that Bering could hardly speak, he was glad for the company and happy to listen. Dutch Kavanagh had a peaceful way about him. He seemed hurt by Bering's suffering.

"You know it was never my plan to become a pastor. Noooo... not by a long shot!" Dutch Kavanaugh grew up in Philadelphia, the only son of a single mom who worked two jobs to provide for him. Their rented house wasn't fancy, but it was home. "Mom was gone a lot, always at work, and I had too much time on my hands. There were plenty of kids on the block to play with, which was great at first, but as we got older there were drugs and alcohol to experiment with. And girls... lots of girls! I was having the time of my life... loved being drunk and high and staying out late! It was better than being bored, and way better than doing homework!" He laughed and took a sip from the can. Dutch was a passionate and prolific storyteller. "You know what I mean, Dan? Not sure if you were ever much of a partier, but I can tell you that I sure was." A nurse came into the room to check Bering's vitals; Kavanaugh stepped out while she worked.

Dutch Kavanaugh's mom was Catholic— Irish Catholic to be exact. And except for getting pregnant out of wedlock and having a baby at 19, she followed the church teachings to the letter of the law. She named her son Benedict Peter, hoping that a proper church name would give him a fighting chance in the world in spite of his mother's unholy past. His childhood friends called him, Benny.

Young Benny Kavanaugh was one of the lucky ones. The night one of the older kids overdosed on a mixture of heroin, LSD, and alcohol, Benny watched the ambulance arrive. They tried to resuscitate the boy, but they couldn't bring him back. He had puked all over his black leather jacket and choked on his own vomit.

Benny watched as the medics strapped him to a board and pulled a sheet over his head. "I bet you're wondering how in the world I ended up being a pastor after all that..."

If Bering could have smiled and laughed, he would have. But the burns on his face had his skin pulled tight, and pain told him to keep still. " So what happened was," Benedict Dutch Kavanaugh continued, "is that there was a guy who came around, said he used to be just like us. Sometimes he brought his guitar and sang, and we all just hung out, except no drugs or alcohol. This guy— J.R. is what he went by— talked about God all the time, like he was some sort of friend. He loved God, talked to God, praised God, and on and on. And he had a kind of peace that none of the rest of us had. When he came around I thought I would be happier if I had peace instead of fear... fear of the streets, fear of being alone, fear that my mom wouldn't be able to take care of me. Long story short, I started spending more time with J.R. and his friends and found that God was the best thing that ever happened to me... changed my world completely. I got saved right after I turned fifteen on the very same street corner where that other kid died. Yup... I was sure one of the lucky ones."

Dutch Kavanaugh couldn't tell if Bering was still awake. The nurses kept him pretty medicated... a blessing considering the severity of his burns and the pain he was in. "Hey Dan... I need you to do something for me. Are you awake? Will you at least give it a try?"

"Grmmmr" Bering mumbled, in a barely audible tone.

"You've got to pray. You've got to talk to God about your situation, Dan. I mean, even if you don't have faith— and I'm not even sure if you believe in him— but He believes in you. I can talk your ear off about my relationship with God, and I can pray, but I can't take away your suffering. You can't make it through this on your own." Bering had hit rock bottom. "Just say, 'God please help me.' You can say it quietly in your heart and I promise, he'll hear you. That's a great little prayer. It would be a perfect place to start."

"Oh. And I guess I forgot to tell you how I got a nickname like Dutch. As I said, we were really poor and we couldn't afford the prices at the barber shop. My mom did the best she could with my haircuts, but after an especially bad one, I looked like the boy on the paint can. The guys on the corner came up with the name, and it just stuck."

Linda Lewis

Max's Fish

The ocean was placid and bright when it greeted Miranda that day. In contrast, the sky was breathing fire with shades of carnelian and gold, slicing through the sunrise like a knife, blood thirsty and burning with contention. Dominic had been having some health issues and recently switched from red wine to vodka. Like the sea, he was uncharacteristically quiet, enjoying breakfast by the pool on Ocean Drive. Miranda had on a swimsuit that Dominic ordered from the Victoria's Secret Catalog. He reminded her that since he paid all that money for breast implants, she could at least show them off so he could get his money's worth.

They were finishing breakfast when the doorbell rang. Miranda stood up and wrapped herself in a long, silk sarong. Its crimson and wine folds moved silently as she passed through the kitchen and down a grand hallway to answer the door. A tall black man in a brown uniform stood waiting for her, a package in one hand, clipboard in the other. Every Friday Dominic got a UPS delivery with his Michigan newspapers, catalogs, and credit card statements.

The driver, Jean-Luc, was working two jobs to earn enough money to bring his family to America. Even though they could barely understand each other, they chatted companionably and enjoyed their brief visits. "So, my friend... how many days till Rosaline and the children come to join you?"

His big smile grew even wider. "Days? Hmmm. You know I keep count." He chuckled. Miranda grinned and nodded in an exaggerated way, teasing him without saying a word. "It would be 188 for my family, and maybe 400 for all the relatives. You know it is very coincidence, then there's the gouvenman depatman yo, of course." They both laughed. Jean-Luc reached for his wallet and pulled out a worn photograph. It was a picture of two young children with fat cheeks and big smiles just like their dad's. Miranda had seen it every week since they came to Miami and always made a fuss.

"I'm happy for you, my friend. You're a good man to take care of your family this way." She knew he was supporting three generations of Rosaline's extended family along with his own. There still wasn't much she liked about South Florida, but Jean-Luc was the exception. Miranda signed the clipboard, gave him a high five, and wished him a wonderful day.

"Guess what came today?" she called out to Dominic when she got to the kitchen. "Can I bring you something to drink?" Miranda got ice and water from the refrigerator door, stepped outside and handed Dominic the package. She noticed that he got himself something to drink. Even though vodka is said to be odorless, the wife of an alcoholic can smell it a mile away. Dominic tore open the package, put on his reading glasses, and pulled out a newspaper.

"Here's a story for you. Seems Daniel Bering had a little problem aboard the *Good Shepherd* last weekend. Good thing I fired him when I did."

Miranda knew that Bering actually quit but knew better than to say anything. "Oh really... what happened?"

"Galley fire. Expired fire extinguisher. Very sloppy." Dominic chuckled. "That's the way he did everything."

"Was the boat in Harbor Springs?"

"No, the island. Of all the dumb places to set a boat on fire. It says there were two children on board... the Dockmaster saw the flames and got them out. Lucky bastard." His tone reflected more amusement than empathy. Dominic handed Miranda the newspaper as he went inside to refill his glass. In Al-anon she learned it's not healthy to count the alcoholic's drinks. This was number two. "Why don't we get dressed. I'll take you someplace nice for lunch."

Miranda suggested *La Petit Maison,* one of his favorite places downtown. There was easy parking at the Four Winds Hotel and some nice boutiques nearby. Maybe she would do some shopping.

"I was thinking of that restaurant with the good eggs benedict where they make it with salmon and bacon." Dominic took the last sip of his vodka. *Norwegian*

Benedictines with sautéed onions and capers. Miranda knew the restaurant well but tried a different tack. She suggested a nice place in Hialeah. Then Dominic remembered: "La Boulangerie, just past Deeny's Cafe in Key Biscayne."

11:00 am

Miranda climbed the back staircase to her dressing room. It was critical that she stay calm. *There is no reason to panic. There are lots of good places to eat, and some of them happen to be on Key Biscayne.* She took a deep cleansing breath but struggled to exhale. *It's a coincidence and that's all.* In case she lost her ability to reason, which occasionally happens under extreme duress, she switched her brain from manual to auto pilot. Even Smart-Miranda had been known to fall apart during a panic attack, and this one would be a doozie. She took rehearsed, measured steps down the hall and into her dressing room, while remaining mindful of the time. Then right on schedule the symptoms began.

11:02 am

She glanced at the clock. Sweat was beading on her face. There was an outside force pressing on her chest that was making it hard to breathe. Auto-pilot sent an alert that it was time to pick out a dress and keep moving.

But what if Dominic does know? What if he's baiting me, trying to get me to confess that I go to meetings because I married an alcoholic and I can barely stand to be in a room with him? But knowing she went to Al-

anon wasn't even the worst of it. What if he knows that I talked to Deen Jr.? He had to know the ladies were at the cafe for one reason. Who else sits around an talks about the disease of alcoholism for two solid hours on a Thursday? She had said some very unflattering things about her husband, and now he knows everything! Damn it! And if he didn't get all his information from Deen, then who? Could Lucille be a spy? Is that how he found out? Oh, no... not you, Lucille... how could you do this to me!

The situation in the dressing room was rapidly declining from panic to paranoia. Bordering on delusional, Miranda stood by the window looking out, still in her swimsuit, unsure of what to do next.

Oh my God, it had to have been Deen Jr.! Why, why, why did she insist on going in there for lunch when she should have known better? How many people in America are even named Deenie? Why would she ever take such a chance? She should have known!" Miranda stumbled over a shopping bag full of new clothes she forgot she had, hit the floor, and put her face in her hands. The room was spinning. She had vertigo. *Did Dominic even know Deen Jr.? Deeny's Hideaway in Traverse City wasn't exactly his kind of place. But...if Charlie Fine knew Deen, and Charlie was a regular at Tommy's Gotcha, and during the season when Dominic's boat is at Mallard Point, he's a regular there, too... well, that pretty much explains everything!"* It's all the proof she needed. Given this new piece of information, Dominic would be on the attack and she would have to be ready.

Miranda heard herself sucking in air, wheezing, and gasping for breath as if inhaling through a straw. But no amount of oxygen could contain the situation or offer her one ounce of protection. Where the fuck was auto pilot? Just then she got an alert, thank God. Floral halter dress from Cache. Black sandals. David Yurman. Chanel bag from Charlie. Pounding, pounding... faster, faster! She could hear her heart beating outside her body, and her hands had gone numb. She was having a heart attack and was sure she would die.

11:06 am

Dominic didn't like to be kept waiting. She pulled on the dress, sprayed some deodorant and got most of it on her face. Crap. She was making stupid mistakes and better slow down. Smart-Miranda cleared her throat and blotted the deodorant off her cheek. All she had left to do was put on some necklaces and be on her way.

The jewelry box is right here. Somewhere. Or at least it was before the night of the dog show. Oh my God, where is it?! The panic attack was now calling the shots. No amount of effort from auto-pilot or Smart-Miranda would change that. Not only was she having a heart attack, she was going insane.

It was the night before last when I stayed up late watching TV. Yes, there was a curfew that Dominic strictly enforced. And yes, it was a stupid thing to do, but what were the odds he'd get up to go to the bathroom and find me in the living room disrespecting him and breaking the rules. It was the night of the Westminster Dog Show, and with so many categories... Best of Breed, Best of Group, Best in Show... and with seven different divisions it takes forever for the judges to decide. Is that my fault? I just wanted to see if the Yorkie won, which he didn't even though he was the cutest dog there. The next day he said he was taking all her jewelry back to Sak's, that Claire was expecting him.

Think, think, think, muttered Smart-Miranda, who got up from the floor and was rubbing her temples. She was a warrior and never gave up. *David Yurman does not just get up and walk away, now does he...*

Debilitating symptoms of a panic attack are amplified as fear and confusion set in, proof that your thoughts can make your body very sick. Even with the thermostat in the house set at a crisp 68-degrees, Miranda's hairline was drenched, and sweat was dripping down her back. The clingy fabric was sticking to her skin, making her feel claustrophobic and anxious. She tore off the dress... SHE COULDN'T BREATHE! Smart-Miranda was about ready the pass the baton to Panic-Miranda who was waiting in the wings. She was an adrenalin junkie and loved this sort of thing... a pretty good athlete, too. Regardless of who was in charge, they knew one thing. If there was a way to make their husband suspicious, going to lunch without jewelry would be it.

11:11 am

Smart-Miranda was in charge of the jewelry, and with good reason: It was worth a small fortune. She knew that if she sold everything she would have enough money to escape from Dominic, buy a car, and a house, and start a new life, hopefully in the witness protection program where he could never find her. David Yurman could buy Miranda her freedom. She knew it, and Dominic knew it, too. But for now, the clock was ticking and she needed to find that jewelry fast! Sometimes she dumped everything out of her jewelry box and onto the dressing room floor as a matter of security and maintenance. Each piece was wiped down with a special cloth she got from Claire, then wrapped in a Kleenex…a pave heart here, a carnelian bracelet there. Each item was individually sealed in a small Ziplock bag, labelled, and hidden inside the zipper compartments of her handbags. If Dominic Manos was going to steal her nest egg, it wasn't going to happen on her watch. She invented a code using numbers that translated into letters that told her which handbag had jewelry inside. The code was based on the science of linguistics and speech sounds which she studied in college, and would be impossible for Dominic to translate. The information was written on an expired DSW coupon which she kept inside a pair of Lucite stilettos, still in the box they came in. In all their resplendent beauty, Miranda loved the shoes the way an art collector loves a Tarkay. They were little more than a vivacious Pucci scarf, wrapped and twisted across the toe, in hues so saturated and juicy they were sweet enough to eat. The scarf continued around the forefoot, then crisscrossed high on the ankle where a hint of Lucite peaked through a single, elegant bow. The shoes were the pansies that bloomed along the streets of Charlevoix in the summer, a procession that exploded with color and danced with possibility. Miranda swayed to and fro with the flowers, eyes closed, her face tipped toward the sun, waiting for a handsome boat mechanic named Drew Becker to kiss her in a way she would never forget. They were the shoes for an imaginary life, the ones that might carry her back to Drew someday.

She searched the black Chanel. No jewelry inside. The Burberry Bucket bag, also empty. *Crap!* She untied the drawstring of the Louis Vuitton Petit Noe, reached in and found only a handful of old marbles from Charlie. *Crap. Crap.!!!*

11:21 am

WHAT ARE YOU DOING AND WHY AREN'T YOU DRESSED?! Smart-Miranda scared the hell out of her! The day after Westminster, the jewelry in the small Ziplocks had been removed from the handbags and taken to the kitchen. It was an emergency relocation reserved only for the most dire circumstances and security threats. All the jewelry was stacked on a big piece of foil that was measured and prepared in advance. The foil was wrapped round and round until it was roughly the size of a Lake Michigan smallmouth bass. Stuffed inside a larger Ziplock bag, it would blend with the other things in the freezer. Written in Sharpie, the bag was labeled *Max's Fish.* She hid it behind a row of Lean Cuisines where Dominic would never find it.

Miranda could hear Dominic in the kitchen finishing a phone call, and while the plan was brilliant, she would not be able to remove David Yurman from the freezer at this time. Miranda pulled on a skirt and floaty pink blouse with a long, feminine bow at the neckline, no necklace required. He wouldn't suspect a thing. She stepped confidently down the back stairs. Bruised-Bloodied-Miranda was tagging along, always expecting the worst. Smart Miranda would make her sit in the back seat where Dominic wouldn't notice her. If he sensed her presence, he would exploit her weakness and turn violent.

Smart-Miranda grabbed her keys from a bowl on the counter, took a bottle of water from the fridge, then went out the back door to get the car. She put the top down, started the engine, and checked the time... 11:29, not bad considering all she'd been through. She pulled the car around and saw Dominic waiting at the grand entranceway between two concrete lions at the top of the marble stairs. His face was crimson and angry... she could see that he was drunk. He made a fist and started punching his hand in the air when he saw her. "WHERE THE FUCK HAVE YOU BEEN? DO YOU KNOW WHO I AM?"

He staggered down the first step, almost fell... then another and another, hanging onto the brass railing for support. With one more step he would be close enough to slap, or punch, or strangle her. Panic-Miranda grabbed the water bottle. She took careful aim as if it were the final pitch of the World Series. Then, with all her might, she threw it at Dominic and hit him square in the head! With her foot on the gas she tried to pull away, but Dominic was standing in front of the car with his hands on the hood. Blood was pouring down his face. He was laughing at her.

She turned hard, accelerated, and drove across the lawn. She would have to leave Miami forever.

Linda Lewis

Bitterness

Drew turned hard, accelerated, and felt the load shift in the back of his truck. He was heading home from Traverse City with two heavy-duty, belt-driven overhead door openers that he'd install that afternoon. The new workshop behind the boathouse on Lake Charlevoix represented not just his dedication to his work, but his commitment to serving his town and the Up-North boating community as a whole. Lake Michigan was the place he loved most in the world, and that is the place he would stay. He swore to honor the craft of boat building just as his grandfather had taught him, only better. The new facility had room for four cradles, better equipment, and a workbench that ran the length of the building. It was all the space he needed to do a complete rebuild.

Drew did his best thinking out in the shop, breathing in the clean smell of fresh sawdust, and surrounded by his grandfather's ancient tools and the secrets they carried. Wooden handles were stained with oil and sweat, but a good awl could last forever. Having money was no reason to stop being frugal. Drew wasn't bitter about being alone, living alone, and feeling alone. He had his own thoughts to keep him company... in the shop by day, and in the boathouse among his books, by night. He pushed a broom to match the rhythm of a song that was playing inside his head... maybe Fleetwood Mac, but he couldn't be sure. Currently, he was reading his way through the biographies of the U.S. Presidents, developing his own rubric for what defined greatness. The outlier was a man named Jimmy Carter, a one term president whose measuring stick for success was different than the others. Drew read about all the things that went wrong during his time in office. His handling of the Iran hostage crisis, energy crisis, and the Soviet invasion of Afghanistan earned him a below average score from historians and political scientists. However, even though crisis may have defined much of his Presidency, it by no means defined the man.

It was Carter's contributions since he lost re-election to Ronald Reagan that tipped the scales in his favor, at least on Drew's scorecard. Carter's work with Habitat for Humanity was inspiring and generous for an old man who was once leader of the free world, and didn't have to work another day in his life. Drew felt a curious kinship to the old man, whose love of hard work mirrored his own. Carter once wrote that he gets more out of building houses for people in need than he puts into it, and the only thing that makes him different from any other volunteer is the Secret Service agents standing nearby.

Drew read that Carter's first work project was restoring a burned-out Manhattan apartment building. The volunteers slept in a nearby church basement, with room and a bed reserved upstairs for Jimmy and his wife. When Carter learned that a young, married couple had postponed their honeymoon to volunteer, he insisted they take it. Drew loved building things. Any boat builder worth his salt was a carpenter at heart. Jimmy Carter was a carpenter, too. There was something deeply satisfying about that. Through Habitat, like-minded people from all over the world were teaming up to build houses. They pitched in on the framing, the siding, and all the finishing work inside. Drew loved working on boats, but his work was solitary. Miranda wasn't coming back, he was always alone, and would always be alone. He wondered whether he might be depressed, or even bitter?

Bitter? Bitter doesn't even begin to scratch the surface of the emotions he had about all the times he got cheated. Drew shoved the broom a little too hard and knocked over a trash can. *Even though he wasn't close to his parents, losing them in the plane crash when he was still a young man made it impossible to ever set things right. Drew wasn't especially fond of religion, even though Miranda had a Bible she read sometimes. But he had to wonder, what kind of God does that to a kid? What had he ever done to be punished that way? Living parents are always better than dead parents. Did anyone know what that was like? Did anybody care? Even though he didn't cause the crash, he blamed*

171

himself. He could have tried harder to respect his dad, maybe even gone to work for him at the Bridge Street Marina. That would have meant everything to him. Instead, he just wanted to work on boats with his grandfather, so that's what he did. But none of that mattered now...

Of course, when Hank Becker died, that was the end of the line, and Drew's last connection with someone who actually loved him. No brothers or sisters, no aunts or uncles, and nobody to go with him to the boat show in Hessel. He always hoped for a life with someone he loved, but obviously that was asking too much. Miranda left without even saying goodbye, then ran off and married Dominic Manos. Manos?!

He despised Jim Tiller for his affair with Miranda and playing Drew for a fool. He hated Miranda, blamed Miranda, but still loved Miranda. What kind of man is he to hold onto hope for a life with someone who treated him so badly? (That's a lie. He hopes he never sees her again. Which is also a lie, because if she came twirling and spinning through the door right now, pushed aside the book about Jimmy Carter and kissed him, he would hold on tight and never let her go.) Yes, he hated her. And as for Daniel Bering... that's the person he hated the most, not just for being the messenger of bad news, but for the joy he found in telling it. Had he died in that boat fire at the island, the world would be better off.

"Bitter?" he shouted out loud. *"Hell yes, I'm bitter."*

Shoes for an Imaginary Life

Clarence Goodhart

"It was a big investment, alright," Drew would say when questioned about the new service building. "Now I just need some boats to work on to pay for the darn thing, so please tell all your friends!" The local folks were harmless. Drew always played along for entertainment. If they thought it was a stretch for him to pay for a new shop, then so be it. He didn't want people to know his business, or anything about where his money came from.

There were plenty of old timers in town, folks who knew Drew from the time he was a kid. Most were happy to see his success and wished him well. Others were just busy bodies bored out of their wits and looking for something to do until spring finally arrived. They all came around, curious and eager to watch the progress as the new shop was going up. When the season ended in September, the well-to-do summer residents went back to their respective cities, and there just wasn't much to do except eat pancakes at McDonald's in the morning, and play bingo at St. Mary's at night. There were some who considered themselves repositories for everything that happened between Traverse City and Harbor Springs, and two of them were heading down Drew's driveway. He hadn't even finished his morning coffee when the questioning began.

The women wore ordinary dresses in muted shades that emphasized their stooped shoulders and plain faces. "I remember your grandfather from when I was just a girl," said the first one. "He was always on the docks, working on that old boat of his. Supposedly it was the fastest woody on all the Great Lakes. My father said he was up to no good, and the whole town knew it! What do you think about that, Drew Becker?"

"Yes, uh huh... well, that certainly is interesting." Drew gathered up his tools and set up a 26-foot extension ladder.

The other woman stood with arms folded, eager to put in her two cents worth. "Well, my mother said Hank Becker was a womanizer... had girlfriends all over the place." As the secretary-treasurer of the Bridge Street Garden Club, she was obviously an expert. "And if a man wanted to hang onto his wife, he better keep her far, far away from your grandfather. You know there were girls all up and down the Great Lakes pregnant with his babies...that's what my mother said. And they never heard from him again. It's no wonder people didn't trust him."

"All we want is the truth," demanded the first one, while the second one twisted up her mouth and nodded indignantly.

Drew wanted to have the garage door openers installed and functioning before the sign shop arrived that afternoon. He could barely hear their chatter over the sound of his drill. With his lips pursed tight around four long screws he said, "Agmm Hmmm Rmmm..." The ladies didn't like his reply and walked away feeling rejected. At their next stop they would tell people how they talked with Drew Becker and what an impolite so-and-so he turned out to be— Just. Like. His. Grandfather!! Drew took a break, got a bottle of water, and considered their comments as they walked away. He already knew Hank was a lady's man, and it's true that the Hacker was the fastest boat on the lake, and would be again!

"And a happy good morning to you, Drew Becker! I remember old Hank... knew the man personally." It was Clarence Goodhart, the old man who ran the Charlevoix Pump-n-Pantry filling station out on US-31. It seems he took a detour on his morning walk to see Drew. He was a civic minded community leader and served four terms on City Council. More than the women who came around digging for information, Clarence Goodhart was truly the eyes and ears of the town. He was known to be ethical and discreet, a benefactor for some good causes, and not one to gossip. He looked like he had to be the oldest living person in Charlevoix County. Leaning on a cane for support, he moved slowly and cautiously, taking measured steps as he made his way down the gravel path. His hair was sparse and fine, barely covering the scars that remained after skin cancer was removed in several places. Drew noticed purple blotches that covered the tops of his hands. "That's what happens when you get old like me, son. Life goes by quick as a whistle. Before you know it, you'll be an old man, too."

They sat at a picnic table beneath the trees, looking out at the watery layer that had formed on Lake Charlevoix.

"You know, there's a real estate lady in town who's offering a nice prize if you can guess the day the ice melts," remarked Clarence.

"I guessed the 13th, but it doesn't look like that's going to happen." What about you, Clarence?

"It wont be till the 5th... gonna be a late thaw."

Drew whistled in disbelief. "The 5th? That's awfully late. How do you figure?"

"I have my ways. I won last year... came in second the year before that. Sometime we'll compare notes, share our secrets about the lakes, hmm?" Drew would welcome that conversation. Clarence was a character.

"How do they even call it? Is there a judge? A committee?" Drew had a feeling Clarence would know the answer.

"Four by eight sheet of plywood with a cement block on top... just outside the boat basin," the old man replied, nodding his head.

It was a chilly day, unseasonably cold and windy. Drew excused himself, went inside, and came back with two cups of coffee, the blueprints for the new shop tucked under one arm. "All I've got is black."

"Black is fine." Clarence took a sip and said, "Ahhh." He was small and frail, and far too old to be on a ladder. He did, however, enjoy studying the plans while Drew finished his work. "You know you're the most eligible bachelor in the county." The comment caught Drew off guard.

Drew chuckled. "So I've heard."

"I suppose you know your grandfather never married." said Clarence.

"Yes. He always said he was not the marrying kind."

"Even so, there was a very special lady in his life once." Clarence studied Drew, waiting for a reaction. Drew's ears perked up like at dog at dinnertime listening for the kibble to hit the bowl.

"Hattie," Drew spoke her name in a whisper, like a prayer. His grandmother's name was Hattie...

"Yep... timing was never right. You know how those things go. But if there is such a thing, I believe Miss Hattie was definitely *the one*. What about you, young man? Is there someone you plan to share this beautiful place with? Someone willing to fetch your tools and hold the ladder?"

The correct answer, of course, was yes! But Miranda wouldn't do it in a boring, predictable way like a common fishwife. She would hold the ladder with one hand and trace the back of your bare leg with the other until it reached the hem of your shorts! You could either shoo her away or fall off the ladder... but either way, if she happened to be wearing nothing but a sheer bra and those sexy panties, well... whatever project was at the top of that ladder would just have to wait. *(Not a lie, but a fantasy, where things like this happened all the time.)* The only thing he liked better was watching her change the oil on the twin 454s down at the boat basin, typically wearing the same thing. *(It is true that Miranda could change her own oil, but his version of the story always ended differently.)*

"Nobody special, Mr. Goodhart. Thanks, but no thanks."

"Well, when you meet her son, follow your heart. Always follow your heart."

Drew was distracted.

"We should sit down sometime and reminisce. You'd indulge an old man and listen to some stories, wouldn't you?"

Clarence reminded him so much of his grandfather; the men were cut from the same cloth. "You are welcome anytime."

Linda Lewis

Becker Boat Works

Drew put away his tools and brought in the ladder, always mindful of safety, just as his grandfather taught him. He was finishing a sandwich and a handful of cookies when a late model utility van pulled up beside the picnic table. The letters on the door read, YOUNG BROTHERS GRAPHICS AND SIGNS. Two clean cut teenagers in work shirts jumped out of the vehicle, set up a ladder, and got right to work. It was a proud day for Drew Becker as he watched the boys install a simple fascia sign above the door of the service building— BECKER BOAT WORKS, MASTER BOAT BUILDERS SINCE 1919. That was the year his grandfather got the HackerCraft. Fraternal twins Ben and Nate Young were the great-grandsons of Charlevoix native Earl Young, who built the first of his famous Mushroom Cottages that same year. While Hank was busy modifying the engine of his Hacker Runabout to transport bootleg up and down Lake Michigan, Earl was gathering rocks to construct the first of his 31 structures. It is said that Earl

Young saw beauty in nature that others overlooked. Turning rocks into places for people to live was his way of expressing that. Young lovingly arranged the rocks to form magical courtyards and fireplaces that tourists still treasure today.

Old Hank, on the other hand, recognized beauty in the lake, as it splashed over his bow and carried him through his workday (or work-night, as was the case in his profession.) While Earl was chiseling and building, Hank Becker was arranging cases and bottles of whiskey in the hidden compartments behind the dashboard, within the upholstery, and beneath a trap door under the engine room. Young left a legacy for all generations to enjoy, while Hank Becker left Drew the old HackerCraft, an immense fortune in cash, and a lot of unanswered questions. There were times Drew wondered if his inheritance was a blessing or a curse. Why were people still so curious about his grandfather's affairs? Drew was becoming curious himself.

"What do you think, Mr. Becker?"

"Looks great, Ben. Good job you two."

"That sure is a nice building. My dad says you've got an old boat in there." Nate was right. Drew moved the Hacker into the new shop as soon as the paint on the floor was dry. Once the boys took down the ladder and secured it on top of the van, they stood silently, side by side, like bellboys waiting for a tip.

"Would you like to come in and have a look around?" Drew grabbed the door and pulled it open just in time, as Nate and Ben sprinted to see who could get there first. When he flipped on the light they froze in their tracks.

"Gentlemen... behold, the 1919 HackerCraft 26-foot Runabout, designed and built in Detroit by John L. himself." In its current state the boat was in roughly the same condition as Clarence Goodhart— extremely old, not very attractive, but valuable and worth restoring. She rested in a sturdy wooden cradle that Drew built himself to protect the boat throughout the restoration. It would take the better part of the winter. The boys were sophomores at the high school and worked for their dad after school and on weekends. They would presumably take over the business someday. For their age they were surprisingly mature and responsible. Ben and Nate slowly walked the perimeter of the Hacker, arms folded in front of them, nodding their heads in approval. "Six were built, one remains." That was true as far as Drew knew. It would be remarkable to hear of another one like it. When they spotted the engine, well secured in a sturdy cradle, they gasped.

"Damn," whispered Nate, leaning in to get a closer look.

"I'm telling Mom you swore," said Ben.

"I'm telling Mom you're an idiot."

"Am not."

"Are too.

"At least I'm older."

"Dude, you are NOT older, I'm older." *(Not a lie, Nate was older.)*

"Well you're still an idiot and I'm still telling Mom."

"Don't be an idiot, Ben!" A skirmish of rib poking and play fighting ensued. No one was declared the winner and Nate called a truce.

"Do you know anything about the engine, Mr. Becker?" Ben was taking a second look and wanted to hear more.

Drew raised one eyebrow and replied, "Have you got a minute?" He took a sip from his water bottle and thought about where to begin.

"Well for starters, and before we can discuss this engine here, we need to talk about the model that came with the boat. It would have been one of two types: The Hall-Scott four-cylinder which was guaranteed to do 30 mph or better. Not bad for 1919, right?"

The brothers grew up with boats on Crooked Lake. Drew was speaking their language.

"Now, if you wanted to go even faster, they also offered a six-cylinder that was guaranteed to do 40! Keep in mind that Hall-Scott wasn't even in the business of building boat engines. They were a company based clear out in California building engines for rail cars, of all things."

"Rail cars?" Ben looked puzzled.

"Way before your time, my friend." Drew chuckled and continued.

"Hall was a mechanic and engine builder... the brains behind the operation in my opinion. Bert Scott took care of the business side. You may already know that in 1919 a famous HackerCraft named *Miss Los Angeles* was the speed boat everyone wanted to beat. She was powered by a new Hall-Scott engine called the *Liberty.* They were running the same motor in *11ᵗʰ Hour, Stroller,* and *Kitty Hawk* which were also prize-winning racers. Impressive, right? But the bigger story is, where did those extreme machines come from?"

The boys turned over a couple of paint buckets, got comfortable, and were listening intently. Ben said he'd like to own a Liberty; Nate wanted to build one.

"Going clear back to 1917 when the U.S. entered the war, the big car companies in Detroit started producing Liberty engines for American combat planes. That's when Elbert Hall of Hall-Scott teamed up with the design engineer from Packard..."

"Packard?" questioned Nate.

"Before your time, dude... we can discuss it later."

Charlevoix had the best high school in Northern Michigan. They even had clubs where you could study Japanese and zoology. Drew couldn't believe that with such an impressive curriculum they didn't have a class about the history of the American car." He shook his head in despair. "If kids could spend an hour watching a tortoise inch his way across a classroom, they could certainly make time to learn about the Packard. After all, it was the big auto makers that put Detroit on the map.

"Scott-Hall and Packard teamed up hoping to get a government contract to produce the engines. The men made a brilliant team... came up with a design and production facility in just five days. Even so, their companies were too small to compete with the likes of Ford, Lincoln, and Buick. They were contracted to produce only a limited quantity... and that's where John L. Hacker came in.

"Long story short, boys, when the war ended two years later, there were thousands of leftover Liberty engines that were never going to see the inside of a war plane. So if you were wondering how so many ended up in America's best speedboats and championship racers, well, there's your answer! Boat builders bought the engines for pennies on the dollar— bad for Detroit, good for John L. and HackerCraft!"

"Now, don't get me wrong. The engines made by the Hall-Scott/Packard team were outstanding. Losing the bid was by no means a reflection on the quality of the finished product, none whatsoever. When it came to mass production, it was a little tough to compete with The Ford Motor Company..." *the understatement of the century*, Drew chuckled. "Well, years passed and Hall-Scott continued to do great things. In 1931 they came out with an engine called the Invader 168, which was your basic, straight 6-cylinder marine engine... most popular product they ever made. Then in '37 they put two of those straight-line sixes together to make a V-12 which they called the Defender!"

"Is there gonna be a test?" asked Ben.

"Should we be taking notes?" asked Nate.

Drew enjoyed their sarcasm. "Yes. A test, and a 2000-word essay." He went on. "Like the Liberty, this engine was produced for the U.S. Military, primarily for Army and Navy crash boats. Well, this time Hall-Scott won the bid and produced 5000 units! And when the Navy said they needed more power, Hall-Scott bored the engine and gave them a supercharged 700 horsepower machine, strong enough to power a 63-foot craft. This was a superior product, boys... truly ahead of its time. Imagine an engine with the best possible power-to-weight ratio with aluminum pistons and crankcases. It was lighter than any comparable product of its day. And while weight was an important factor, the real key to Defender's success, in my opinion, was a little innovation called the *hemispherical combustion chamber*, also known as..."

"A Hemi!" they shouted in unison!

Drew could talk about boats all day, but he needed to wrap things up. He wanted to take a ride up to Alanson, maybe stop at Bob's Place for lunch. "In 1945 the Defender was retooled for general marine use, and the rest was history."

"So what kind of engine is this?" Ben gestured at the machine in the corner.

"This engine right here? Well fellas, it was a tough decision. Of course, I looked at a lot of Hall-Scotts... even drove clear to Vermillion, Ohio for a boat show where one was for sale. At one point I considered a Sterling Petrel— a real nice engine, but the guy wanted an arm and a leg. I'm not made of money, y'know. *(A huge lie!)* I even flew out to California to check out a Hispano Suiza V-12. Now that's an impressive machine, but fitting her in the engine bay would have taken a lot of extra work. Nothing wrong with it, just not the right one for the Hacker. Then, just out of curiosity I went to

Kenosha to see a 1942 Scripps 302, one that a man took out of an old Chris Craft. It was basically two inline sixes, but the configuration was really awkward... nothing like the Defender. Then there was the V-12 Kermath Sea Raider Special... it ran good, but where on earth would you get parts for a Kermath if something broke?

Drew glanced at his watch. He could tell by the looks on their faces that the twins were so overwhelmed with information that they'd never guess which engine would power Hank's old boat. Drew never planned on telling them anyway.

"Any questions?"

"My dad says you're rich. Is that true?" Nate was just a kid, he had no idea...

"Richer than God, Santa Claus, and Michael Jordan combined. Next question?"

"Your boat doesn't have a name... why not?" asked Ben.

"Truth is, I'm still thinking about it." *(Another lie. Drew knew exactly why there was no name on the transom. Hank Becker was a rumrunner during Prohibition. Why would a man who is breaking the law make it easier for the police to find him?)*

Shoes for an Imaginary Life

McDonald's

"They say the early bird catches the worm, Drew Becker, and this old worm got up early to watch the ice melt!" Clarence Goodhart chuckled, still sure he would claim the prize.

"Like watching paint dry, I suppose?" Drew was happy to play along.

"Like watching paint dry, only colder."

For all the years Drew and Clarence lived in the same town, Drew was amazed that they had crossed paths twice in two days. That was quite a coincidence! Drew was at McDonald's already enjoying his second cup of coffee. The old man's cheeks were rosy from sitting outside at the Boat Basin."

"Why don't you take off your coat and stay awhile, Mr. Goodhart?"

"What?" It was loud in the restaurant.

"LET ME TAKE YOUR COAT!"

"Of course I vote! It's our civic duty!"

Drew helped the old man out of his quilted Carhartt, a Realtree camo, threadbare at the collar and cuffs. Clarence must have been a hunter. Drew was surprised to see a successful business owner in a tattered jacket and broken-down shoes. He wondered if the old man was struggling financially. If he needed a hand, Drew would gladly help Hank's old friend. "So Clarence, it looks like you did some hunting back in the day."

"Hunting?"

"YES, HUNTING. I NOTICED YOUR JACKET!"

"Well, of course we did some hunting!" His face brightened. "In fact, we hunted every weekend during duck season, me and your grandfather... that's if we weren't working. We'd go down to that club in Manistee... finest duck hunting in all of Michigan! We always said they must pay the waterfowl to light there just so we could shoot 'em." He was holding an imaginary 20-gauge and aiming it at people in the restaurant. "Pow! Pow!"

"I didn't know you and my grandfather worked together. Did he help out at the gas station?" Clarence didn't answer and went on with his story.

"Do you know what it cost to join that place? Well, I can tell you that when we were young men, a lifetime membership cost more than my 26-foot boat and my Ford truck combined."

Drew whistled in a way that old men do. "That's a lot of money..."

"It's funny the things you remember," Clarence went on. "There was a young Russian who helped his father in the kitchen, a boy named Sergei... a disagreeable youth if there ever was one. It's true he made the best duck and goose sauce in the county... couldn't complain about that. Trouble is, he never washed his hands after he went to the bathroom! We never knew if we were going to die of the typhoid on the ride home, or live to see another day! And here's another thing." Mr. Goodhart lowered his voice to a whisper. "I can tell you for a fact that young Sergei used to swing both ways, if you know what I mean. You wouldn't think that a bunch of men with guns would be into that sort of thing. We just kept our distance, except for the duck and goose sauce, of course. Clarence Goodhart laughed, coughed, and let out a long sigh. "I miss those days, Drew... I really do."

Two things stood out about Goodhart's story. "I'd really like to hear more about your boat, Clarence."

"My what?"

"YOUR BOAT... YOU SAID YOU HAD A 26-FOOT BOAT!"

"Yep... a 26-foot HackerCraft... prettiest little lady on all the Great Lakes."

"What did you call her?" Drew asked.

"Never gave her a name, son. A man needs to be discrete." Drew didn't mean to pry, but his answer certainly raised some questions.

"I've got one just like it sitting in my shop waiting to be restored. It was my grandfather's." For the first time, Goodhart's expression turned serious. He began to cough and couldn't catch his breath.

"Mr. Goodhart? Clarence... are you okay?" The couple at the next table looked up from their hotcakes and sausage.

The old man put on his coat, grabbed his cane, and thanked Drew for the coffee. "We need to talk, son. Your place, tomorrow morning, 9am." He hobbled out the door and was gone.

Linda Lewis

Boca Town Center

Heading north on A1A out of Miami, Panic-Miranda's driving skills were unparalleled. No road was too narrow, no stop sign too intimidating to cause her to break her stride. She ran the light at 6th Street, just missing a lady with a Zara shopping bag, and at 7th she nearly mowed down a group of tourists exiting a restaurant after lunch. The streets were packed. How many times did Smart-Miranda have to warn her about driving on the sidewalk before something bad happened?

"Give me the damn wheel!" Smart-Miranda knew that as drunk as her husband was, there was no way he'd venture out in traffic to look for them. *What would be the point of finally escaping if the three of us ended up dead?* Bruised-Bloodied-Miranda was asleep in the back seat. She was suffering vicariously from Dominic's water bottle injury. The blood on the front of the car frightened her.

"You drive too slow! We'll never make it to Boca before the stores close with you behind the wheel!" Panic-Miranda shook her fist at a hippie in a VW bus waiting for the light to change at the Royal Palm Hotel. She was determined to escape for good this time, or die trying. That's the part that really troubled Smart-Miranda. Getting arrested for homicide or reckless op wasn't going to end well. They'd been in prison long enough.

Finally, a sign for 41st Street and 195 West. They passed the hospital, stayed in the lane for the Expressway, then merged onto Tuttle Causeway. There was an accident ahead. Mid-day traffic was heavy. Panic-Miranda was putting on lipstick in the rearview mirror, blotting, and making sure none got on her teeth. Smart-Miranda reached into her handbag and took out a bottle of pills.

"Where's my water? I brought that along for a reason! Do you expect me to chew a Xanax or should I just swallow it whole?

"I threw it at Dominic to save our lives, remember? If you didn't take so damn much medication you would know that." If Smart-Miranda didn't regain control of her car, it was going to be a long drive back to Michigan. But where would she go? Of course, her first stop would be Charlevoix. She needed to find out why Drew Becker dumped her— never called, never tried to find her. Not that she was bitter, (a lie, she was bitter as hell and heartbroken). She just wanted him to tell her the truth.

From the right lane they caught I-95 north— just 1600 miles and 24 hours from home. They'd take 10 west at Jacksonville and drive through the Osceola Forest, then 75 north at Lake City. She was concerned about

Panic-Miranda going without her medication for a few days. It's not like they had time to pack even the essentials. Smart-Miranda couldn't be sure if the manic symptoms were just a surge of excitement knowing they may have murdered their husband, or if this was a full-blown bipolar episode coming on.

She turned on the radio. Most of the stations in Miami were crap: country, soft jazz, sports talk... Spanish talk, light rock, money talk... static, static, static... Christian contemporary, and religious talk radio. That's all she needed... somebody to judge her for injuring her husband then leaving him for dead— no thank you. She settled on BIG 105.9. It was classic rock from a happier time, and good entertainment for the long ride home.

"It's amazing how a song can stay in your head forever, and when you hear it years later, the words come right back," she said to no one in particular. Miranda turned up the volume. It was Stevie Nicks, Fleetwood Mac, and that song with the words nobody could understand.

"Cannon rings like a bell inside a wooden hearted lover.
Hey, oh why like a pillow fight, it's one way or the other.
On a lie you see a woman, fakin', taken by the wind,
Would you say she promised you a seven. Will you let her win?
Will you let her win..."

Panic-Miranda was singing at the top of her lungs with the top down. People in the carpool lane were staring.

"Next exit, Pompano Beach," she shouted, "Woo hoo!". On the left they passed the Festival Flea Market...best place in the world to buy knock off jewelry that looks totally real. A fake Yurman bracelet was twenty dollars. She thought about all the money Dominic spent on her jewelry through the years. He was very generous. *Maybe leaving was a mistake. If he was badly injured, he would need someone to take care of him. What if he had a concussion, or worse yet, a skull fracture with internal bleeding?! A blood clot between the skull and the surface of the brain was often enough to kill a person! If he did have a subdural hematoma and had to go to the emergency room, he was all alone with no one to drive him. Oh my God, it was all my fault!*

Miranda's mouth was dry as cotton. She was panting like a Boston Terrier, barely able to speak, and the pain in her chest was growing by the minute. She knew this was cardiac arrest and she was going to die! She also knew it was just another anxiety attack and reached in the glove compartment for a paper bag, one she kept in the car for this very reason. Another Xanax and a few deep breaths later, and the terror started to subside. For being the smart one, her thinking was beginning to unravel. *Oh my God, we have to go back!*

"We ha-a-a-a-d none...
A ca-a-a-a-nyon...
Banan-a-a-a-na...
Compa-a-a-a-a-a-anion..."

"We're not going back," Panic Miranda stated sharply.

"We *have* to go back. I don't have my jewelry."

"We're not going back."

"We need that jewelry. *It's our nest egg.* We. Need. David. Yurman!!" This was not negotiable. It was their future.

"We'll figure it out later." Panic-Miranda cut off a Palm Beach County school bus and changed lanes at the Deerfield exit, then signaled to get off at Palmetto Park.

"What are you doing?!" Smart-Miranda was at her wit's end.

"The gas tank is on empty and we haven't had lunch. If we don't eat soon you'll get a migraine then use it as an excuse to make me do all the driving. The low gas light came on when we were still in Miami."

"Then why are we turning onto Saint Andrews?"

"Because there's food at the mall, and a gas station on Glades Road."

Panic-Miranda turned into the lot at Boca Town Center, and parked near Bloomingdale's. They had arrived at the *Promised Land.* Smart-Miranda felt a wave of serenity wash over her, a sense of peace she had not experienced since her last Al-anon meeting. Food from the nearby Capital Grill and New York Prime smelled juicy and expensive. Surely, they could make time for a steak. Then reality set in. "What the hell are you thinking? WE ARE NOT GOING SHOPPING!! The car door flew open. "You idiot! Get back here, NOW!!"

Panic-Manic-Miranda was halfway to Bloomingdale's when she stopped next to a Mercedes and was talking-baby talk to a pair of Yorkies inside. This was not going to end well. Panic-Manic-Miranda knew she was being watched and ran the rest of the way in her good Christian Louboutin's, scraping a heel on the curb. It's exactly what happened that night at Castle Rouge in Detroit. Why did she have to be so careless?!

When Smart-Miranda caught up with her she was in Bloomingdale's trying on handbags in front of a full-length mirror where a clerk was suggesting she buy two. "How many good handbags do we have in our dressing room already?" asked Smart-Miranda, trying to calm her down while flashing a limited production Cherry Cerise Speedy 30 by Takashi Murakami. Louis Vuitton's collaboration with the Japanese artist was one of the company's most successful ever. From the time Dominic got her the bag, its value had increased by nearly a thousand dollars. The right LV earned status and respect for the woman who carried it, or silent ridicule from anyone wise enough not to throw away their money. Like the Queen of England, Miranda placed the bag in the crook of her arm, adjusting the angle to show off the details. Like all her LV's, it was worth more than her first car.

Arm in arm, they strolled through Bloomingdale's, a unified front, at least for now. Miranda stopped in the shoe department, kicked off her stilettos, and tried on some black calfskin boots by Jimmy Choo... vexing and confrontational, with heavy brass eyelets, waxed laces, and a five-inch flare block heel. A layer of crystals decorated a sharp toe— Rocky Horror meets Moira Rose meets the Wicked Witch of the West, all for just $1495. The boots belonged to somebody's imaginary life, but no longer her own.

There was another pair she liked by Sam Edelman. They were the same shade of brown as the trapper's hat she practically lived in on her boat that winter, the hat with the real fur lining. The boots had a chunky heel with a lug sole, padded collar, and red plaid laces. She slipped one on and turned the other around in her hands to see if her ice cleats would fit. They made her heart smile.

Miranda paid for the boots and exited the shoe department with an iconic Medium Brown Bag at her side. She passed through costume jewelry and dodged the ladies in cosmetics who try to convince you that a $50 eye shadow is worth it. With the entrance to the mall in view, she stopped at the fragrance bar just long enough to spritz some Chanel No. 5. It reminded her of the first (and only) night she spent with Drew, and the white hot, glass breaking, Oreo eating, quilt snuggling time they shared. "One hour," the girls agreed, "then back on the road."

Linda Lewis

Jungle Red

Around the perimeter of the mall she flew, playing connect the dots between the anchor stores and smaller shops. One lap, then another, the mannequins and window dressing became one fabulous, shiny blur. The teenie little clothes in BeBe looked even smaller than last year, and the window display at Cache was a splash of mixed metals, Lycra, and skin, twisted and molded in some sort of bizarre swimsuit/cover-up ensemble that every woman in Boca was probably already wearing, including the fat ones. From the time they were married, Dominic assured her she would grow to love South Florida, but that never happened. Once she got out she was never coming back.

Miranda always did her best thinking in a retail environment. By her third lap, a plan for the trip home was in order. Her feet, however, were killing her! No one in their right mind goes shopping in red-bottoms! *(But "right mind" is such a blurry way of defining mental health, perhaps even risky...)* She strolled into Neiman Marcus like she owned the place, and breezed past the ladies selling $50 eyeshadows. She would not be intimidated. The perfect pair of Miu Miu sparkle diamond flip-flops practically jumped off the table and landed in the hands of a nice young man who quickly returned with her size. They had rubber bottoms and padded insoles for comfort, and graceful straps covered with big fake diamonds! They were $995, not on sale, but what at Neiman Marcus ever is?! It's not like she was buying something she didn't need. These were well made, quality sandals she could wear all year long! There was a huge value in that, right? *(Not a lie, but not exactly true, either. Manic-Panic-Miranda was a big spender. Impulse buys were her specialty.)* She slipped them on, handed over her credit card, and explained that she was getting the Miu Miu's to go! He boxed up the Louboutins and wished her a pleasant day.

On her way out she spotted a collection of fragrances by Jo Malone. *Wait. Isn't this what Oprah wears?* And Neiman's was the only place that carried it! Miranda spritzed one called Blue Agava and Cacao. If sparkle and fizz was a smell, this would be it! She bought two to qualify for the free gift with purchase. It's not like Dominic would even know she was using his credit card, especially if he was at the ER getting stitches. Just ahead, neon signs indicated she was approaching the food court. She would dash into Sephora, grab what she needed, then eat! *(That's a lie. Miranda had no intention of having lunch that day, even at the expense of her health. Seems like her judgement was slipping.)*

It took nearly an hour to sample every lipstick in the store, not including glosses and plumpers. After drawing a few dozen choices on the back of her hand, wrist, and halfway up her forearm, she left with a single tube of Nars Jungle Red— her crisis lipstick standby. Thank goodness it was in stock! She hadn't considered this in a while, but what if someday it was discontinued? Sure, the shade would be easy enough to duplicate, but the texture? That waxy, deeply pigmented formula that stains your lips could never be matched exactly and she would be miserable without it! She was stricken with grief. A familiar old black crow landed on her shoulder, whispering hateful words to discourage her. The emotion was far out of proportion to her actual circumstances, but the symbolism was real. *What was she waiting for?!* She raced back into Sephora and bought the remaining three. It was responsible to have a plan and be prepared for every eventuality. She exhaled. The bird was gone. *Thank goodness.*

She stopped beside a giant potted plant to organize her purchases, putting the little bags inside the bigger ones. Manic-Panic-Miranda seized the opportunity, grabbed the shopping bags, and pulled out a tube of Jungle Red. She threw the tissue paper on the ground and expertly applied it without using a mirror. She gave herself a big high-five.

"Well, what do we have here?" she blurted out in a loud, smarmy tone, punctuating each word for effect. She was creating so much drama people started to stare. *Given how many kooks go to this mall every day, a girl in sparkle flip-flops talking to herself should not come as a huge surprise.* "Move along! Move along!" She spoke with authority, as though she were queen of the manor shooing away unwanted guests.

Smart Miranda was exhausted, hungry, and mortified. She was afraid this might happen. Manic-Panic-Miranda was on the move, greeting a woman with a Pomeranian in a baby carriage, nodding a quick hello to Claire from Sack's who was coming back from lunch, then pushing her way through a group of matronly women dressed in St. John, probably next in line to meet the Rolex Bandit. "Snooty and Quinn Art Gallery... must be something new!" Smart-Miranda kept her distance as Manic-Panic-Miranda studied her reflection in the glass store front. She had lipstick on her teeth and was speaking in a fake British accent... a younger, cuter Mrs. Doubtfire. She bragged about being bilingual. Manic-Panic glanced over her shoulder and shouted, "I can take it from here, thenk you veh-ree much!"

A uniformed guard greeted her and pulled open the door; she entered talking. "I doo so love how certain wooks of aht lit-rah-lee hold memories in a way we keh-not explain. When I see a favorite pehn-teeng, it is a clandestine gathering of old friends and shed secrets." The gallery was empty except for two associates dressed all in black. The clack-clack of her sandals echoed as she crossed the marble floor. "An exceptional pehn-teeng is not just a wook of aht, ladies... it is a powerful relationship, curated over many yehs like a tapes-tree between the ah-tist, the ken-vis, and the one who cherishes it most." Manic-Panic-Miranda loved art. It helped calm her down if she was off her meds. It was she who formed the closest bond with the women in the Tarkay painting. Unfortunately, in all the excitement, she forgot to place the Cherry Cerise Speedy in the crook of her arm where it would be noticed. Now they'll think she's just another kook spending her day at the mall.

"Would you like something to drink while you enjoy our collections? Champagne or Perrier, perhaps?" The women were straight out of a scene from Pretty Woman where Richard Gere gives Julia Roberts a credit card and tells her to go shopping. Manic-Panic-Miranda detected a fake British accent.

"Shem-peen would be grend, thenk yoo," said Miranda. *One glass can't hurt.* She took a sip and slowly placed one foot in front of the other, viewing the thoughtfully displayed pieces, and nodding occasionally with an ooh and an ahh. The fake British woman followed closely.

"Is there an artist you especially like, Miss...?"

"Ghislein." It was a French name but the best she could do on short notice. It was better than Lola.

"So nice to meet you, Miss Ghislein... I am Elizabeth, the gallery manager."

Miranda sipped her Shem-peen. "Well, I doo love Tarkay."

"Then follow me!" Fake-British-Betty led the way through a bright open space with floating display panels hanging from a rod overhead. One side had a collection by a young man from New York. The paintings were all black and white, each with rows of small shadowy men marching about, possibly a political statement. The other side displayed the work of an artist whose paintings looked like wrapping paper— early 20th century Hallmark. They stepped through an archway into a room showcasing a collection of modern sculptures... giant swirls of twisted metal, and jagged edges that would snag your dress if you walked by in a hurry.

The third room was smaller. The walls were on sliding rails so the space could be altered to suit the collection. Miranda took the last sip of Shem-peen; the glass was very small. *(A lie. It was a standard six-ounce flute with a four-ounce pour. Manic-Panic-Miranda had been a heavy drinker back in the day, and could always find an excuse to justify having another.)*

She looked up from her glass. Miranda spotted the Tarkay and was overcome with emotion. It was even more stunning than she remembered! Her friend Tommy Blum, an old man who owned a restaurant in Traverse City, had a Yiddish word for that— *verklempt.* It means feeling deeply emotional but not comfortable showing it. Miranda didn't expect the painting to affect her in such a mercurial way, but it did. It was a gift from her late husband, Harry Stowe, on her birthday. It was their first year as man and wife, living in a castle and sharing a privileged life. She was smitten, with both the Tarkay and with Harry, her very own Prince Charming. Miranda sensed a growing tightness in her throat. She swallowed hard and took some long breaths struggling not to cry. The painting was the only thing she took with her when she left, and the only thing she had left of Harry.

When she moved aboard the old Marinette, the vintage craft she called *Seeking Miranda*, the painting was placed in storage at a Charlevoix art gallery just two blocks from the Boat Basin where she stayed. They offered to take care of the Tarkay indefinitely, provided it could be displayed for guests to enjoy. She was confident the ladies would be safe there, and she could visit anytime. When Miranda bought the little house in Petoskey, the Tarkay was displayed in a prominent space behind the sofa, opposite the red dining room. Now, face to face with the serigraph, Miranda was inundated— first with joy, then longing, then sadness. She reached in her bag for a Kleenex.

"I see you like the Tarkay. Lovely, isn't it? Let me just see what this one is called..." Miranda dabbed her eyes, trying to contain herself. "Just to be clear, this is a serigraph... a very nice piece, but not the original."

"I'm aware of that," Miranda said nonchalantly. She didn't mean to sound coarse.

Fake-British-Betty raised an eyebrow and scoffed. "I see! And how could you possibly know that? Are you an authority on fine art? A dealer, perhaps?" Miranda was aware that her new sandals were a bit much for daytime and probably undermined her credibility.

"I know it is a print because I own the original."

Linda Lewis

Reunion

"You *own* Blue Mood? The painting? That last sold for..."

"Yes."

Miranda moved closer. The women in the painting never looked better... a bit older and a few pounds heavier, perhaps, but what a comfort it was to see them again, especially after all they'd been through together. How many years had it been?

Elizabeth brought another glass of Champagne and invited Miranda to stay as long as she liked. "If I can help in any way, Miss Ghislein, don't hesitate to ask."

Miranda watched droplets of crimson and wine fall from the painting, its hues so saturated and juicy they were sweet enough to eat. At least that's what her imagination told her whenever they were together. In the painting there were three ladies seated at a table. The girl in front was the pretty one, her face turned away, her eyes averted. Was she shy, or was something else wrong? Miranda could see that even though the women were together, the pretty one was all alone.

211

Her companions were seated behind her. They wore ordinary dresses in muted shades that emphasized their stooped shoulders and plain faces. The pretty one, however, was a vision of grandeur in a long chiffon skirt that draped across the canvas. Pleats and gathers of crimson and wine softly caressed her delicate frame, floating and falling as she moved about, cautiously guarding her secret. But what was it? Her yellow blouse was sheer, and a royal blue scarf draped casually over one shoulder. It had a design that looked like waves on the sea, placid and bright till a storm set in. Her clothes were adorned with painted flowers, some blooming, others starting to die... because life is that way sometimes.

The pretty one had posture that was regal and erect. Her collarbone and long graceful neck gave her a striking appearance, and perhaps a show of strength that belied her true nature. The painting also revealed her small waist, shapely breasts, and a spritz of Chanel No. 5. Her pale skin and lightly applied make-up were the perfect palette for painted ruby lips. Her appearance made her desirable, more than the girls seated behind her.

Even on Miranda's worst days the painting spoke to her. In Providence with Harry, the women were there to quiet the storms of her illness, the ups and downs still not diagnosed. In the living room at her little house in Petoskey, they cheered her on as her friendship with Drew Becker grew, deepened, and turned to love. She sipped her Champagne, slower this time. Manic-Panic-Miranda was already drunk and sitting on an imaginary barstool somewhere. Her attention span was short; her interest in fine art fleeting.

When she married the man in the navy blue blazer (her name for The Dominic before they officially met), he convinced her that making a clean break from her life in Petoskey would be the best thing for her. It would allow her to move forward with no encumbrances with her new husband. The Marinette was already gone. Miranda joked that she sold it on the day that everything worked! At the time, she and Drew Becker were already a couple, (sort of), and secretly hoped they would end up together, (maybe even forever), presumably on dry land. Dominic also wanted her to sell her car, the old Lincoln Continental with its smooth ride and gigantic trunk that served as a storage locker while she lived on her boat.

Miranda had big plans for her little house in Petoskey, the one she and Drew worked on every weekend. *It would be great to keep the house, rent it, and essentially have the tenants make the mortgage payments,* she suggested to Dominic. Keeping the house was a good business decision and would give her some financial independence if she needed it someday. But Dominic firmly disagreed. *It doesn't make sense to become attached to one's possessions,* he told her whenever the subject came up. *And besides, if the roof leaks or the toilet won't flush, who's going to drive to Petoskey and make repairs in the middle of the night if you're in Miami? Being a landlord is no life for you.*

When Dominic asked her to marry him at the end of that summer, everything happened so fast! They were already in Greece when the house sold. Dominic's people took care of the details and wired the money to her bank account. Miranda asked her husband repeatedly about the painting. He told her she was ungrateful for all he had done for her, and stated she should not ask again. *But where was the painting now?*

Miranda ran from the gallery, urgency in her voice. "Oh my God, I've got to find it!!"

Shoes for an Imaginary Life

Rolex Bandit

There was a Godiva Chocolate Boutique just before Bloomingdale's where she would make her exit... not exactly real food, but a bite of chocolate would tide her over and help her stay focused. Once she was back on the road she would stop for dinner in West Palm Beach. She chose the four-piece sampler and handed the young man at the counter her American Express. He slid the card, then tried again. Then a third time. "I'm sure it's nothing...this just happens sometimes," he said, sparing her the horror of what she already knew to be true. He tried her Mastercard, then her other Mastercard, and a VISA. "We also take cash and personal checks," he said politely, sharing in the awkwardness of the moment.

There was a surge in her gut, then a familiar burst of adrenalin. The fight-or-flight response hit her fast. It was the same reaction that gave her the strength to heave heavy furniture in front a closed door when Dominic was chasing her. Miranda had been a fool to think she could actually escape this time. Even drunk with a head injury and all that blood, Dominic had the presence of mind to cancel her credit cards. *Crap.* There was enough change in the bottom of her bag to purchase a small bar of dark chocolate. She bit off a piece and was disappointed. It was bitter. As soon as she swallowed the last bite, a familiar pounding set in... squeezing, throbbing... the sensation of a knitting needle stuck right in her eye. It was the migraine that had been threatening to strike since they left Miami, and it showed up at the worst possible time.

Miranda dragged herself through Bloomingdale's and out to her car. The sunlight accelerated the pain, driving it deeper into her skull. The heat radiating from the parking lot made her nauseous, and the smell of hot asphalt made it worse. *Good thing her medication was hidden on a shelf behind the books in her bedroom where no one could find it. For all the good it's doing me now, it may as well be in the freezer labelled Max's Fish.*

Miranda turned the key— sputter, sputter, sputter. *Damn— no gas. Leave it to Manic-Panic-Miranda* (who was sleeping like a baby in the passenger seat) *to prioritize shopping over a full tank.* With her phone battery nearly drained, she called the number on her AAA card. They promised service within twenty minutes; they showed up two hours later. Service was horrible in South Florida. Thank goodness she'd be back in Michigan soon.

Dominic didn't know Miranda had a bank account with some money set aside for emergencies. She would withdraw some cash once she reached West Palm. She tried again, heard the engine turn over, then checked the mirrors. She glanced over her shoulder just in time to see a uniformed officer approaching. Miranda was not a rule breaker. She obeyed traffic laws and didn't have any points on her driving record. She didn't even jaywalk, for Pete's sake! Then it hit her. He was one of the Sheriff's Deputies stationed at the mall to protect women from the Rolex Bandit, just like she heard on the news!

So far, the Rolex Bandit had committed 42 robberies at Boca Town Center. Even in broad daylight with security cameras in every parking lot, law enforcement had no leads. The Rolex Bandit watched expensive-looking women walk away from their expensive-looking cars. When they returned, distracted by keys and shopping bags, he held them at gunpoint and took their jewelry. Once he waited ten hours for his victim to return to her car. He got her Rolex watch, a ten carat round diamond solitaire, and a diamond tennis bracelet, (the trifecta of everyday jewelry for well-heeled women in Boca.) That heist was worth $130,000. Another robbery netted a diamond solitaire and Cartier watch valued at $40,000. Women who resisted were pistol-whipped, some badly injured. Miranda was grateful the officer was checking on her. She didn't need one more bad thing to happen.

"License and registration, please.

"I made it safely to my car, Officer...no trouble from the Rolex Bandit, thank God, but I do appreciate you checking on me."

"Step out of the car." She handed him the paperwork. "Is this your car, miss?"

Miranda didn't know what any of this had to do with the Rolex Bandit, but she needed to be on her way. "Of course it's my car! Whose name is on the registration?"

He paused to make sure he read it correctly. According to this, the owner of the vehicle is Dominic Manos. The car was reported stolen."

Oh, crap... this is going to be bad.

"And what is your relationship to the owner?"

"My husband," she said in a small, deflated voice. "Dominic Manos is my husband."

"According to the report, he stated he will not press charges if the car is returned to his residence within 24-hours. Otherwise, you'll have to come with me."

First the credit cards and now the stolen vehicle... it happened every time she tried to leave him. She knew better than to tell the officer about the abuse, the alcohol, the threats, and the knives. The police had been to the house so many times, she had become the girl who cried wolf, just like the fairy tale. Every time they handed her the clipboard to write her statement, she declined to file charges, knowing he would kill her. A restraining order was only as good as the person told to follow it. Miranda was painfully aware that money talks, and even more aware that her migraine was affecting her vision.

"I need a decision, ma'am. You can return the vehicle or go to jail. We don't do arraignments till Monday morning, so you'd be there all weekend.

Miranda was too broken to speak, and in too much pain to cry. "Return the car. I will return the car." She wasn't going to Michigan; she was going home.

"I'll follow you to Miami just make sure you get there okay."

Shoes for an Imaginary Life

The Long Road Home

Interstate 95 south to Miami was no picnic even under the best conditions. Had Miranda not been drunk on Champagne, wasted on Xanax, disabled by a migraine, and bitter from the chocolate, the drive might have been manageable. But with the sheriff on her tail, an angry husband waiting, and rush hour traffic, she was frantic.

One, two, three... arrows on green overhead highway signs counted as one. Three and two and two more is seven... arrows on yellow exit signs counted as two points each. Counting felt right. It gave her peace when life was out of control, and it was never more out of control than right now. When Miranda focused on the arrows instead of her life, she could step out of reality and the fear would stop, at least for a while. It's why she kept going back to Alcatraz with Harry.

Solar powered LED signs with programable messages counted as ten, but only when lit. These would be the giant overhead signs with unique messages like an Amber Alert or detour instructions. South Florida was such a detestable mess! There was always some new warning, like the time the sign spelled out ZOMBIES AHEAD... obviously, someone's idea of a joke. Miranda counted it as ten points anyway.

Predictable, rhythmic counting... steady and slow like a heartbeat. On the road there were signs; in the kitchen, the cutlery. Counting was a powerful defense mechanism. It allowed her to watch her husband's lips move and never hear a word. Just like the proper ladies in Harbor Springs counted their good silverware after a holiday meal (to make sure there were no missing forks in the garbage disposal or resting on a dessert plate in the living room), Miranda counted. In the beginning she counted silverware while unloading the dishwasher. She took a special interest in the knives... the knives in the butcher block, the knives in the drawer, and any knives in the kitchen sink waiting to be washed. The chef's knife, the Santoku, and cleavers were the easiest to count, and posed the greatest threat because of their size. Utility and boning knives were equally dangerous because of the sharp points and blades. Controlling and counting... foolishness for some, but relief when you can't find it elsewhere.

Fifty-six, fifty-seven... aaand two points for a yellow exit only arrow, two more green arrows at one point each, and the airport exit sign with two yellow arrows makes four, for a grand total of... sixty-five. It had been a long day, and the counting started to fail her.

At midnight, when other people are safe and sleeping, visions of the knives consume you. You wonder if the count was correct. If you got distracted, there was a chance you missed one. What if it was the Santuko? Oh my God, how could I be so careless?! Dominic was passed out on the living room floor. How likely is it that he would get up out of a deep sleep and go to the kitchen for a knife? If he was going to kill her, it would be in broad daylight, which makes more sense, right? The house sat on a huge waterfront lot, a good distance back from the road. She had never even seen their neighbors. He wouldn't hide her body or clean up the mess. Men like Dominic Manos pay people to do that. It was late. All the knives were accounted for. You tell yourself it's foolish to dwell on it.

You *climb in bed, fresh sheets, feeling peaceful, tired enough to fall asleep, sort of. But thoughts of the Santuko spring to life! Don't get up don't get up don't get up!! Even knowing your thoughts are irrational, you must reverse the tiresome bedtime routine and go to the kitchen. You secure the small canister of pepper spray to the side elastic of your underwear, then confirm that the fireplace tool is still under the bed, in the spot where you can grab them without looking. You make sure your Lithium and migraine medication are hidden on the shelf behind a row of books, lightly tapping each one just to confirm. Knowing your good jewelry is safe in the freezer is a time saver, one less thing to check when every minute counts. A surge of energy, well past midnight, awakens your thin legs and back as you wrap your torso around a giant wing chair and heave with all your might, shoving it away from door just enough that you can squeeze through the opening. In the dark you silently move toward the kitchen, which you do by hugging the walls and counting your steps. You know the lamp on the right has a wobbly base and could easily fall so you use extra caution! Where the carpet ends and the cold tile floor begins, you know you've reached the kitchen. From there it's three giant steps to the center island, and the first drawer on the right holds the steak knives which you count by touching each one. Two more steps and on the right is the butcher block that holds all the others. Each handle has a slightly different size and contour which you have memorized, allowing you to take precise inventory without making a noise or turning on a light. As you trace your steps back to your bedroom— the tile floor, the carpeting, and through the small crack in the door, you feel a sense of accomplishment much like the night of the head butting. You can stay calm in a crisis and systematically check your body for injuries. You can walk silently and memorize the way kitchen knives feel in your hand. Moving heavy furniture puts you in the same league as women who use that surge of energy to lift a car off a child in an emergency. It's that same adrenalin rush that makes it all possible! Satisfied that all is well, you touch your medication behind the books, place the pepper spray on the nightstand, double check the fireplace tool, and fall asleep.*

Miranda put on her turn signal and pulled into the driveway. Mentally exhausted and physically drained, she pulled into the garage, got out, and pushed the door shut with a barely audible *click.* Knowing her fate was already sealed, she walked to the front of the house and looked down. A thick pool of sticky brown blood had congealed on the driveway; a corpse without the body. A million hungry ants were feasting.

Shoes for an Imaginary Life

The Carousel

The Palm Beach County Sheriff waited for a moment, did a U-turn, then drove off. It was getting dark earlier now, and the house was pitch black except for the front porch lights, one above each lion. The shorter days were a happy reminder that it was almost time to go home.

Under the pressure of counting and scoring highway signs, the throbbing in Miranda's left temple had intensified and crept through her jaw into the roots of her teeth. Even so, it was the least of her concerns. Just as Dominic's blood spilled onto the driveway that day, an equally abhorrent story of victory and defeat played out in her weary mind where the damage had already begun. Yes, she won the battle, a solid victory with a plastic bottle, like David's stone in the face of a drunken Goliath. But now the win had lost its zeal. Fear set in and there was nowhere to turn. She heard a voice screaming, "No, no!!" She was a child again, a girl who escaped a pirate's grasp at a dim, derelict amusement park, where the carousel was dark and the painted horses turned to ash when she tried to climb on. The music and the smells of midway food were whispering her name, but it was all a lie, a terrible lie!! She had ridden that carousel before, and remembered how the majesty of the rotating jumpers and their jeweled faces drew her close then deceived her. She ran as fast as she could, looking for a place to hide.

Then footsteps... heavy footsteps, and the smell of cigarettes. Park Security found her hiding in the House of Mirrors, curled up on the floor trembling. A pirate held her face in his nicotine stained hands and kissed her cheek. "I miss you, darlin. Come home with me." A scar under his eye reminded her of someone, or maybe she was mistaken. "The Code Adam has been located," said the man into a hand-held radio, his gravelly voice so familiar. "Subject is unharmed, returning to guest services."

Of men and horses, who's to say
The day Miranda went astray
And sold her heart, a compromise,
A wretched truth, her choice unwise.

And like a ship on raging seas
The Pirate Ride will always be
A place where captives scream and say,
"I'm not unharmed! I'm not okay!"

The carousel goes round and round
Her thoughts and dreams are tightly bound
To memories and mortal fear,

A kitchen knife that disappears.

Bloody Friday, ghoulish sight,
To run away or stay the night?
Trinkets of the masquerade
"I'M NOT UNHARMED, I'M NOT OKAY!"

Painted horses, spinning, falling,
Bleeding, dying, gasping, calling
Chasing gold, a true disaster,
No brass ring shall be your master.

"Only I can calm the sea,
Take my yoke and lean on me."
In brokenness she humbly came,
"Will God in heaven know my name?"

But Miranda was not a girl, she was a grown woman living under the rule of a madman, all because she didn't want to mow her own lawn or pay her own way. There. She said it. She married Dominic for his money. It was the easy way out. *(Not a lie, that is the truth.)* She tiptoed through her day, waiting to offend her husband with some small infraction that no one could possibly anticipate. And she stayed awake at night with a chair in front of the door, waiting for him to kill her. The rules were strict, and the punishment harsh. Worse than that, the rules frequently changed without notice. She would never be good enough to please Dominic, and now she wondered why she should even try! It was inertia with no one to stop the ball from rolling. Something had to change.

The fear was so deeply embedded, so disabling, that the other Miranda's (the one's who helped her when life was too much to handle alone), evolved to ease her belief that she would die under the weight of Dominic's mighty hand. She had grown to depend on them the same way abused children make it through childhood by compartmentalizing the scary places and escaping into personalities that could better manage the pain. It was an involuntary condition, the result of severe, repeated trauma. Though Miranda wasn't aware of the dissociation, it was saving her from complete madness.

Her tears sparkled like diamonds on the surface of Dominic's blood. What irony. It was getting late and Miranda knew the driveway was not the best place to make a lifechanging decision. As she turned to walk away, she thought about Lucille's short prayer. Until now, she had been too proud to say it, and too self-involved to care. But having reached rock bottom alone again on the carousel, something changed. In the quietness of her heart, and the stench of hatred all around her, she whispered a small prayer.

Hello, God? It's me, Miranda, from Thursday morning Al-anon. I'm a friend of Lucille M. She said if I prayed you would help me. I'm afraid my husband might kill me tonight. It's been a really bad day. Please help me.

She stepped through the door and felt her way through the dark, touching the walls, counting her steps. The knives in the butcher block, the knives in the drawer, the knives in the kitchen sink, all accounted for. The chef's knife, the Santoku, and cleavers were exactly where they were supposed to be.

"Twas grace that taught my heart to fear
And grace my fears relieved
How precious did that grace appear
The hour I first believed."

From the song Amazing Grace, by John Newton.

Shoes for an Imaginary Life

Linda Lewis

The Rumrunners

Drew Becker heard the rumble of an old truck coming down the gravel driveway. The new shop was turning out to be a real gathering place whether he liked it or not. And although he was looking forward to talking about old boats with Clarence Goodhart, he had a bad feeling about their meeting.

"I'm afraid we need to get right down to business, Drew, because time is of the essence."

Drew poured two cups of coffee from his new coffee maker, an upgrade from the Black and Decker that he had in the old shop. He handed one to Clarence, black. He wasn't sure what could possibly be a matter of urgency for an old man during the off-season on Lake Charlevoix. Clarence walked up to the Hacker. "Ah, yes... I remember her well. May I?"

Clarence gestured at a step ladder resting against the wall. "Can you give me a hand?" This was a side of Clarence Goodhart he hadn't seen. Drew opened the ladder and set it beside the boat, curious to see what the old man was going to do next.

"Bet you can't wait to check her out, right? Go ahead and take a look! The 1920's... those were my grandfather's best years, or so he used to say." Ignoring Drew's attempt at conversation, Clarence reached the top of the ladder and was about to climb aboard. "Whoa, hey there, my friend. Let me just give you a hand."

As if Clarence were a much younger man, he threw one leg over the gunwall and onto the upholstered bench seat, followed by the other leg which landed squarely inside the cockpit. "Not bad for an old man," he shot back in a gravelly voice.

"Clarence...I have to ask. What is going on here?"

"It's like this, Drew. Your grandfather and I... we had a lot of fun in our day. But we also worked very hard and made a good bit of money." Clarence leaned forward, grimacing as he strained his back and reached behind the simple mahogany dashboard. He furrowed his brow as he moved his hands an inch at a time, from left to right and back again. He brushed off the dirt and shook his head.

"Drew, Drew, Drew... I wish you'd have told me."

"I don't understand."

"What I'm trying to say is, either you found Hank Becker's fortune and are a very wealthy man today, or the boat was robbed before you had the chance."

Drew wasn't prepared for this conversation. "Sounds like you know a lot more about all this than I do." Drew suddenly wondered whose side Clarence was on, and whether he was being set up. Yes, he found the money...

in the Hacker, the truck, and all over the boathouse! But he never told a soul! And except for putting up the new building, he had lived the same modest life as before.

"Maybe this will refresh your memory." Clarence pulled a worn leather wallet from the zippered breast pocket of his coat, slowly opened it and removed a single bill. He looked Drew in the eye and held his glance, curious about how Drew would react when he saw the money. "Does this look familiar?"

There was always a low, steady current of impending doom burning inside Drew's law-abiding head where his grandfather's fortune was concerned. It was ironic that Hank successfully stashed millions of dollars over who knows how many years, and Drew was the one about to get caught.

He handed Drew the bill. "There are only 336 of these still in circulation my boy," Clarence said in a quiet tone, never taking his eyes off of Drew. "I've got half of 'em, and I got a sneaking suspicion you've got all the rest." Drew studied the image of Salmon P. Chase, President Lincoln's first Secretary of the Treasury. The denomination was $10,000. He had a stack of them in a rubber band in the back of his underwear drawer, the same place he hid his condoms.

Drew handed back the money. "So what do you want from me, Clarence?" still not willing to show his hand.

"It's not what I want from you, Drew Becker. Whether you like it or not, you and me just became partners in this thing just like when I worked with your grandfather, God rest his soul."

"Suppose my grandfather *did* leave me some money. If there's a problem with that, I'm listening."

"Let's just say I hope you enjoyed your days as a millionaire... million, billion, who knows."

"I haven't even finished counting it! I have no idea how much is there!" Drew couldn't hide the fear in his voice.

"Million, billion... it doesn't make much difference, except to the Feds. Those sons of bitches will count every last penny when they find us." Drew was sure he was in the middle of a very bad dream; actually more like a nightmare. "Not to worry, Drew... I have a plan to beat the Feds!" Clarence spoke in a whisper, with a twinkle in his eye. "We're gonna take all that money and give it all away!"

"Slow down, Clarence...slow down." Drew refilled their coffee cups and got the old man a chair. "Have a seat, Clarence, and start at the beginning."

"Well, I suppose I can either tell it to ya here or in prison." Drew held back a grin. It couldn't be near as bad as Clarence made it seem, but the expression on his face suggested otherwise. The story began with a fifteen year old boy who went to work as Hank's helper running whiskey.

"The first five years of Prohibition were the best because the authorities weren't watching your every move. But once the authorities caught on, there were all sorts of laws, and the Coast Guard, too. It helped to have a second set of eyes out on the lake. My uncle was Charlie Ursani. He ran the docks in Detroit...that's how I got on with your grandfather. He taught me the job, loaned me the money to get my own boat. He was very good to me. Uncle Charlie promised my mother he'd keep a close eye on me and keep me out of trouble, and every month we paid him out of our profits for helpin' us out."

"It was a complicated time for two young men trying to make a living for themselves. The Volstead Act was real strict and the feds tried their damnedest to put people like me and your grandfather out of business. We stayed ahead of them best we could, but then there came a law that made it easy for them to charge you on a smaller crime, like transporting, then find out your business and send you up with something more serious. That's how we ended up at Leavenworth. They got us on transporting, but nothing else. We never knew for certain, but I'm pretty sure Ursani had our backs. Otherwise, we would have done serious time."

"Leavenworth? Federal prison?" Drew couldn't believe what he was hearing. Did that mean Hank Becker was a criminal?

"Not as bad as you think, son. Leavenworth was full of characters who committed far worse crimes than we ever did. My neighbor across the hall was a bootlegger name of Kelly. Talk about a man that was full of stories! But he wasn't in under the Volstead Act this time. This time, they got him for kidnapping... something about a rich oil man and a real high ransom. My opinion, he was a bit greedy. I'd say, Ya greedy bastard... you could have been a rich man living on the outside today.... might of done some things different and gotten away with it." Clarence sipped his coffee. "This has gotten cold son... can I trouble you to fix me another?" Though spring was just around the corner, it was a cold day in hell for an old man.

Drew brought Clarence a fresh cup. A kidnapping. Something about that rang a bell. Kelly. *Machine Gun Kelly.* "Oh my God, my grandfather did time with Machine Gun Kelly?!"

"Of course, four years was a long time," continued Clarence, as he wrapped his hands around the warm mug. "And it was no picnic... food was all right...not many creature comforts, and worst of all, no women! I was a man in my twenties, and let's just say I missed the ladies somethin' awful! It was during those years that Hank lost track of Hattie... you know, your grandmother." Drew thought about the black and white photo taken in front of the train station. Other than the old trunk in the living room, it's all he had to remember her. "I suppose I don't need to tell you the kind of money we were making at the time. But making it was the easy part. The tricky part was making it all look legit, which wasn't exactly legit either. The money had to move around, slowly from place to place, in and out of businesses set up just for that purpose, then in and out of accounts to clean it up again, if you know what I mean."

"Money laundering," Drew mumbled under his breath. "I think I see where this is heading." Drew leaned over and put his head in his hands and sighed. He rubbed his temples, anticipating the kind of headache he was in for.

"Hank was very careful. He was a rum runner after all, and much smarter than most...resourceful on the job, discrete when he needed to be, and very skilled at managing his affairs. He knew when to keep his mouth shut which got him out of more than one mess." In spite of the risk, it was clear that Clarence had fond memories of those days. Drew could see in his eyes that he missed Hank, too. "Eventually our number was up and we were charged with money laundering. Maybe we got a little sloppy, because we had no idea how that got traced back to us, but it did. It was no small crime, Drew, but everyone did it. All I can say is we'd have done serious time, up to twenty years, had we been convicted. But my uncle had a man in Detroit, an accountant supposedly working for a big three auto maker. He had a little side business helping men with their finances. There were others in the same line of work, but not like this guy. The Feds asked questions but could prove nothing. One day we were facing felony charges, and the next day it just all went away. No tellin' how much dirty money he was moving through the system. You'd be shocked if I told you all the men he did work for."

"Please don't tell me, Clarence, I don't want to know,"

"Whenever the Feds came around asking questions, they could talk all day but never prove anything. Uncle Charlie used to say, as long as our man in Detroit is alive and well, we've got the Feds by the ass." Clarence Goodhart roared with an old man backwards laugh, revealing century old teeth stained with a century of bad coffee. "Funny when you think about it, isn't it?" His laughter led to an episode of prolonged coughing, and Drew decided it might be time for a break. "When our man in Detroit passed away suddenly, God rest his soul, it left a power vacuum in the industry. The Feds came around talking to people. Other than the dock workers, our only connection during the years we were running liquor was Charlie Ursani, and he had also passed on, God rest his soul. I just needed a safe place to stash what I'd earned fair and square, and your grandfather did the same. Hard as it was, Hank and I agreed it was better not to stay in touch. If the Feds came after either one of us, we didn't want the other to be found out as well. All those years and we never got caught."

"Until now."

"Until now."

"So what happened?" Drew had no plans of spending twenty years in federal prison. Whatever he had to do to get out of this mess he needed to know now. Drew never cared that much about the money. The only good it might have done him was to impress Miranda. And even then, he didn't want a girl who wanted him for his money. He'd leave that to men like Dominic Manos.

"So here it is half a century later. I have a regular customer at the Pump-n-Pantry... nice older fella, retired from a government office. The other day he stops for gas and a slice of lemon pound cake, and he asks me,

"Clarence, you ever been up to Hessel? I hear you had a real nice HackerCraft at one time. You wouldn't still happen to have that old boat, would ya?"

"Clarence, that doesn't mean they know about the money. Maybe your friend just likes old boats and wants an invitation to the boat show in August."

"Maybe so, Drew... maybe so."

Shoes for an Imaginary Life

Galileo Figaro

"Here's a story for you!" Dominic was by the pool drinking coffee and reading the Harbor Light, a newspaper from up north. "You know that fund raiser they have every year for the Humane Society..."

Miranda sat down in a lounge chair opposite her husband, just close enough to notice the stitches in his forehead. The wound was bruised and swollen. "The Look-Alike Dog Contest... of course! I remember the lady who won last year; older gal, white hair, and a long pointy nose... just like her Samoyed." They both laughed. Smart-Miranda was an early riser and sat by the pool to keep an eye on Dominic. *Now is not the time to let our guard down, not even for a second! He has played Mr. Nice Guy too many times before.*

When Miranda got home last night, Dominic was passed out on the living room floor. Common sense told her to go quietly to her room, check the fireplace tool, and move the heavy chair in front of the door. But a flicker of compassion— a whisper, a pause— made her reconsider. She took a pillow from the couch and gently placed it under her husband's head. A lady at last week's Al-anon meeting said she didn't do this because her husband deserved it, she did it to honor God. She was glad he didn't remember anything this morning.

"Take a look at this year's winner." Miranda leaned forward to grab the paper.

"Hah!! Look who it is," she exclaimed! "The great Warren Puckett from the Hatteras on C-Dock, and his little Chinese Crested. I didn't realize that dog had such a full head of hair."

Dominic chuckled. "I didn't realize *Warren* had such a full head of hair!" They roared! Warren looked ridiculous with his hair moussed all over the place.

"Looks like he had it styled for the occasion." Dominic wasn't especially fond of Warren Puckett, who had a bigger boat and a bigger plane. "He looks like Albert Einstein... the dog, too! What was that dog's name?"

Miranda squinted in the sun and studied the article. "Stoli. As in vodka."

"Stoli!!" They both laughed. It was a stupid name for a dog. Everyone knew Warren Puckett drank too much, but there was no need to advertise. Dominic and Miranda sat companionably by the pool while Dominic finished his coffee. No mention of the water bottle, the blood, or the stitches in his head. *He is taunting you with his silence, hissed Smart-Miranda. Remember, he is the reason you count the knives every night!*

"I'd like to run the car up to Joe's this morning. There's a vibration in the steering wheel and I want him to take a look at it. "Dominic folded his newspaper and stood up. "I need you to follow me up there. Why don't we get dressed. I'll take you someplace nice for lunch." *This is a trap,* cried Smart-Miranda... *don't do it, don't do it!* Without hesitation, she put on a pretty dress, reached into the freezer for some jewelry, and breezed out the door with a bottle of water in hand, just in case. Smart-Miranda was outraged. *Don't say I didn't warn you.*

"Galileo! Galileo! Galileo Figaro..." Miranda's headache was still a ten on the pain scale. *"Magnifico-oh-oh-oh."*

"Oh my God, is Freddy Mercury trying to kill me?!" She slammed the power button on the radio. Even with medication a migraine could last for days, and she wasn't looking forward to a long drive in traffic. Dominic backed out of the garage and she followed him. Miranda braced herself for what would happen when he saw the blood on the hood of her car. But when she pulled out into the sunlight, the blood was gone! Puzzled, she buckled her seatbelt and turned on the radio.

"I'm just a poor boy! Nobody loves me!" Crap!! She pressed seek and found Spanish talk, light rock, money talk... static, static... Christian music, religious talk and sports.

WRMB 89.3, talk radio. Miranda leaned back into the soft leather upholstery and took a deep breath. At least the station was quiet and didn't have an opera section. From what she could gather, there were two girls on the radio talking with a man about what it was like to be... a prostitute? *Not what I was expecting, but why not.* One of the girls was Lola. (Probably not her real name, either.) She said she got into the business when she was just seventeen. Her stepfather was a drug addict. He smacked her around when he got high, and her mother was too afraid to do anything about it. She ran away and started working at a strip club. When she found out what some of the girls were making on the side sleeping with their customers, she wondered. It didn't seem like that big a deal. She was doing private dances in the Champagne Room every night, which was almost the same thing. She left the club and worked through an agency, or at least that's what they called it. Her clients were politicians, businessmen, and professional athletes. She went to the nicest hotels, road in limousines, and drank champagne all night. Her fee was $2000; more if they wanted something extra. Which was fine until the night a client drugged her and she ended up in the hospital, where she eventually learned she could never have kids. She spent three days on a respirator— they were the worst three days of her life.

The second girl was Jasmine (also not her real name). She spoke with an accent in a soft, exotic voice. She started using drugs when she was fifteen. Her parents were both in prison for trafficking, so she lived with her grandmother. "Some people could use and then quit when they wanted. For me, I could not stop." The more she used, the more money she needed, and her dealer figured out a way for her to get it. "He was my pimp, my dealer, my savior. I literally could not live without him. If you've ever used heroin and tried to quit, I promise you, you'd be better off dead." She said she needed some extra money for her grandmother's care, so one night she kept a little back. Her pimp counted it and shot her at point blank. She feels lucky to be alive. At the emergency room a police officer recognized her from the streets, and said it serves you right. "It took a long time for the gunshot wound to heal, but what that officer said to me never went away."

Miranda considered their plight. It was tragic that anyone should have to put themselves in harm's way just to have money to live. She understood there was give and take in any relationship, whether you're selling sex or something else. Each party contributes something of relative or equal value. Both parties recognize this, but it's never discussed. Equity could be based on money (like in the case of those girls) or something else. It's the reason you see short, bald men with tall, beautiful women who look like super models. What does he have that she wants? Maybe he's a charming conversationalist, or a brilliant scientist with six patents pending. But most likely, it's because he's got money. Charlie Fine is the perfect example. Of course, Miranda hated Charlie Fine, hated the ground he walked on. Even so, she wondered what he was doing these days... whether he'd be at Mallard Point when she and Dominic got back to Michigan, which couldn't happen soon enough. The conversation in her head was going nowhere, and with Smart-Miranda at home by the pool, there was no one to shut it down. Spinning and twirling, her thoughts danced around the elephant in the living room. She was so close to learning its name and gaining new insight... maybe even learning the truth about her own marriage, an opportunistic union if there ever was one. Instead, she dismissed the elephant, pushed away the thought, and looked at the new ring on her finger—the Blue Topaz Albion! The faceted stone nearly blinded her.

When the announcer said they were out of time and would finish the conversation the next day, Miranda was disappointed. She pressed the radio pre-set and made a mental note. She wanted to know how the story ended.

Linda Lewis

Meanwhile in Traverse City

Drew Becker had a feeling there was something Clarence Goodhart wasn't telling him. With all the talk about Prohibition and going to prison, he wanted to know how the story ended.

"Well, it sure has been nice getting caught up, Drew Becker. This is a fine repair shop you've got here. Your grandfather would be proud." Clarence handed Drew his empty coffee cup and pulled on his coat. Clarence had been there all morning, and as much as Drew enjoyed his company, he had work to do. He walked the old man to the door.

"Stop by anytime, my friend. I'm always here, and there's always coffee."

"Oh, and Drew..." Clarence turned toward him, a serious look on his face.

"There's one other thing. There's a fellow down at Traverse City... some kinda big shooter. He keeps a boat at Mallard Point... at least he did until he got caught."

"Caught doing what?"

"I don't exactly know, Drew, but if can't be good."

"But Clarence, you can't go jumping to conclusions just because somebody got caught breaking the law. Everybody at Mallard Point has money, and they all think they're big shots. I can tell you from experience that most of it is bullshit. Who knows what this guy was doing? He probably had a party that got too loud and someone called the cops, or maybe he got drunk and punched a guy. Happens every weekend. Heck, Dominic Manos once got so drunk he streaked all the way down E-Dock before anyone could catch him! And that was in broad daylight! Streaking is a violation of the law, too, you know..."

"It was a financial crime, Drew," he said under his breath. "Money laundering, possession, tax evasion... something like that."

"Where are you getting all this information? So far it sounds like a rumor dreamed up by some local folks who are bored stiff and trying to stir up something."

"I heard it at Tommy's"

"Tommy who?

"You know...Tommy!!"

"Tommy Blum?

"At Tommy's Gotcha, right after I had coffee with you at McDonalds."

"How does he know?"

"One of his customers told him."

"And who was that?"

"Ramono. He's a lawyer."

"I know who he is!" Drew was losing patience.

"I stopped in for some lunch. And I overheard everything."

"Who is he then... the guy that got busted?"

"That's the part I don't know."

Drew grabbed his keys off the hook, and shouted, *"Let's go!"*

It was obvious that Drew hadn't looked at his morning paper, or the New York Times, Wall Street Journal, or Investor's Business Daily. If he had, the rest of the story would have been clear... all except his part in it.

Linda Lewis

Traverse-City Record Eagle

HEADLINE:
Financial Crime Finally Solved

A decades -old federal investigation came to an end Saturday when a sting operation led to the arrest and seizure of material possessions related to a Prohibition money laundering crime. A timeline of events was reported to the Record Eagle's Carson Kramer by an undisclosed source who is familiar with the investigation.

Thursday, May 10   Elena Finello Fine dies of old age (allegedly) at approximately 2300 hours at Whispering Pines Nursing Home in Lavonia, Michigan.

Federal Bureau of Investigation Field Office in Detroit is notified of the death and launches operation PIRATE TREASURE. Subpoenas are issued for medical records and visitors logs from the care facility. Twenty-four hour surveillance on Grosse Pointe resident Charlie Fine (son of Elena Finello Fine and mob boss Charlie Ursani, also deceased) is assigned to Special Agents Alexis Romanov and David Singh on the ground, with

Special Agent Analysts PJ Conrad and Jillian Hightower conducting analysis from Detroit. Romanov reports that in the week following his mother's death, target leaves residence once to go to the Village Market, 18333 Mack Ave. and twice to Parkies Liquor Store, 17259 Mack Avenue. Singh reports the target exits residence each night for King of Diamonds Gentlemen's Club, 141 Eight Mile Road and leaves alone each time at 0200 hours.

Agent Gino McCord prepares subpoenas and coordinates interviews with Elena Fine's known relatives: a brother, Benito Carbone of Cleveland, Ohio; a niece, Lucille M. of Key Biscayne, Florida; and Sophia Carbone of Bensonhurst. Further, the visitor's log the night of the tongue incident was signed by Baldassario Castoro Carbone, who may be living or deceased according to Bureau records.

Sunday, May 20   Special Agents Romanov and Singh follow target to Mallard Point Yacht Club, 5900 Mallard Point Drive, Traverse City, Michigan. Working undercover and posing as husband and wife, agents establish strategic operational surveillance aboard a 50-foot Sea Ray Sedan Bridge Motor Yacht, Registration No. MC-3717-ZW, located at C-dock slip 24. At 1300 hours Agent Singh receives voice activated audio recording of a conversation between Charlie Fine and Dock Master Orson Ford, discussing Charlie's request for an extension to be constructed at the end of B-dock to accommodate his new yacht. Fine states that money is no object.

Wednesday, May 23 at 1100 hours. Special Agent Singh observes Charlie Fine boarding a 92-foot Sunseeker Predator Motor Yacht which he purchases for $4M U.S. dollars at Flagship Marine in Bay Harbor. The brokerage immediately submits IRS Form 8300 which flags a cash purchase in excess of $10,000, as required by law.

Friday, May 25 at 1300 hours. Target motors down Old East Channel to Mallard Point Club on said watercraft, call sign *Big Hook,* no registration number affixed on bow, and moors vessel at the end of Mallard Point Yacht Club B-dock where an extension has been constructed and installed. Special Agent Romanov alerts Agent Hightower that the target is in place and the tactical team is notified. Coastguard Ninth District assigns three Maritime Enforcement Specialists and a Boatswain to the operation. Additionally, six Traverse City Police Officers are alerted and assigned to provide back-up and secure the scene. Romanov and Singh confirm that at 1900 hours target exits the vessel and walks to the main dining room for dinner. Audio surveillance records conversation between Charlie Fine and Stella the bartender with target requesting information regarding Miranda and Dominic Manos' arrival date. She states that the couple is scheduled to return to Mallard Point sometime the following week. Romanov and Singh report target returns to vessel at 1100 hours alone and hasn't deboarded since.

<u>Saturday, May 26 at 0800 hours.</u> Special Agents Romanov and Singh deploy operation PIRATE TREASURE. Traverse City law enforcement officers advance down B-dock with weapons drawn. Coast Guard secures the vessel port side in two Defender-class Response Boats to prevent escape by water. Romanov knocks on the door, gets no response, knocks again, and shouts, *FBI open up*. Special Agent David Singh breaks down the door, Romanov and four officers board the vessel, guns drawn. Target is asleep on the sofa in his underwear, his lucky marbles spilled onto his lap and his wirey red hair badly in need of a trim. Alexis Romanov reads Fine his Miranda Rights, unaware that poetic justice is fully being served.

"You have the right to remain silent. Anything you say can and will be used against you in a court of law."

"Well look at you, young lady… aren't you a hot piece of ass." Charlie yawns, stretches his arms, and lights a cigarette.

"You have the right to talk to a lawyer and have him present with you while you are being questioned. If you cannot afford to hire a lawyer, one will be appointed to represent you before any questioning, if you wish.

"I'm not sure why you're here busting my balls this morning, darlin', but you've got the wrong guy. And by the way, I can afford my own damn lawyer. Now get off my damn boat!"

"You can decide at any time to exercise these rights and not answer any questions or make any statements. Do you understand each of these rights as I have

explained them to you? Having these rights in mind do you wish to talk to us now?

"I'm not talking to you or anyone else. AND TAKE OFF YOUR DAMN SHOES!"

"21 U.S. Code 853 states assets derived from unlawful activity shall be subject to forfeiture to the United States."

Charlie Fine is handcuffed, the Boatswain and Maritime Enforcement Specialists proceed with securing and searching the yacht, and the police officers exit the boat to manage a growing crown of rich people looking aghast on the dock. Yellow barrier tape is installed at the perimeter to protect the crime scene and to prevent curious weekend boaters from coming aboard.

Tuesday, May 29 at 0900 hours. Charlie Fine is arraigned after spending an extra day in jail since Monday was Memorial Day and the Courts enjoyed a three-day weekend. Fine is charged with violation of 18 U.S. Code 1961, known as the RICO Statute.

It is unlawful for anyone employed by or associated with any enterprise engaged in, or the activities of which affect, interstate or foreign commerce, to conduct or participate, directly or indirectly, in the conduct of such enterprise's affairs through a pattern of racketeering activity or collection of unlawful debt. 18 U.S.C.A. § 1962(c) (West 1984). The Racketeer Influenced and Corrupt Organization Act (RICO) was passed by Congress with the declared purpose of seeking to eradicate organized crime in the United States. *Russello v. United States*, 464 U.S. 16, 26-27, 104 S. Ct. 296, 302-

303, 78 L. Ed. 2d 17 (1983); *United States v. Turkette*, 452 U.S. 576, 589, 101 S. Ct. 2524, 2532, 69 L. Ed. 2d 246 (1981). A violation of Section 1962(c), requires (1) conduct (2) of an enterprise (3) through a pattern (4) of racketeering activity. *Sedima, S.P.R.L. v. Imrex Co.*, 473 U.S. 479, 496, 105 S. Ct. 3275, 3285, 87 L. Ed. 2d 346 (1985).

A more expansive view holds that in order to be found guilty of violating the RICO statute, the government must prove beyond a reasonable doubt: (1) that an enterprise existed; (2) that the enterprise affected interstate commerce; (3) that the defendant was associated with or employed by the enterprise; (4) that the defendant engaged in a pattern of racketeering activity; and (5) that the defendant conducted or participated in the conduct of the enterprise through that pattern of racketeering activity through the commission of at least two acts of racketeering activity as set forth in the indictment. *United States v. Phillips*, 664 F. 2d 971, 1011 (5th Cir. Unit B Dec. 1981), *cert. denied*, 457 U.S. 1136, 102 S. Ct. 1265, 73 L. Ed. 2d 1354 (1982).

An "enterprise" is defined as including any individual, partnership, corporation, association, or other legal entity, and any union or group of individuals associated in fact although not a legal entity. 18 U.S.C.A. § 1961(4) (West 1984). Many courts have noted that Congress mandated a liberal construction of the RICO statute in order to effectuate its remedial purposes by holding that the term "enterprise" has an expansive statutory definition. *United States v. Delano*, 825 F. Supp. 534, 538-39 (W.D.N.Y. 1993), *aff'd in part, rev'd in part*, 55 F. 3d 720 (2d Cir. 1995), cases cited therein.

"Pattern of racketeering activity" requires at least two acts of racketeering activity committed within ten years of each other. 18 U.S.C.A. § 1961(5) (West 1984). Congress intended a fairly flexible concept of a pattern in mind. *H.J., Inc. v. Northwestern Bell Tel. Co.*, 492 U.S. 229, 239, 109 S. Ct. 2893, 2900, 106 L. Ed. 2d 195 (1989). The government must show that the racketeering predicates are related, and that they amount to or pose a threat of continued criminal activity. *Id.* Racketeering predicates are related if they have the same or similar purposes, results, participants, victims, or methods of commission, or otherwise are interrelated by distinguishing characteristics and are not isolated events. *Id.* at 240, 109 S. Ct. at 2901; *Ticor Title Ins. Co. v. Florida*, 937 F. 2d 447, 450 (9th Cir. 1991). Furthermore, the degree in which these factors establish a pattern may depend on the degree of proximity, or any similarities in goals or methodology, or the number of repetitions. *United States v. Indelicato*, 865 F. 2d 1370, 1382 (2d Cir.), *cert. denied*, 493 U.S. 811, 110 S. Ct. 56, 107 L. Ed. 2d 24 (1989).

Continuity refers either to a closed period of repeated conduct, or to past conduct that by its nature projects into the future with a threat of repetition. *H.J., Inc.*, 492

U.S. at 241-42, 109 S. Ct. at 2902. A party alleging a RICO violation may demonstrate continuity over a closed period by proving a series of related predicates extending over a substantial period of time. *Id.* Predicate acts extending over a few weeks or months and threatening no future criminal conduct do not satisfy this requirement as Congress was concerned with RICO in long-term criminal conduct. *Id.*

As to the continuity requirement, the government may show that the racketeering acts found to have been committed pose a threat of continued racketeering activity by proving: (1) that the acts are part of a long-term association that exists for criminal purposes, or (2) that they are a regular way of conducting the defendant's ongoing legitimate business, or (3) that they are a regular way of conducting or participating in an ongoing and legitimate enterprise. *Id.*

When a RICO action is brought before continuity can be established, then liability depends on whether the threat of continuity is demonstrated. *Id.* However, Judge Scalia wrote in his concurring opinion that it would be absurd to say that "at least a few months of racketeering activity. . .is generally for free, as far as RICO is concerned." *Id.* at 254, 109 S. Ct. at 2908. Therefore, if the predicate acts involve a distinct threat of long-term racketeering activity, either implicit or explicit, a RICO pattern is established. *Id.* at 242, 109 S. Ct. at 2902.

The RICO statute expressly states that it is unlawful for any person to conspire to violate any of the subsections of 18 U.S.C.A. § 1962. The government need not prove that the defendant agreed with every other conspirator, knew all of the other conspirators, or had full knowledge of all the details of the conspiracy. *Delano*, 825 F. Supp. at 542. All that must be shown is: (1) that the defendant agreed to commit the substantive racketeering offense through agreeing to participate in two racketeering acts; (2) that he knew the general status of the conspiracy; and (3) that he knew the conspiracy extended beyond his individual role. *United States v. Rastelli*, 870 F. 2d 822, 828 (2d Cir.), *cert. denied*, 493 U.S. 982, 110 S. Ct. 515, 107 L. Ed. 2d 516 (1989).

Linda Lewis

Tommy's Gotcha

Drew Becker and Clarence Goodhart pulled into a full parking lot at Tommy's Gotcha in Traverse City, just up the road from Mallard Point . It was Drew's usual lunch spot when he was working on boats at the marina and he knew most of the regulars. There was a good chance Joe Ramono would be there. They stepped inside and sure enough, he was sitting at his usual booth. Ramono looked at his watch and greeted Neil Lipman with a curt, "You're late." Although Neil rarely arrived anywhere on time, he had recently studied and passed his Private Investigator Exam, Level 1. It was a big step up from the winter he spent stalking Miranda and taking pictures of her on the dock. Although Lipman inquired, Ramono never disclosed that Dominic Manos was the client. Joe opened his menu and ordered a Diet Coke.

"Just the two of you today?" asked the waitress.

"There's gonna be four... the other two are on their way." She put down four place settings just as Joe's friends walked in. Drew and Clarence sat down at the booth right behind Ramono, Drew with his back to the attorney.

"Lexi!"

"Hey, Joe!" He stood up and greeted her with a kiss on her cheek. "I'd like you to meet my partner, David Singh, the surveillance master."

"My lead investigator, Neil Lipman," said Ramono. Lipman beamed.

As introductions were completed, Drew nearly spilled his beer! Did he just see Miranda walk right past him and sit down at the next table? His heart skipped a beat, but only for a second. It was just last week that Deen Jr. phoned in a Miranda sighting on Key Biscayne... said she stopped by the Cafe with some friends. The girl in the next booth could be her twin. "Damn," he said at the thought of it.

"The fish and chips is good here. I can also recommend the turkey Reuben." Clarence was looking forward to a nice lunch, but gathering information and learning how they could avoid prison was paramount.

"So Lexi, I hear congratulations are in order. When did you get assigned to the case?"

"Detroit got tipped off the night the mother died. They had us up here early the next day, but our analysts have been working the case for decades."

"You people don't waste any time," said Neil Lipman, who was so accustomed to operating at a snail's pace, any level of efficiency baffled him.

"We've had eyes on the target's father, clever genius that he was, since the 1940's. When he died we knew the mother had all the money. The Bureau ran surveillance on her for years, but nothing moved. For the entire time she was in a Detroit nursing home, the only visitor was her son, and possibly a brother. We're looking into that. Charlie Fine had no power of attorney over her finances, but we believe Elena supported him his entire life. Even so, it's hard to prove money laundering until the funds start to reenter the economy. Charlie made our job easy the day he bought a new yacht."

"Right, right." Ramono's law practice specialized in getting the summer boating crowd out of their DUI's, a profession that made him a lot of money. He knew from the time Lexi worked as his intern, and then his associate the year after law school, that she was destined for bigger things. She quickly grew bored with drafting wills and reviewing real estate documents. Joe was proud to write a letter of recommendation when she applied to the Academy, and thrilled when he learned she got in.

Alexis Jo Romanov was a straight A student, a feisty tomboy who didn't realize the advantages of being a knockout till she got to Quantico, and learned how to use it to her advantage. Joe assumed she was still single, not because she wasn't extremely desirable, but because she scared men to death. When you combine the attributes of a swimsuit model, a razor-sharp intellect, and the tenacity of a hungry pit bull, not many guys could keep up. Even before hand to hand combat training, her right hook could kill a man. Joe always said her aggressive side could get her in trouble if she wasn't careful. So far, it's the very thing that had driven her success.

Drew was nervous. For all he knew, David Singh had his eye on him right now, waiting for a full confession! And the way his hands were sweating, he'd fail a lie detector test even if he was telling the truth.

"They put David and me out on C-dock in a brand-new Sea Ray— a fifty footer— just a little something we seized from a bad guy selling drugs to teenagers. It was our home away from home, wasn't it, dear..."

David Singh was young, just a year out of school in Bangalore, when he joined the Academy. Joe wondered if this was his first big case. Regardless of whatever training he got at Quantico, no man could be prepared to live aboard a boat with Lexi, especially a man his age. Lexi grew up in Cheboygan, the daughter of an attractive bartender who served drinks to a young attorney, and married him shortly after. Lexi Jo was not a descendent of Russian royalty, but life in Cheboygan was good.

While in high school, she spent summers teaching kids at the sailing school in Harbor Springs. She was nearly six-feet tall and a natural athlete. In Joe's opinion, she drank too much, but it didn't seem to get in her way. She was a good student, but it was a volleyball scholarship that landed her in the nation's capital where she spent four years at George Washington University.

From there she attended law school at the University of Michigan, the same place her dad got his law degree.

The waitress brought lunch and refilled their drinks. "We sat in front of 221 Sudbury Way, thinking Charlie might run, but nothing happened."

Joe wiped barbeque sauce off his fingers. "Yeah, until he ran up to Bay Harbor and dropped four million dollars on a boat. Way to be discrete, dip shit." Everyone roared.

"Once David had everything set up, my job was easy. We had eyes and ears on the target 24/7. But he was clumsy, and stupid... made a lot of careless mistakes. He really believed he was going to collect his family fortune, no questions asked."

"So you set him up."

"It was more than that. We could have seized all his property the day we showed up. All we needed was suspicion that his boat and vehicle were bought with dirty money. The boat was nice enough, but an old black Volvo?"

"Criminals will often drive a low-profile vehicle to avoid suspicion," David added. "That was the case with this guy. But as we expected that all changed in a hurry."

"How could you seize his possessions before you had any proof of a crime? Wouldn't he at least have to be charged," asked Neil Lipman in an uncharacteristic academic tone.

"Good question, Neil." Lexi knew Lipman was trying to impress her. She smiled at him. "The general rules for civil forfeiture proceedings allow us to seize property that we believe has been involved in certain criminal activity. The charges are against the property; the owner doesn't even necessarily have to be guilty. In this case, the crime was money laundering."

"So why did you wait?" asked Joe.

"We needed to hold off till he started spending the money. It only strengthened our case to get things moving. You realize the Bureau has been chasing this money for decades. We figured we'd give him enough rope and let him hang himself, which is exactly what he did." They all chuckled. Lexi was a good storyteller and liked being the center of attention.

Clarence was enjoying his fish and chips. The restaurant was loud and he couldn't hear a damn thing, but he trusted Drew to get all the information he could. They were partners in this thing, whether he liked it or not. Drew was moving French fries back and forth on his plate, but still hadn't taken a bite. All he could think of was, damn, damn, damn, I am going to jail. He also wanted to get a better look at Lexi, but couldn't risk it. It was better that Ramono didn't know he was there.

"Charlie Fine fashioned himself quite the ladies man," Lexi continued, "and for whatever reason, women saw something in him that I did not. From the people I talked with, he had a long history of girls he 'dated'… usually married, bored, and very attractive. His wife died two years ago, but he had been cheating for decades. She's not implicated in any of the crimes. He obviously had her fooled, too."

"So Lexi, are you saying you didn't fall for the guy? Mr. Bigshot didn't have enough to offer a girl like you?" Ramono couldn't resist.

"Whenever I find out my date is just a few weeks out from doing time, it kills the romance, you know what I mean?"

They roared. Joe said if she ever got bored putting away bad guys, she could have a career doing stand-up... or come back to Traverse City and practice law with him again.

"David and I joined the club as Mr. and Mrs. David Cho. Our cover was, we were newlyweds... just bought a house in Eberwhite, minutes from downtown Ann Arbor and the University, where David is an assistant professor of mathematics..."

"... and my lovely wife, Ashlee here, teaches part time at a Pilates studio and volunteers at the Humane Society." Just like a married couple, they were already finishing each other's sentences.

"You two are adorable together, you know that, right?" If Joe kept kidding around, Drew was never going to get the information he came for. So far, they'd given him nothing.

Ramono looked puzzled. "So what's the upshot of all this?" He wondered if Lexi was being secretive because there were more charges to be made, or more individuals they were watching, possibly for related crimes. If Charlie ever worked in the family business, who knows what kind of information he might have?

"What I can tell you Joe, is that the Bureau spent decades watching these people. You gotta remember, this goes all the way back to the 1920s, when laundering was invented by the mob. Bootleggers and rumrunners were making all kinds of illegal money, and there was so much effort to hide it, law enforcement couldn't keep up. The BOI, the Bureau of Investigation, was the FBI's predecessor. Of course, when you're dealing with the mob, there are always more crimes involved, so the role of investigators and enforcers just exploded. In the first six months after Volstead, Federal Agents arrested nearly 300 violators of the liquor laws, and the Bureau of Internal Revenue had another 300 they were watching."

Neil Lipman sighed. "I should have been born 80 years ago, like my grandfather."

"Maybe so Neil, but if a bus was leaving today for 1925, you'd be late and miss your chance. And like always, you'd have an excuse." Joe laughed. It was an inside joke.

"According to our files, young Charlie grew up in a world full of deceit, which might explain why he chose lying and cheating as a lifestyle, even as an adult. Secrets were his comfort zone. How else could you live with yourself, having multiple affairs while married to a perfectly nice wife? The plotting and scheming, the risk... it was an adrenalin rush. He got off on it... perhaps couldn't have sex without it." Lexi took a bite of her sandwich, and offered to finish David's fries.

"His parents grew up in Bensonhurst, New York, got married right out of high school, then took a train to

Detroit. By the time his father applied for a job at Ford Motor Company, he had altered his Social Security Card, changed his last name, lied about his age, and applied for a job in accounting. Even with no degree or work experience, Peter Fine demonstrated an extraordinary, almost savant-like ability with mathematics, and was hired on the spot. My personal theory is that Ford recognized his potential and didn't want to lose him to a competitor. He and his wife, Elena, moved into the house at 221 Sudbury Way in Grosse Pointe Woods. It was owned by a friend of Peter's mother, a Charlie "the Flame" Ursani. Apparently, Vivian Finello made all the arrangements with him. They were very discrete. There's no evidence to show what the connection was between the two, but we have some idea. Miss Vivian wasn't in a line of work where anyone keeps records. Ursani and his family lived in the house next door. The underground tunnel between the homes has since been closed off, but if you take a close look, you can still see where it was." Clarence glanced up at Drew, then back at his plate.

The day drinkers were wondering in and getting settled at the bar for an afternoon of cheap whiskey and mutual sorrow. The waitress took Clarence Goodhart's plate. Drew didn't touch a bite of his food and asked the waitress to take it anyway.

"Elena Fine had a colorful history of her own. Two of her brothers had mob connections. One was a simple Soldato who never did time, but the older brother served a long sentence at Leavenworth... everything from racketeering, extortion, and an embezzlement scheme that got him millions. His cover was a job as bank vice president... held a political office, too, where he managed the city's money, and was the auditor of his own books."

"How convenient," said Joe.

"I know, right?" Lexi agreed with an eye roll.

"Anyone famous?"

"Gimme a second." Lexi finished her ice-tea and gestured to the waitress to bring another. "Carbone. His name was Castoro Carbone. Died in prison, or maybe not. That's a whole other story." This time Clarence was noticeably distraught. He turned over his placemat and took a pencil out of his shirt pocket. In shaky cursive handwriting he scribbled a message then turned it around to face Drew.

My cell mate— Castoro Carbone.

Shoes for an Imaginary Life

Peter and Elena

"Oh my God," Drew whispered. "You gotta be kidding me! "We've gotta get out of here, *now!*"

"Is there anything else I can get you?" The waitress was ready to finish her shift.

Drew reached for his wallet and said, "Just the check." But Clarence had other plans.

"I would like a cup of coffee and a nice piece of your apple pie, please... decaf if you've got it, but don't make a fresh pot on my account." He smiled at the waitress. As she walked away, Clarence Goodhart leaned across the table and addressed Drew in a serious tone. "When we have what we came for we can leave, but not until then. Do I make myself clear?" Filled with despair and trepidation, Drew waited for Lexi to continue.

"It didn't take long for Peter Fine to established himself at his new job. He wasn't just an asset to the company as an accountant, he was professional and discreet, qualities that were prized by the company's top brass. When his coworkers were taking breaks and discussing their plans for the weekend, Peter never stepped away from his desk. And when those same people were sharpening pencils and writing in ledger books, Peter was doing impossibly difficult equations in his head, one calculation after the next, and documenting only what was necessary. He could commit volumes of mathematical information and retrieve it as if he opened a file and read from the page. Just as important, he demonstrated his loyalty when he called the emerging threat of an auto union an unnecessary intruder into Ford's bottom line. News of this boy wonder spread— Peter Fine was making a name for himself.

Victor Kristoff was a retired U.S. Marine and the head of security at the River Rouge plant. He was Henry Ford's second in command and advisor. It was a tumultuous time in the auto industry, and no one hated trouble more than Victor. Demonstrations and picket lines caused unrest among the workers, which made the men on the assembly line nervous and distracted. On a good day, a new Ford vehicle rolled off the assembly line every 53 seconds. That number made Mr. Ford happy, and in turn, made Kristoff happy, too. Victor was a peaceful man, who took pride in serving his country. While in the military, Victor learned that some conflicts could be resolved quietly by reasoning things out, but sometimes solutions required force. At 6'5" and 260, few people wanted to exchange blows with Victor Kristoff, but there was always someone who wouldn't follow the simple rules of their job at the Ford Motor Company. If a man wanted a fist fight, a fist fight he got.

The tables in the lunchroom at the Ford Plant were too close together. Even divided into shifts, thousands of men gathered in the same tight quarters every day. Tables for four were in the center, separated by a narrow isle, and smaller tables lined the perimeter. The wooden ladder-back chairs were uncomfortable, and didn't offer much relief for workers who stood at their stations all day. Each table had an institutional aluminum napkin holder in the center, flanked by a matching salt and pepper shaker.

A shop foreman on the transmission line was a trouble-maker. It was a known fact that he supported unionization, but the cafeteria was the wrong place to talk about it. Victor Kristoff used his time efficiently, and didn't believe in warnings or second chances. He approached the man with purpose. Without a word, he lifted him off the ground by his shirt collar then landed three solid punches to his face. There was a scuffle of heavy boots as adrenaline flooded the room. Chairs hit the floor with a clatter, and tables were overturned. Some men rushed to his aid, while others ran like hell. The blood from those three punches spattered across such a vast radius, the cafeteria had to be closed for cleaning. The foreman suffered a fractured jaw, broken nose, and an intracranial bleed that was probably sustained when he hit the floor several feet from where the incident began. He died in the hospital four days later. The pro-union men not only stopped promoting their cause in the lunchroom, they took to bringing a sack lunch and eating at their respective stations.

It was no surprise that Kristoff was a sports fan and occasionally placed a bet. When James Braddock took on Heavyweight Champion Doc Malady, Victor Kristoff invited some friends to join him downtown at The Olympia for the event. Mr. Ford was invited out of courtesy, but declined. Ford kept a close eye on his workers, insisting they maintain a certain level of respectability even when socializing. He frequently reminded Victor that questionable activities like gambling and drinking could reflect badly on the company. In attendance that evening were Max Mosier, Kristoff's assistant; Peter Fine the accountant and his wife, Elena; their neighbor, Charlie "the Flame" Ursani; and Ursani's associates, Vince Bassett and Hank Becker."

"The pie is delicious," said Clarence. "Why don't you have a piece?"

Drew's face turned pale. Through clenched teeth he said, "Why didn't you tell me any of this?"

"Prohibition was over in 1933, Drew. By the time Braddock fought Malady, your grandfather and I had gone our separate ways... I told you that. Ursani was our man on the dock in Detroit. He took care of the money, handed it off to the Gatekeeper who got it cleaned up, then gave it back to Ursani, who gave it back to us, minus his service fee. If Hank was spending time with the man, I never heard about it."

Lexi expertly applied a fresh coat of red lipstick. "We don't know what came first... whether Peter was the Gatekeeper and started running the books later, or if he really was hired as an accountant and rose to the level of criminal after that. Either way, it was a tremendous opportunity for him to make a lot of money... and he did. The boy genius probably stole millions, but because the books always balanced, he never got caught."

"Until now." Joe and Neil said it at the same time, and they all laughed. Drew looked at his watch and checked the time, while Clarence enjoyed his second cup of coffee. He needed to think about getting his affairs in order.

"The tunnel between the homes of the Fine's and the Ursani's was no doubt built to conceal money and hide from the law. It was a thing in those days. But here's where it gets a little sketchy. At some point, Elena and Charlie "the Flame" had an affair. We know this because a year after the Fines arrived in Detroit, Elena had a baby that was not her husband's."

"But how could anybody possibly know that?" Neil recalled from his studies that human paternity tests weren't developed until 1984, and not made available for use until four years later.

"In those days, paternity could be loosely determined by one of two factors: the parent's blood types, and the honor system." More laughter, then Lexi added, "But wait, it gets better."

"Even without a rudimentary understanding of Mendell's Law of Independent Assortment, or the role of allelles in revealing certain traits, there were physical characteristics that could not be disputed. Charlie "the Flame" Ursani had a big dimple right in the middle of his chin, and a hairline so low it nearly touched his bushy red eyebrows. Even without a test, the truth about Charlie Jr.'s paternity could not have been more clear.

An unfortunate chain reaction was set in motion when the waitress offered to refill Clarence's coffee cup, which, in an effort to be helpful, he lifted by the saucer. Because a small amount of coffee was pooled beneath the cup where not even the waitress could see it, the cup slid off the saucer, hit the table, and in spite of her attempt to catch it, fell to the floor with a crash. The day drinkers didn't so much as turn around, but Joe Ramono and his guests, who understood the importance of situational awareness, looked toward the source of the commotion. Drew Becker expected to be arrested and handcuffed on the spot. Instead, Ramono left cash on the table and the four of them exited Tommy's, leaving Drew and Clarence with a lot of unanswered questions and a broken cup at their feet.

While Drew scrambled for some cash to leave on the table, Clarence pulled out a $25 gift card. It was the grand prize for knowing when the ice would melt.

Linda Lewis

.

Charlie Fine

Lexi Romanov and Joe Ramono got in her black, government issued Chevy Suburban. He was happy to visit a few minutes longer before she headed back to Detroit. She really did bear a striking resemblance to Miranda. "Whatever the Federal Government has in store for Charlie Fine, it couldn't have happened to a nicer guy, am I right?" Lexi pulled down the visor, flipped open the mirror, checked her make-up, and ran her hands through her hair.

"You look amazing, as always."

"Joe..." How many times had they had this conversation?

"No, no... really, I'm just saying you look good, and you just caught the bad guy, and I'm glad everything's going well, that's all." He thought about kissing her, which would really piss her off. "Any other intel on Charlie Fine you care to share? He's always seemed like a sketchy character, but nobody could quite put their finger on it."

"Classified intel on a felon who has already turned state's evidence and agreed to rat out all his father's criminal friends? Is that what you're asking?"

Joe raised his eyebrows and grinned to indicate he was listening.

"Well, given that he was a boy with two fathers, both criminals, a drunk for a mom, and a tunnel connecting their houses, he had an unusual upbringing."

"An understatement," Joe nodded.

"Peter loved Elena, but was married to his work. Elena loved Charlie Ursani, who loved Francesca, his second wife and the mother of his five children."

"Geez."

"Francesca loved little Charlie Jr.— all babies for that matter— and considered him yet another gift from God, one who looked shockingly like one of her own. For all the times Elena came home drunk after a three-martini lunch, Frannie quietly paid the babysitter, scooped up little Charlie Jr. from his crib, and brought him home with her until his mother sobered up. Sometimes it took days."

"It was a time in America, and especially Grosse Pointe, where quality people behaved with the utmost propriety and discretion. You know the type. To question Charlie Jr.'s pedigree would have been gauche, at best. As long as nobody ever gave words to the curious situation, there was nothing to explain. Whatever anger, mistrust, and resentment might have been brewing, there was no reason to be mad at the baby, or behave in an unneighborly way."

"It was a charmed and wildly unsupervised childhood for a boy growing up on Sudbury Way. From an early age, Charlie's life was without structure or discipline. When the phone rang with a call for his mother, he was told to say, *She's not home, can I take a message,* even though she was sitting in the living room in her nightgown drinking a martini. He wasn't supposed to tell Peter about her drinking, so he started cleaning up the evidence by finishing the last sips from glasses she left around the house. An early taste of alcohol created a craving, and by the time he was a teenager, Charlie Jr. had the tolerance of an adult."

"Hey, kinda like you," chided Joe.

"Look who's talking." They laughed as old friends do.

"Dinner at 221 Sudbury Way was prepared by an old black cook named Opal, and served by her adult son, who had also made a career of working as a domestic for the wealthy. Blacks made up less than 1% of the population in Grosse Pointe, and the ones that worked there were bussed in from downtown to their jobs each day... racist bullshit. Family dinners at the Fine residence became less frequent, Opal was let go, and Charlie Jr. was left to fend for himself at mealtime. To make things worse, Frannie had had another baby, and the Ursani's listed their home for sale. Maybe they needed the extra room, or perhaps Frannie decided she was done sharing her husband with the drunk woman next door."

"Holy crap... no wonder he's a mess"

"As you're probably aware, Joe, the easiest 1950s car to hotwire was the Chevy Bel Air."

"Way before my time, dear."

"The majority of auto thefts in those days were committed by boys younger than sixteen who weren't even legal to drive! They would just pull off the wires one at a time, connect the hot wire to the coil, the starter wire to the coil wire, and crank the engine. Remove the starter wire, leave the coil wire where it's at, and you're good to go!" Joe raised an eyebrow.

"Hey... I grew up in Cheboygan, everyone did it! And besides, my dad's a lawyer!"

"How many times did you get shocked?"

"Once. Something a girl never forgets."

It reminded Joe of the first time he saw Miranda at Tommy's Gotcha the night before she took her boat to Charlevoix. Nobody believed a pretty girl could restore an old boat with rented tools and elbow grease, but sure enough, she did it. She could have done so much better than Dominic Manos. Joe would always regret the day he accepted the assignment to have her followed, with photos of her personal life and everything else.

Lexi continued. "Charlie was driven by two things: perfection and luck. Practice and repetition improved his car theft skills, and with every car he stole, he streamlined his craft. In his early teens he could hotwire a car faster and better than most men, except for the one time he got caught. Charlie Ursani got him out with a phone call. For the first time, he recognized his son's potential and offered him a job in the family business. Of course, he was only a runner at first, but in time, Charlie Jr. knew everyone on the docks, and every man transporting hooch on Lake Michigan. There's a lot of money that's never been recovered. We suspect Charlie Fine knows where it's at."

"How much?" asked Joe, wishing he was a Federal Agent instead of lawyer who babysat drunks all summer.

"When he hands over the names, I'll track down the money, count it, and let you know." She laughed.

"What else have you got?"

"Well, Charlie had a strange affection for good luck charms... thought they were the key to his success in the business. To this day, he keeps a collection of Italian coins, marbles... there's also a gold ring."

"And you know this how?"

"I interviewed a handful of the girls he slept with over the years. Every one of them was happy to talk. It's no surprise that while Charlie was cheating on his wife to cheat with them, he was sleeping with more girls on the side."

"And the ring is significant?" asked Joe?

"Possibly. It's a heavy gold ring with an insignia that appears to be Neptune King of the Sea... very old." Lexi took a file from her bag and handed a photo to Joe Ramono. "Apparently it was a gift from Charlie Ursani. The Bureau has documented similar rings, but I don't know details. Apparently he never takes it off so everyone will know he is his father's son. Supposedly there are more like it floating around out there... or maybe it's just an urban legend."

When Drew Becker and Clarence Goodhart arrived back at the boathouse, Drew extended his hand to help the old man out of the truck. "This is the last time we'll see each other this side of heaven." Drew looked puzzled.

"I'm not going anywhere, Clarence. We're gonna figure this thing out and everything's gonna be fine."

"I'm afraid it doesn't work that way, son. Just as your grandfather and I had to end our friendship for the sake of the other, you and I must go our separate ways as well."

"But, what about..."

"Do as we discussed, son. Be careful, be discrete. I wish you all the best." And with that, Clarence Goodhart got in his truck and was gone.

Drew didn't waste a minute. He headed for Petoskey. He already had a plan.

Shoes for an Imaginary Life

Peter's Party

Lexi enjoyed Joe's company, but it was getting late and she had a four-hour drive back to Detroit.

"So whatever happened to Peter? Nice wife, money, house in Grosse Point… sounds like he had the world by the ass."

"Ah, yes… Peter." Lexi and Joe were great as coworkers, good as friends, but romantically it just never worked. She knew Joe would stay in her car forever if she let him. She would give him one last story, but not one more kiss.

"Peter Fine didn't like celebrations. He shunned corporate life, and preferred working quietly at his desk with the door closed. At the completion of the new administrative building, he received a nice promotion and an office with his name on the door. He declined the offer for an additional assistant. Peter's work had always required discretion. But as the years went on, and the years turned to decades, secrecy dominated his role at work and consumed his life in general. Money laundering is the lifeblood of organized crime, and Peter was the ringleader. He shuffled and shifted obscene amounts of illegally generated income. He concealed it, disguised it, and returned it to his client clean as a whistle, ready to rejoin the general economy without a trace. Throughout his 45-year tenure, his performance was stellar— Peter Fine never got caught. In addition to Ursani and the bootleggers, he processed money for dozens of organized crime fronts with cash businesses: a food truck and catering giant, a trucking company, gambling outfits and casinos, strip clubs, prostitution... even a businessman with a coin-op laundry who brought his proceeds in pillow cases full of loose change. He earned the trust of the industry's most important men, names he could never repeat because they would all go to prison— and Peter would go down with them.

His work required intense precision; a single error would cost a client his fortune and his freedom. For Peter, it would cost him his life. The 'atta boys' and accolades that were spoken in his name only added to his stress. Even with Peter's irrefutable genius, his workload was immense. As far as the Feds could tell, it worked something like this. Once the money was handed off to Peter Fine, a complex structuring process was set in motion. Huge sums of money were broken down into smaller, less discernable chunks, then deposited into various institutions to avoid suspicion.

"We've actually found smaller amounts of money— that's anything less than $10,000—at banks in Cheboygan, Midland, West Haven, and clear across the bridge in St. Ignas," said Lexi. "Once the money hit the bank, money orders could be purchased and deposited anywhere as clean cash. If so much as one account raised suspicion, tracing money back to the source (or Peter) it would all be over. The cost of paying off bankers, tellers, runners, and dirty cops was exorbitant, the personal cost, soul crushing. There were no vacations, no days off. Retirement was out of the question. Peter avoided his family and worked late to protect them from what could be his personal fall. Peter Fine wanted out. During Prohibition, tax evasion laws were put in place to prevent money laundering. However, once the offender started paying taxes, *the law couldn't touch him.*"

"Government inefficiency... never changes," chuckled Ramono.

"Peter managed that with ease. But in the 1980's things started to change. New track and seize laws were put in place to target drug crimes, but anyone who was suspected of receiving money from an illegitimate source was fair game. This included every person Peter ever did work for, living or dead. The new law meant you were guilty until proven innocent. The Feds could swoop down and seize all your assets until you proved your innocence."

Ramono never stopped thinking about Lexi Romanov, and wondered what kind of idiot would not have swooped down and grabbed her when they had the chance. *Why didn't he?*

"When the Money Laundering Control Act made concealment a federal crime, Peter didn't want anything to do with a $500,000 fine or 20-years in prison. He lied and told Ursani he had a heart condition, that his doctor insisted he get out.

"And that somehow explains how Charlie Fine's boat disappeared?"

"The day he came down the channel in the new Sunseeker, his first mistake was paying Mallard Point to build an extension at the end of D-dock so there'd be a place long enough to dock it. It was a good tip. He called the new boat *Big Hook*... always trying to impress the ladies.

"Oh brother." Joe shook his head in disgust."

"The broker is required to file a Form 8300 for any cash purchase over $10,000. When Charlie made his grand entrance last week, we knew he was coming."

"Couldn't have happened to a nicer guy," mumbled Joe.

"Peter Fine hated surprises. He learned of his retirement party the day before the event, and dreaded the pressure of socializing with a roomful of coworkers he barely knew. Given that he was the only man alive who knew the financial dealings of every mobster in the state and beyond, he might have been concerned for his personal safety. But Peter didn't dwell on that. He was more interested in the trip to Hawaii he and Elena were planning; a celebration for getting his life back. It was finally over.

The catering staff prepared an impressive spread of traditional Hawaiian fare, with tacky grass tablecloths and plastic mugs made to look like pineapples adorned with fancy straws. A man sang and strummed a ukulele.

Fortunately, by the time Peter arrived, the party was well underway and most of his coworkers were drunk. He could say a brief hello and be on his way. A gal wearing a coconut bra and grass skirt approached him with a plate of appetizers and a pineapple mug filled with sweet blue punch prepared for the occasion.

When Peter got home, he went straight to bed, where Elena was drunk and already asleep. Exhausted from the party and a vague sense that he might not live long enough to see Hawaii, Peter drifted off to sleep.

It seemed, in fact, that he slept better than ever— not because he was finally retired, but because he was dead. When Elena found him beside her that morning pale and cold to the touch, she shuttered and screamed, never to speak another word. When police questioned the party goers about signs of foul play, word had already spread that Peter Fine had a heart condition, God rest his soul. No one questioned the waitress in the pineapple bra and grass skirt. Her role in the party was insignificant. What could she possibly know? When the waitress arrived home that night, she was greeted by her boyfriend who pulled her onto his lap, ripped off the pineapple bra, and devoured her full, young breasts. She giggled as his wild red hair tickled her chin. It was Charlie Ursani.

The coroner was an associate of Ursani, and on his payroll for a number of reasons. The toxicology report revealed Ethylene Glycol, Methanol, and Propylene Glycol. Peter Fine died from antifreeze poisoning. The report, however, stated he suffered a fatal heart attack— case closed.

Shoes for an Imaginary Life

Elena was diagnosed with Stuporous Catatonia due to the shocking circumstances of Peter's death, and Wernicke-Korsakoff Syndrome, a type of brain damage caused by years of hard drinking. While people with Catatonia rarely communicate, a condition called echolalia may allow the patient to repeat what they hear, without necessarily knowing the meaning. Wernicke-Korsakoff is so debilitating, that while speech is possible, the words are rarely coherent. Injections of Lorazapam failed to improve her condition, and electroconvulsive therapy offered no results.

Elena rarely had visitors at the nursing home, so when a man showed up one evening and stated he was her brother, the staff was happy to show him to her room. The visit was brief. The staff invited him to come again. An orderly checked on her at bedtime and found Elena— the sheets and the carpeting covered in blood. The nurse on duty was called to her room and discovered that her tongue had been severed and removed from her mouth. Even though Elena wasn't likely to reveal any family secrets, cutting out her tongue was a guarantee.

Linda Lewis

West Marine

"Good afternoon to you, Drew Becker!" The store manager at West Marine was a jovial, good looking sailor who retired after running charters and sailing all over the world. Taylor Russell wasn't one to brag, but according to Cruising World Magazine, he sailed all the Great Lakes, plus the Caribbean, Mediterranean, and north to Nova Scotia. No one knew why an adventurer on such a grand scale retired young, or how he ended up with a day job in Petoskey. Russell was apparently the *other* most eligible bachelor in the area, according to Deen Jr.'s sources, and may have even earned a spot on Miranda's Thirty-Dates-in-Thirty-Days list had he been in town sooner. Drew cringed at the memory of Miranda's mental state that led her to such foolishness.

"When you gonna come to Charlevoix and see my new shop?" Drew's question was sincere. Taylor Russell would be a great source for referrals, and seeing the facility would be a plus. Drew found a display of dock boxes and quickly made his selection.

"Probably whenever you invite me. But with all the construction down on M31, it could be awhile. The summer crowd is trickling back in town, tying up traffic as usual." Taylor laughed.

"Well consider yourself invited, and bring beer! And not the cheap beer you drink, I'm talking about good beer, something imported or better." It was a known fact that Taylor wasn't working at West Marine because he needed the money. He owned a place at Windward just outside of Harbor Springs... upscale and very secluded. Becker was well aware he could afford to drink whatever he wanted. He never flashed his wealth.

"I drink PBR because I'm a traditionalist, Mr. Becker. You know it's making a comeback... I'm just ahead of my time." The sophomoric conversation and friendly jibing could have gone on all day, but Drew had business to tend to.

"I'll take three of these," Drew said, gesturing to the big dock box on the end. And I need to take 'em with me today."

"I'll go in the back and get those down for you," Taylor said as he copied down the part number. "And Drew, if you've got a minute, we have a new guy in the parts department." He changed his tone and was uncharacteristically quiet and serious. "Someone I'd like you to meet."

Drew was in the race of his life and didn't have time to spare, but followed him anyway.

An old, disfigured man sat slumped over at the counter. His face was shiny and colorless, with the skin pulled so tight he appeared to be wearing a mask. His nose was clearly a prosthesis. Oh my God, thought Drew, what in the world happened to him? The man was making notes on a clipboard as he entered parts into inventory. His hand was gnarled and thick, with purple and blue blotches separating ridges of scar tissue. Two of his fingers were webbed. Drew had to look away. When the man noticed Drew he said, "The left hand looks really bad, but it's better than the one on the other side." He turned toward Drew and pulled back the sleeve of a flannel shirt, revealing only a stump and more horrendous scarring. "I admit I was a real pain in the ass when I was in the hospital. They told me I could lose my right hand, but I didn't think it would really happen." The words were slow and awkward, perhaps fighting the rigid scars on his face to speak. Drew would never have recognized Daniel Bering. He knew there had been a fire on Mackinaw Island and that Bering was found to be responsible, but he was shocked to see the man in person, looking decades older than his former handsome self.

Bering knew he'd have to face Drew Becker sooner or later. Since the accident... meeting Dutch and finding God in a hospital room, and finally getting some peace, Daniel Bering was a changed man. With help from his good friends at Alcoholics Anonymous, Bering was sober for the first time since he was a teenager, and was faithfully working the steps with his sponsor. He survived Steps Four and Five, struggled over 6 and 7, and was now tackling Step 8 and Step 9… *Made a list of all persons we had harmed, and became willing to make amends to them all*, then, *Made direct amends to such people wherever possible, except when to do so would injure them or others.* While the list was long and would take a lifetime to complete, the first name that came to mind was Drew Becker.

Bering wondered how in the world he could possibly make things right when the two someday met face to face. Drew hated the man, hated what he had done and the things that he said that night at the boathouse before Miranda left. Drew understood suffering but couldn't fathom what must have happened aboard *Good Shepherd* to do this kind of damage. Drew's bitterness toward Bering ran deep and he suspected this would be a difficult conversation. He thought about leaving the dock boxes behind and walking out. As Drew always did when feelings of anger began to take over, he took the high road and faced the enemy.

"Daniel Bering. It's been a long time." Drew extended his hand and gasped when he realized Bering's hand was too weak to grip his hand in return.

Bering nodded. "Yes, long time." Taylor Russell turned and walked away toward a case of motor oil waiting to be unpacked, sensing this would be more than a friendly hello.

"There's something I have to say to you, Drew Becker, and I feel just awful about this. Not that feeling bad can make what I did any better. I can't change what happened in the past, although, believe me, I wish I could take it all back... the years with Dominic Manos, the way I treated you on Dominic's boat that summer, and especially about everything that went on when Dominic got involved with Miranda. It wasn't true. I made it up. Not that there's any excuse, 'cause God knows I've made enough of those in my day. For all the years I worked for Dominic, he made demands on me that turned me into less of a man. I fought his battles, kissed his ass, pretty much did as I was told. I got him women, I got him men. They were all paid mightily, and I handled those transactions, too." Bering paused to collect himself. "The fire, my injuries, the pain... I thought it was God getting back at me for the way I lived my life, y'know? The alcohol, the drugs, the men, the sex... it was my punishment, and I deserved it. I often thought that dying in my hospital bed would be the best thing for everyone. I try to accept my life as it is today—life on life's terms as we say in AA." He rubbed his eyes and moaned, wincing in pain. "I hurt so many people. Shit, I hurt you as much as anyone when I lied to you that night about Miranda..."

Drew tried not to stare. He couldn't face Bering without seeing that grotesque mask pulling and stretching the features of a man who used to be quite handsome. This was far from the conversation he expected to be having at West Marine that day. There was always talk that Bering was bisexual or gay, and of course, everyone knew about Manos. Even with the lovely and talented Hanna, Dominic's faithful beard by his side, there were always rumors. A boat name like *Neptune's Hammer* should have been a dead giveaway. Bering continued.

"I'm sorry, man. I can never make it up to you, I get that, but I am really sorry. I don't expect you to forgive me. Heck, if our positions were reversed and you robbed me of a relationship that really mattered, we'd be having a fist fight instead of a conversation. But I'm gonna ask it anyway. Please forgive me, Drew Becker. If there's a way I can make amends for what I did, for the lie I told you that night, I hope that you'll tell me now." Bering spoke in a whisper. His hand was trembling and he lowered it to his lap to hide this show of emotion.

Something wasn't clear. Drew remembered that night well. He had played that scene over and over in his head to keep his hate for Daniel Bering fresh and steady. Let's face it— learning that Miranda had been sleeping with Jim Tiller the whole time they were together was a knife in his heart. He would never forgive Bering for that. Drew recognized that he played the game... never told Miranda that he loved her... that he wanted to be with her and only her... maybe even forever! Even though he would never forgive her, *(possibly a lie, only time would tell),* he was curious about something Bering said. Drew chose his words carefully. "You said you lied about something, something that had to do with Miranda... but I'm not sure what you're talking about."

"I'm talking about her and Tiller!" Bering was staring right at him now, his eyes bulging through the deep crevasses of their sockets. She wasn't sleeping with Jim

Tiller! That never happened. I just said it that night... said it to convince you to stay away from her. That's what Dominic sent me to do, and I made it up. I'm telling you the truth. I made it up, and she went off and married Dominic. I'm sure her life has been hard. That's all I can say about that now. But between me and you, Drew, I'm sorry for what I did and I apologize." Bering was coming apart, quietly blowing his nose into a handkerchief. Drew had a lot to think about. "Please go now, Drew Becker. Please go!" Drew paid for the dock boxes and left without saying a word.

"One of society's most difficult decisions is whether to extend forgiveness to someone who has committed a crime or made a serious mistake. In every case it is necessary to assess the offense, extenuating circumstances, evidence of reform or restitution, and the willingness of victims to forego continuing punishment of the guilty." From *Time to Forgive Pete Rose,* a book by Jimmy Carter.

The willingness of victims to forego continuing punishment of the guilty. Hmph. Drew didn't even know Carter was a baseball fan. In the spirit of his favorite President, Drew recognized that Bering is truly a changed man and decides to forgive him. He would finally stop punishing Daniel Bering, and stop punishing himself.

Drew Becker leaves West Marine with three Model #11952116 dock boxes with stainless steel lockable

303

latches and built-in storage for fishing rods and tac. Drew's intent, however, is not recreational. From the parking lot he places a call to Neil Lipman and offers to pay him $10,000 in cash to transport three dock boxes full of "important papers" to the Jimmy Carter Library, 441 John Lewis Parkway Northeast in Atlanta. He will state that the contents are a gift from an anonymous donor, to be given to Carter's beloved work project, Habitat for Humanity. Also, that the keys were lost in transit, so feel free to cut the locks off. Joe Ramono was so preoccupied thinking about Lexi that he didn't even realize Lipman was absent from the office that day.

Shoes for an Imaginary Life

Saving Miranda

Part two of the interview with the prostitutes started right on schedule. When the announcer came on and introduced everyone, it became clear that this was Christian radio, and right away Miranda worried that some angry church people would jump out of her car stereo, shout insults, and condemn her. She wondered if they would ask for money at the end of the program, demand she confess a lifetime of sin, or maybe even tell her how to vote. There was always an agenda with these people.

The thought of advancing from Lucille's short prayer to a bunch of hyper-religious hoopla was not appealing, regardless of how things turned out for these girls. Church people scared her with all their finger pointing and demands. There were so many "religions," and each one was more correct than the last, or so they claimed with the conviction of a politician serving his own agenda. Miranda considered the pastors of her youth who turned out to be hypocrites, swindlers, and chronic breakers of the Ten Commandments. That was all the church she needed to know that religion was not for her.

What about the famous television preacher whose wife wore all that make up? Didn't he have an affair, or several? Worse yet, was the former president of the National Association of Evangelicals who admitted to paying male prostitutes for sex, while condemning homosexuality from the pulpit. He represented more than 45,000 congregations nationwide, sending the confusing message, *do as I say, not as I do*. And who was the guy who stole all that money? Tune into any late-night cable channel to see "God's financial deliverers" boasting about their special anointing for understanding stocks, bonds, and Wall Street. He made a plea, insisting that their seed money would come back to them multiplied and with fast results. His target audience was believers who lacked financial literacy and were desperate to heal their financial woes. While the preacher made millions on the donations, many of his victims lost everything. What does God say about that? Though not an expert by any means, and from her limited experience, Miranda knew that God was not a con artist or a hypocrite. It wasn't in his nature.

The girls finished their conversation, telling the interviewer how happy they were with Jesus in their lives today, and describing a peace they had never known. They had been beaten up, threatened, cussed out, and raped. Though faith had not escalated them to the ranks of rich televangelists, their message was pulling at Miranda's heart. Whatever happened to them, and however they came to know God, it was really real, like the night in the driveway when she prayed the short prayer. These women were not hypocrites; they had nothing to gain by sharing their stories. How could Miranda be so certain? Somehow, she just knew.

Were there others who knew about this? That God was kind and approachable? Just from what she had learned from the short prayer, she had an odd sense that God liked her. Determined to find out, Miranda listened to the radio wherever she went, and even found excuses to try some new places just to spend time in her car. She found herself eating lunch on her lap because she didn't want to miss anything. One day she heard something so important she needed to write it down. It was from the Book of Hebrews and seemed like it was directed right at her!

Those who love money will never have enough. How meaningless to think that wealth brings true happiness!
Ecclesiates 5:10

It had been so long since Miranda was free of fear, she could not imagine how God could possibly do that, even if he wanted to. And there it was again… that same verse later that day. The announcer called it the Moody Bible Verse of the Week. Still driving, she rummaged through her purse. There were six lipsticks, a shimmer gloss from Sephora, and no pen. Keeping her eyes on the road, she felt around the center console and found something to write with. At A1A and 6th Street she pulled off and scribbled down the words on a yellow paper napkin from Wendy's, not even aware she was parked in front of Zara and bypassing some very cute things. Miranda didn't intend to make this a habit— she had her life to live, after all— but the verse on the radio really spoke to her.

A man named Dr. D. James Kennedy was next in the program line-up. He began his show by asking listeners to think about their sin life. *Oh boy, here we go.* The lesson was about forgiveness. It sounded good in theory, like a lot of things, but Miranda didn't see a practical application. It wasn't she who was doing the sinning... it was Dominic! When Dr. Kennedy prayed at the end of the show, it didn't sound like her simple prayer at all, but made her curious. Was she making this all too complicated? Maybe she would talk to God about forgiveness, or maybe not. Miranda was out of her comfort zone but couldn't figure out why.

She wrote down more verses, frantic to capture the best ones for her collection. There were so many programs, so many topics and speakers on Christian radio, that she could barely keep up! She was writing down verses on yellow paper napkins at traffic lights and on the Florida turnpike, which is treacherous even when you're watching the road. She listened to a likeable, straight-forward woman named Joyce Meyer, who was as funny as she was wise. Hard to believe that stories about a red dress and chickens at the grocery store could have Biblical impact, but somehow she made it work.

If you say, "The LORD is my refuge,"
  and you make the Most High your dwelling,

no harm will overtake you,
  no disaster will come near your tent.
For he will command his angels concerning you
  to guard you in all your ways;
they will lift you up in their hands,
  so that you will not strike your foot against a stone.
You will tread on the lion and the cobra;
  you will trample the great lion and the serpent.

Psalm 91:9-13

Miranda scribbled this down at a drive-thru window while the cars behind her honked. Though Joyce didn't know Dominic or how horrible he was, she apparently had been through some things in her own life, and found meaning in these words. She drove with her knees to write down some powerful words from Erwin Lutzer, and made a note to order Charles Stanley's series, Advancing through Adversity. Adversity was a topic she knew all too well, but how to Advance and survive the nights with her husband was a mystery. She had seen many of these verses in her little white Bible over the years, but for some reason they all seemed new and alive. She lost interest in Dominic and his hateful words. Even though she was his wife, she could choose a life of peace and joy in spite of him. Miranda kept driving, talking to God, and listening to the radio. The yellow napkins in her car were piling up.

Through Al-anon, she was learning to keep the focus on herself, and not on the alcoholic. One way to do that was by going to the Thursday morning meeting on Key Biscayne, another was to leave the house at dinner time and bring home carry out. Dominic was always hungry when he drank. It was no coincidence that Miranda arranged to pick up carry-out at the same time Tony Evans was on the radio. He was a wise and ferocious man, with a booming voice preaching hellfire and brimstone. He also had a warm, riotous sense of humor that made him strangely endearing. On a night she ordered sushi from Wabi Sabi, Miranda spent ten minutes listening on the way to the restaurant, ten minutes listening on the way home, and ten minutes parked in the driveway, fully focused on the message. She was starving. She snuck a few bites of spicy eel roll out of the bag, trying hard to keep the sticky sauce off her fingers.

She listened intently as she searched for a yellow napkin with no writing on it, but there were none. The Prayer of Salvation was something she had heard many times before, but this time there was an urgency to pay closer attention. There was no denying it anymore. Her selfishness, her drinking, her bad decision to marry Dominic, and all of her millions of sins that led up to this moment were ruining her life. She was sick of all the years she spent lying to cover her tracks, the whole time hating the girl she was covering for. She was a sinner— of course she was! Why had it been so hard to put words to that simple truth? She hurt people and she did it with ease, as if sin were the most natural thing in the world. Miranda didn't know how it got to be so bad, but it did.

Her cheeks burned with shame and for once, she was truly sorry.

Unlike the day Miranda first tuned in to hear the hookers, she no longer rolled her eyes at the radio when she didn't like the message. If she felt convicted, it was time to meet that feeling head on, not run away from it. Tony Evans was winding up for his big finish. He was shouting at the congregation and the folks in the church pews were shouting back at him.

"Being religious doesn't earn you an acceptable status with a holy God... you know that, right?" he began.

"Mm hmmm," said the people in agreement. These were the folks that were about to become Miranda's brothers and sisters.

"No one is good enough to meet God's standard."

"Amen," they called out.

Tony Evans shouted the prayer, the one that really mattered. And Miranda shouted it back at him.

"God I'm a sinner."

"God I'm a sinner...."

"I can't save myself, but I believe Jesus Christ died to save me. And I now place my eternal destiny into your hands."

"I can't save myself..." *Oh my gosh, why am I crying?* Miranda was distracted, but why? For all the years she was married to Dominic she had shouldered the burden of his hate all alone but rarely shed a tear. The police lost interest long ago so there was no point in calling them for help. The women of Thursday Morning Al-Anon believed her, but she was too ashamed to call anyone.

Tony Evans repeated, "I can't save myself, but I believe Jesus Christ died to save me."

Miranda took a deep breath, dried her tears, and rejoined the conversation. "I can't save myself, but I believe Jesus died to save me."

"And now I place my eternal destiny in your hands."

"I do… I really do! I place my eternal destiny in your hands."

Evans concluded, "Thank you for the free gift of salvation that you promised to give me if I came to you for it."

Miranda cleared her throat and finish the prayer. And that was it. Amen.

There were no angels singing, no trumpet fanfares. It was a quiet night; a decision had been made. It wasn't a burden, but a relief. Miranda would be doing it His way from now on, or at least she would pray about it and try. She gathered up a handful of napkins… some suitable late-night reading for when Dominic went to bed. She grabbed the sushi, closed the garage door, and went inside. She couldn't wait to tell someone about what she had just done.

Linda Lewis

Maris

Like the girl in the painting, Maris was the pretty one. She placed a donut and a cup of coffee on the table across from Miranda and took a seat. She smiled good morning and set her bag on the table— a Louis Vuitton Denim Neo Speedy, new this season, very rare, made only in Japan in limited quantities. It was even more scarce than the Long Hair Goat Trans-Siberian! The zipper for the side compartment was trimmed in red patent leather with a double row of flawless top stitching, and the solid brass hardware was so chunky and overstated it was practically obscene! The price? Miranda had no idea; there were none to be had! Somewhere in her dressing room there was a Louis Vuitton Vernis Shoulder Bag, Conte De Fees Pochette crafted with a disturbing image of an owl's head. It was a Japanese LV she picked up at a consignment shop in Palm Beach... equally rare, but nothing compared to the treasure before her.

"Hey," said Miranda.

"Hey," said Maris.

Miranda was so distracted by the presence of the elusive Louis, she missed the delicate gold cross around Maris's neck. The Thursday morning meeting was crowded. There were still people standing in line to get coffee when Lucille rang the little bell and began reading The Welcome. After the formalities were complete, the ladies began to share.

"Hi everyone, my name is Maris, and I'm a grateful recovering member of Al-Anon."

"Hi Maris," said the ladies.

Maris explained that she and her husband had just arrived at their home on Key Biscayne from their penthouse in Manhattan, after checking on the home they're building in Colorado. The chaos was maddening, she explained, and was causing her husband to drink more to relieve the stress. She went on to thank her Higher Power, whom she chose to call Jesus, for the many blessings in her life. She had her diamond ring turned upside down as a courtesy to the women whose diamonds were less than three carats. Miranda had started to question whether a big diamond was a blessing or a curse.

"I'm embarrassed to even admit this," Maris continued, "but when my husband gets drunk, he gets angry, and sometimes he's violent." Miranda wondered if Maris was hiding bruises under her sheer yellow blouse, a blue scarf draped over one shoulder. "He hits me, then he's sorry. He buys me something nice, and I accept his apology. He promises it will never happen again, and I believe him. Things are peaceful for a while, and then it starts all over. I've lived like this for ten years and I hate it. And yet here I am, sharing my story and doing nothing about it."

The lady beside Maris gave her a gentle Al-Anon hug and the room said, "Keep coming back."

Maris deserved more. Miranda deserved more!! There had to be better men out there... men like Drew Becker who would never mistreat a woman the way Dominic had mistreated her! As the sharing continued around the room, Miranda wondered what Drew was doing right now...

Linda Lewis

Drew's Habitat

Drew Becker adjusted his new green ballcap and shouted, "Good morning everyone, and welcome to Habitat for Humanity! Anyone here ever built a house before?"

Among the teenagers from the Alanson High School Marching Band, some had used hand tools before; many had not. No one had built a house or even a shed. He promised this would be an excellent adventure. Drew learned from his grandfather that it was good practice to learn the basics of carpentry before moving onto the more refined skills. That all began with a screwdriver, hammer, and tape measure. Lessons for using a table saw and miter box would be reserved only for the students who proved they were capable. For now, they were only interested in clowning around, flirting, and cracking jokes. After a week of training with Drew, the new Lead Carpenter for the Habitat for Humanity house on Valley Drive, they would be proud junior craftsmen, just like he was at their age.

When the crew quit at 4:00, Drew was tired and sore. He had to laugh at himself. Winters were always hard on the bones, but every year he felt it a little more. Maybe it was arthritis, or maybe he was just out of shape. Either way, working on the house would help. It wasn't just the physical boost he needed. There was a sense of community among the volunteers that he really enjoyed, all in the spirit of a common goal for a worthy cause. It was the closest thing to a family he had known.

Drew hadn't been to any of the antique stores in town since he and Miranda bought the chairs for her red dining room. How many years had it been? He never drove past her old house in Petoskey. It was more haunted than a graveyard, and more depressing. After he and the students swept up and put away their tools, Drew headed down Route 33 into town, and on a whim he pulled off at the Alanson Antique Mall and Auction House. Maybe he'd find a nice baseball card or antique tool for his collection. Among the old photographs and framed advertisements for vintage boats, there was a piece that didn't belong. Miranda's prized Tarkay was dusty and the frame was cracked, but otherwise the ladies were in good condition. "Ha!" he exclaimed loud enough for the owner to hear.

"A hundred dollars seems like a lot. It's not really in very good shape. Would you take $85?"

"It's been here a long time… kind of an oddball piece if you ask me," said the man.

"It really is," Drew nodded.

"I can do $85," said the man.

His memory caried him back to the house in Petoskey... watching Hitchcock movies and eating Oreos with Miranda in his arms, getting crumbs on his shirt and kissing her neck, while the ladies in the painting looked on in approval. Drew always suspected Miranda was the pretty one. Heading south on 33, he drove through Petoskey, stopped in front of her old house, and felt the sting of loss all over again.

Linda Lewis

Lovely Pave

"Something terrible is going on." It was Lucille's turn to share and she was noticeably distraught. Even the little flowers and swirls on her nametag looked out of sorts.

"My aunt passed away in a nursing home and now the FBI is involved. What this has to do with me I have no idea."

The ladies raised an eyebrow in unison, shocked by the news.

"A man came to my house and told me. He looked like someone from CSI Miami... had a badge and everything."

"What about her family?" asked Estelle, breaking the sacred rule of no cross talk during meetings, although everyone was curious and didn't care.

"She has only one son, my cousin Charlie Fine. But I haven't seen him since we were kids at the Feast of Rosalia in Bensonhurst."

"What do they want you to do?"

"They want me to answer some questions. I fly out of Fort Lauderdale on Tuesday. That's all I know."

"Az s shreklekh," said Estelle.

"Keep coming back," said the room.

Oh my God, thought Miranda, *that has to be Aunt Elena!* But she was so lost in the amazing craftsmanship of the Louis Vuitton Vernis Shoulder Bag, Conte De Fees Pochette that she missed an important detail. Lucille never did tell her what happened after Elena and Peter got married and took the train to Detroit, and today would not be a good time to ask.

Miranda was familiar with The Al-Anon Statement of Purpose that says, *The group conscience requests that all present refrain from gossip, dominance, and discussion of religion.* Even so, when it was her turn to share, she told the story about Lucille's short prayer, the one she said in the driveway that night right before she expected Dominic to kill her. Lucille shot her a half smile, and winked. And even though he was still abusive, he had calmed down a lot since she started going to meetings, working the Steps, and putting the focus on herself. Taking her husband's inventory night after night never improved the situation and only made her bitter. Miranda shared about her adventure with Tony Evans— the radio show, the sushi, and the prayer! Several of the women at the meeting were Jewish; many were Christians, like Maris. She wondered which rules she had broken and who she might have offended. But when Miranda finished speaking, all the ladies clapped. She looked across the table at Maris, who had a tear in her eye. She was no stranger to Miranda's trials and Miranda's joy. Maris whispered, "Do you wanna have lunch?"

They went to a swanky restaurant on the island where they would have some privacy. Deeny's would be packed, and Miranda really wanted to hear this woman's story. The conversation was as pleasant as the day; two girlfriends sharing their experience, strength, and hope. Maris's husband was a lot like Dominic—wealthy, older, with a really bad temper. He blamed her for everything that went wrong in their privileged lives, and Miranda said it was the story of her life, too.

"So did he buy you that Trefoil Disco Ball," Maris asked, gesturing at Miranda's necklace. "It's nice, by the way... love the pave." Apparently Maris knew her David Yurman.

"NOBODY *does pave like Yurman,"* stated Miranda in her best snooty voice.

Maris met her tone. "I see you've met Claire at Saks Fifth Avenue. My husband uses her, too. She's complicit, you know, with all her *lovely pave.* What about the other pieces?"

"The disco ball, the Confetti Ice ring, and the matching bracelet... all delivered right on schedule after our last big fight." Suddenly all her treasures were reduced to foolishness when she considered the sacrifices she made to get them.

"What about the bag? The Neo Speedy from Japan," questioned Miranda.

"Good eye," Maris grinned. "He bought me one in Fuchsia, too, when we were in Tokyo. They nearly laughed till they cried.

"Carry each other's burdens, and in this way you will fulfill the law of Christ." Galatians 6:2

For the first time, as far back as she could remember, Miranda wasn't alone. Maris finished her sumptuous crab cake salad and apologized for having to run off. She had reports to turn in at the hospice center where she volunteered, and new assignments to pick up. Maris invited Miranda to come along. "You would bring joy to so many people. And the patients would be a real blessing to you." It was the craziest idea Miranda had ever heard—crazier than living aboard an old boat, crazier than working for Tiller, and crazier than staging that big kiss on the dock with a boat repairman she didn't know. Maybe that wasn't crazy after all.

Whether it was Maris's beauty, the cross, or the handbag resting properly in the crook, she knew from listening to the radio that God sometimes speaks to his children through others who know him. This was all too farfetched to be an accident. Though it seemed unlikely that Miranda would take an interest in caring for someone other than herself, she smiled and said yes.

Shoes for an Imaginary Life

Karla

Karla was reading the morning paper when Miranda arrived at the nursing home. It was her first Hospice visit since she completed her training. Karla appeared much younger than her 89 years, and didn't even look sick. Before Miranda could begin her cheery repartee of encouragement and small talk, Karla had a specific request. She needed to tell someone her story. Whatever it was that was so urgent, Miranda was honored to be her confidante and compassionate listener. The distress in her voice was palpable. Miranda prayed for grace and wisdom; that she could be a source of comfort whatever Karla had to say.

"Bear one another's burdens, and so fulfill the law of Christ." Galations 6:2

They sat in badly stained armchairs facing a window that overlooked a garden. "I have felt guilty every day my entire life." She spoke with an accent. "I grew up in Germany during the war. I had one brother, one sister, both older...we were Jews. We heard about the camps and knew it was only a matter of time before we were taken. My brother knew a lot of people and used his connections to get us papers that would allow us to leave the country. My parents, my brother and his wife and their child, my sister, my fiancé, and me. We started packing right away, just a few things we would need to travel. We held onto hope."

"I said, Mutti, Mutti, why aren't you packing? In one day we have to leave and you need to be ready." She said she and my father were not coming with us. Their life was in Germany. They were too old to start over in a new place. Everything would be okay, they would stay safe. I said, "No Mutti, no, no!!" and opened the suitcase on her bed. I packed only what she would need so the suitcase would be light, while she sat in the corner and wept. And I knew we would be leaving without her." I asked again, and again. "Mutti, we need you to come with us because we are a family. We must stay together. We have the papers, see?!" I showed her the document. "See? Your name is right here!" I was yelling at my mother, demanding that she use good sense and prepare to leave in the morning. "If you don't leave now there will not be time. You will not get another chance, and the Nazis will take you and you will die!"

"It will be okay," she persisted.

"It will *not* be okay! Please, Mutti... please!"

"We left in the morning but my parents stayed behind. It was the worst moment of my life, all of us driving off while they stood there. The other worst day was when I learned they had been taken. Because of their age, I knew they were shown the way to death as soon as they arrived. They were of no use... not young, not able-bodied. I've thought of this every day, the angry conversation, boarding the boat without them, news of their passing. Once we were in America my fiancé and I were married. We never talked about our lives in Germany. But those times never left me... how it was my fault my parents stayed, that I couldn't convince them, that the Nazis took them just like I said. For my whole life I have had no peace because peace is not what I deserve. I have never told this to anyone, not another living soul."

"If our hearts condemn us, we know that God is greater than our hearts, and he knows everything." 1 John 3:20

She spoke with urgency, but without shedding a tear. It was more like a proclamation than a memory. Miranda said she was so sorry, that it must have been very hard to live under the weight of that burden all these years. She asked God to give this woman peace, to take her guilt and lay it before the cross where it could not torment her anymore. An aid tapped Karla's shoulder and said it was time for lunch. Miranda promised she would come back the next day, gave her a hug, and watched her walk away.

The next day a nurse told Miranda she was gone... not taking a walk or having breakfast in the dining room. She was really gone. Karla died in her sleep that night. The nurse said her passing was peaceful.

Shoes for an Imaginary Life

Linda Lewis

Francis Speck

Miranda was purposeful with her words, careful to never call any of Dominic's houses her home. She had faith that she wouldn't always be his prisoner, whether on this earth or in heaven. There would be a life without flashing blue lights, and a kitchen full of knives she would never count again. When Miranda studied her Bible, she didn't see an angry God who was watching, waiting, and ready to drop the hammer. She only saw a reminder that she was loved and forgiven. Loved and forgiven.

"For I know the plans I have for you," declares the Lord, "plans to prosper you and not to harm you, plans to give you hope and a future." Jeremiah 29:11

She was heading out Route 27 to visit a lady in Haileigha Springs, a 94 year old retired school librarian named Francis Speck. She had a terminal diagnosis and a Do Not Resuscitate order, and was spending her final days in a decrepit old nursing home. The paperwork from the hospice home office stated she was violent, non-communicative, and having hallucinations. It also said she was tearing off her diaper and throwing feces all over her room. Full PPE was advised. The mattress was on the floor for fear she would fall or throw herself out of bed in an attempt to end her life. The drapes were drawn, it was hot in her room, and the smell was horrendous.

Like many of the widows in south Florida, she was rich, useless, and abandoned by her family, who waited patiently on the sidelines for the will to be read. Miranda knocked on the door, introduced herself, and crouched down on the floor beside her. She made a mental note to leave her good handbag at home next time. The souls of the dying people she ministered to in their final days were the treasure she carried with her now, not just during her visits, but in her heart and in her prayers. The time she spent with her husband was also impacted by this part of life she had never seen before.

"You don't have to talk if you don't want to," Miranda said calmly to Francis, who made an angry face and screamed. "If it's okay, I'd just like to stay here with you awhile and pray... quietly to myself, you don't have to do anything. Would that be okay? Just a few minutes?" The woman studied her through crinkled skin and squinting eyes. She didn't have her teeth in, and since she was refusing food, it didn't really matter.

Miranda visited the nursing home again. By the third day the room was in much better order. Francis had on fresh briefs and a clean nightgown.

"This is a horrible place. Why are you here?" Francis asked, as she gurgled to spit out the words.

Miranda had warmth in her smile and peace in her heart. "I found out no one was here to help you and it made me so sad. I thought you could use a friend."

"Yeah, well after what I've been through, having a friend is not going to make any difference."

"It sounds like you've been through a lot." Miranda needed to find a way to reach this woman.

"Why are you really here? No one can even stand to be around me, not after the terrible things I've done."

Miranda had asked God to give Francis peace before she died. "I've done some terrible things, too," Miranda whispered. Sometimes I thought the shame and guilt were going to kill me."

"Hmph," the old woman mumbled indignantly. "You're young and beautiful. You have no idea what goes on in this life."

"I was a drunk. I cheated on my husbands." Miranda wondered why on earth she was saying all this. "I've been married three times. I hurt a lot of people and didn't really care until I couldn't stand myself anymore. Thank God I found God and he forgave me."

Francis Speck almost chuckled at how silly that sounded, but something about the comment reached her.

The voice was barely audible. Miranda leaned in close to the woman's face so she could hear. They were side by side; the woman on her mattress, Miranda on the floor beside her.

"I did a very bad thing," she began. "I was young once. I went to church, I was a daughter, a friend. And then there was a baby." There was a long pause. Miranda stayed present, allowing the woman to process whatever it was that was hurting so much. There was pain in the silence.

"There was a baby," she hissed, eyes wide open as if wanting to be understood. "I was so young. My parents would have sent me away. It was a different time then." Miranda thought about her baby, the one she never had with Harry...

Miranda closed her eyes and silently spoke the words from the Lord's Prayer... *Thy will be done.* It wasn't a cop out, but a simple acknowledgement that whatever happened next was between Francis and God. *Thy will be done.*

"I killed my baby!" She was looking into a far-off place, reliving something terrible. She began coughing, and crying, spitting up liquid. Miranda was afraid she would choke on her own vomit. The woman reached for Miranda's hand and squeezed hard. "Call for a priest... please!" Miranda squeezed her hand in return, and assured the woman that she would. A nurse came in, then another. They attended to Francis while Miranda made arrangements with the hospice priest to come right away.

Miranda got a call the next morning. Dominic was outraged that the phone rang before 10:00am, but so what? *Civilized people know better,* he used to say. Miranda found herself less interested in Dominic's childish tantrums and more concerned with the calling she'd been given. It was her supervisor. Francis Speck had died peacefully, surrounded by the priest, and a daughter she hadn't seen in years. That was all the information she could give. It was the best and most wonderful news Miranda could hope for.

"Not only that, but we rejoice in our sufferings, knowing that suffering produces endurance, and endurance produces character, and character produces hope." Romans 5:3-4

There were nights when Dominic came after her that she would just stop right in front of him and pray. Sometimes it was the Lord's Prayer, sometimes the Serenity Prayer that they say in Al-anon. One time she stood at the kitchen counter slicing vegetables for his salad. He picked up the santuko knife; she turned to face him. Drunk and red faced, he raised the knife above his head. He was smiling; an angry, wide eyed grin. Miranda was studying her Bible well enough to know that if God wanted her to survive and continue her work with the sick and the dying, he would protect her. The days of screaming, and running, and shoving furniture in front of doors were over! She had no use for his threats, and took orders from only one man, and it wasn't him.

With Dominic's hot drunken breath on her face and the knife poised to strike, Miranda stood perfectly still, eyes averted. Not even aware that she knew the 23rd

Psalm by heart, she recited the parts she could remember.

"The Lord is my shepherd; I shall not want... yea, though I walk through the valley of the shadow of death, I will fear no evil: for thou art with me: thy rod and thy staff they comfort me." Psalm 23:1,4

Dominic dropped the knife on the floor and ran screaming to his bedroom. He slammed the door and shrieked at the top of his lungs while Miranda finished making the salad. He was afraid of her every day after that, as though she had some kind of power over him that he couldn't understand. And of course, she did. Though he remained angry and vile, he never touched her again. Thank God.

Shoes for an Imaginary Life

Sophie Schoenberg

So many lives were coming to a close. Miranda spent her final weeks in Miami with a dozen patients. Sophie would be her last assignment. "So. You're Miranda-the-hospice-volunteer, and you're here to see Sophie." The nurse looked at her coworker and grinned. "She's in room 116 and she's all yours." They laughed as Miranda walked away and headed down the long hallway. In spite of their ridicule, she knew God was with her that day, and nothing scared her. Miranda knocked on the door and a deep, raspy voice answered.

"Unless you've come to fix my hearing aids, you can get the fuck out of here!"

Seriously? What the heck? Miranda prayed, "God help me."

Sophie was 105 years old. She had survived nearly every type of cancer, and in spite of that, spent most of her days on the patio smoking. Her room was littered with plates of half-eaten food, human waste, and the stench of time. It appeared she hadn't had any personal care in weeks. Miranda prayed for courage and patience. She was going to need it.

"Well hello there, Sophie! My name is Miranda," she said in a cheery tone. "I'm a hospice volunteer and..."

"What part of get the fuck out of here don't you understand?!"

"It was really nice meeting you, Sophie," Miranda said trembling. "I'm going to make sure your hearing aids get fixed, then I'll be back to see you again. Is that alright?"

Sophie snorted, pointed at the door, and shouted, "GET OUT!!" Her anger ran deeper than what she let on. Maybe Miranda could help this woman find her way to a place of comfort, whatever her despair.

"The Spirit of the Lord is upon me, because he has anointed me to proclaim good news to the poor. He has sent me to proclaim liberty to the captives and recovering of sight to the blind, to set at liberty those who are oppressed." Luke 4:18

On her way out the door, Miranda thanked the girls at the nurse's station for their help and wished them a nice day. She was now Sophie's advocate. The nurses knew she would be watching.

She stopped by the next day to drop off some donuts with a note that said, "Thanks for all you do." The following day she popped in again and spotted Sophie on the patio, dressed in clean clothes with her silver paige boy neatly combed. The third day, she brought in a big box of assorted chocolates and thanked the nurses for all their hard work. She peeked inside Sophie's room. It was cleaner, almost tidy, and smelled better than before. "COME!!" shouted the raspy voice, as she motioned with her finger to move closer. Sophie had spotted Miranda dilly-dallying outside the door.

"You're not afraid of me, are you..."

"You look nice, Sophie. How are you today?"

"I'm dying. Didn't they tell you that? However, I am much better now that I've had a bath and I can hear you. Damn hearing aids. Thank you for taking care of that."

"You're welcome."

Born in 1901, Sophie had been a spirited flapper girl, a Manhattan socialite, and the wife of a New York Yankees shortstop. She was the author of children's books, a designer of high fashion apparel, and sadly, the mother of only one son, Orson, who was 80 years old and suffering from Alzheimer's Disease. His photo was on her nightstand; he didn't know his mother. After a life filled with so much sparkle and fizz, she was dying alone— no wonder she was angry. It was raining when Miranda arrived for her next visit. Sophie had grown pale and weak. She complained that she hadn't had a smoke all day and asked for a cigarette. Miranda suggested she should rest, then squeezed her hand and kissed her cheek.

Miranda was already in her pajamas watching TV in the living room when she got the call. Sophie was actively dying and was asking for her. Miranda got dressed and drove out I-95. It was a 15 minute ride to the care center. She prayed the whole way, *God help me, God help me, God help me.* What was she supposed to do? There was nothing in her training about this. *Certainly, there would be doctors and nurses there who knew what to do, right?* She was a good hand holder and listener, but that was about it. She had never seen anyone die. *Was this going to be horrible?!* Miranda ran through the empty lobby, knocked over a potted plant, and spotted an old man and his caregiver seated on a bench. It was Orson.

"You are for Sophie yes?" A girl in a uniform was alone at the nurse's station. She was very young and hardly spoke English. "For her doctor yes?"

Miranda ran down the hallway and realized she was still wearing her slippers. Crap. She was out of breath by the time she reached Sophie, who was curled up in a fetal position, crying, and begging for someone to help her. "Please, oh please, God help me. Just let me die…"

"Sophie, it's me. I'm here." Miranda was choking back tears. It was time for Lucille's famous prayer again, "God help me, and please, please help my friend!"

The girl from the desk appeared in the doorway.

Miranda grabbed a pen and a clean diaper from the nightstand to write on. She printed the words, *Duragesic Patch* then drew a picture of what the package would look like. "I need one of these, quickly please!" Miranda knew that Sophie had been getting transdermal Fentanyl for the past week, but tonight there was only a red mark on her back where the patch had been. There she was, asking God for help one minute, and prescribing narcotics the next. She was breaking the law (maybe more than one), but her heart was in the right place.

Would that make a difference if she got caught? Is there a loophole for good intentions?

The girl in the uniform came rushing in with the small, precious package. Miranda put on gloves and applied the patch to Sophie's back the way she had watched nurses do. Gradually, the medication eased Sophie's pain, and her frown and grimace were all but gone. Miranda kept a cool compress on her forehead, and used a special sponge to keep her mouth comfortable and moist. The verse from Proverbs might have been a stretch, but getting her friend the medication was far more expedient than waiting all night for a doctor to never show up.

"Do not withhold good from those to whom it is due, when it is in your power to act." Proverbs 3:27

"Sophie. You know I would never lie to you, right? Her eyelids fluttered and she looked up. "Sophie, listen to me. This is important. Everything the Bible says about Jesus is true. All the stories, and the miracles, the cross and the resurrection... it all really happened, and God did it all for you." Before Miranda could come up with the words to finish the prayer, Sophie opened her eyes! She was staring at the doorway, looking at something Miranda couldn't see. She extended her arms and leaned forward in bed. With a final surge of energy, she called out a word— "Hemis! Hemis!" Her voice was clear and her face was radiant. It was the happiest Miranda had seen her in there time together.

Sophie passed away while Miranda slept in a chair beside her bed. That afternoon, a call came from the facility's social worker to get an update and complete some forms. Before she hung up, Miranda mentioned Sophie's last words.

"It was something like Hemis, Hemis."

The woman was quiet, then finally said, "*Hamish*. Hamish was Orson's younger brother. He died of scarlet fever when he was a baby. Did Sophie ever talk to you about him?"

She didn't have to... he was with her that night.

Linda Lewis

The Little Church

Miranda couldn't recall how she found the church in Hollywood, Florida. It was in an old part of town, surrounded by decaying strip malls, a liquor store, and kids hanging out on the sidewalk when they should have been in school. Police cars were parked in front of the Subway sandwich shop on the corner, waiting for their next call. Sometimes when she was driving and writing down verses she lost track of time and misplaced her sense of direction. Otherwise, she had no idea how she got there. The church was on a dead-end street, with weeds growing up through the cracks in the parking lot. The white stucco building was in desperate need of repair, its Spanish style archways crumbling. The sign said, "Sunday Service 11:00 am," and she decided to go.

Miranda always pictured God in a giant, gilded cathedral, with beautiful rich people in suits gathered around talking about where they would winter next year and what was happening in the stock market. An acclaimed organist would be performing Buxtehude: Prelude in G minor with a level of skill and perfection worthy only of the Creator. The pews would have plush tufted cushions crafted of fine velvet, and stained-glass windows would gleam around the perimeter. It was a place fit for a king.

Sunday morning at Calvary Chapel. Miranda stepped into a dreary space with boarded up windows where the stained glass used to be. The carpet was badly stained and thread bare, and cracks from floor to ceiling exposed the age of the old, decrepit building. The pews, however, were like sturdy oaks, firmly planted and able to withstand any storm, just like the people who sat in them. Miranda was greeted by two women in colorful dresses with matching hats. One reminded her of Janet from the unemployment office in Petoskey who got her the job with Tiller. She was warm and soft spoken with a cross statue on her desk. The other woman made her think of Mavis, the bartender at the country club in Providence she went to with Harry. Both Janet and Maris were God's faithful servants and always said they would pray for her. Miranda wondered why she hadn't found the little church sooner, then remembered something she wrote a yellow napkin from Wendy's.

"Trust in the Lord with all your heart and lean not on your own understanding; in all your ways submit to him, and he will make your paths straight." Proverbs 3:5-6

Shoes for an Imaginary Life

There was a sign-up sheet in the collection plate. Pastor Chris announced he would be baptizing people at the beach Easter morning, and anyone who wanted to participate should sign the paper and meet with him after the service. Miranda knew from her teachers on the radio that baptism wasn't a requirement to be a Christian, she wanted to make this commitment to herself and to God. Life a best friend who was always there for her, there was finally something she could do for Him.

Miranda was so excited, she didn't know what to do with herself in the days leading up to the event. She was grateful for Lucille and the Thursday morning meeting. She was grateful for the former prostitutes who got her hooked on Christian radio. Was it a coincidence that she heard their testimony that day? Did anything in God's world happen by accident? For all the years she carried around her little white Bible, reading now and then but never fully trusting, was this just finally her time? She accepted that this was God's plan for her along. It was the turning point.

Easter morning. Even at sunrise, it was hot on the beach. The unofficial "season" was over; she and Dominic were flying out in the morning. Dressed in flip-flops, a tee shirt, and swim trunks with a tropical theme, Pastor Chris addressed the congregation. There were sixty people gathered that day, a church family ready to celebrate. Ladies in lawn chairs made a row in the sand, some with colorful tote bags stuffed with beach towels. The younger crowd sat at the water's edge, close to the music. The worship team played acoustic guitars; a man played a single drum with his hands. The music continued as the pastor began his message about the commitment that Miranda and five others were about to undertake.

Pastor Chris talked about the Ethiopian eunuch in Acts Chapter 8, who met up with one of the early Christians named Philip on the road leading out of Jerusalem. He was an important figure in his land, riding in a chariot and reading from the book of Isaiah when Philip approached him. As Philip began to tell him about Jesus, the Ethiopian said, "Look, here is water. Why shouldn't I be baptized?" Miranda liked the eunuch's enthusiasm and marveled at how many years water baptisms had been going on. The church taught that infant baptism was a nice tradition and a way for the church to welcome a family's new baby. However, and she could only speak for herself, she knew that even though she was baptized as a baby, she still had a lot of living to do. It took a lifetime of adventure, deceit, and consequences to know she needed more.

The music got louder, the drummer was singing. As the sun began its ascent, Pastor Chris asked if there was anyone else (besides those who were already on the sign-up sheet), who wanted to be baptized that morning. A lifeguard who was stationed nearby climbed down from his chair. After hearing the pastor's message, he was openly weeping. He walked toward the group wearing only a red Speedo swimsuit, made even smaller with his big belly hanging over the edge. With conviction he replied, "I do."

After a brief exchange, the pastor, the lifeguard, and one of the church deacons walked down into the water, just like Philip and the eunuch. Pastor Chris talked to him about the seriousness of the commitment he was making, then baptized him in the name of the Father, and of the Son, and of the Holy Spirit. The lifeguard held his nose and they dunked him under. The crowd cheered, the beat of the drum played on. The man in the Speedo, our new brother in Christ, came out of the water met by enthusiastic applause, and a smiling lady in a lawn chair gave him a towel and a hug. It was what true beauty looked like.

Miranda stood alongside the five others at the water's edge, eager to take her turn. When she came out of the ocean, dripping wet in an oversized tee shirt (the official uniform of the day), the sun was brighter than ever and a lady with a beach towel waited. It was one of the women who greeted her, whose faith was bright as the day. Did it really matter, the public proclamation of faith via baptism in the old Biblical way? For some people, of course not. But for Miranda, it was important— an outward symbol of an inner change. She wondered if Dominic would notice the difference.

"Rather, it should be that of your inner self, the unfading beauty of a gentle and quiet spirit, which is of great worth in God's sight." 1 Peter 3:4

And so it was for Miranda and the man in the red Speedo on that glorious Easter day of baptism, resurrection, and beach towels. Miranda continued packing.

Return to Traverse City

Some journeys have a beginning and an end. Others are like waves on the sea—whether placid and bright, or blown and tossed by the wind. Miranda had been existing in a hellish purgatory, bouncing along with lies, and waiting for inertia (or something stronger) to shout, ENOUGH! Reality was no place for blue swirl marbles, $10,000 handbags, or skirts that twirled. To see strength and purpose in the journey ahead was a gift Miranda was ready to receive.

On the weeks long journey up the Intercostal Waterway, *Neptune's Hammer* would follow the shoreline on a 1500 mile ride to the St. Lawrence Seaway, and down the St. Lawrence River to Lake Ontario. The boat would go through the Welland Canal (hopefully without incident—it was a treacherous passage) then run the full distance across Lake Erie to the mouth of the Detroit River. They would cruise north past the city, past the old Ford River Rouge plant, motor across Lake St. Clair, and up the St. Clair River to the Blue Water Bridge. On to Lake Huron, the boat would travel all the way north to the Straights of Mackinaw, under the Mackinaw Bridge, around the Tip of the Mitt, and down past Little Traverse Bay. The captain and crew would round Charlevoix, where Miranda left a piece of her heart and often wondered if it would still be there waiting for her. The boat's arrival at Grand Traverse Bay and Mallard Point would end the journey. Dominic and Miranda would take the Learjet out of Fort Lauderdale and land at Cherry Capital Airport three hours later. When they arrived at the dock, *Neptune's Hammer* would be clean, waxed, and ready for their arrival.

Shoes for an Imaginary Life

Mallard Point

Year after year, much of Mallard Point Yacht Club stayed the same— the Pompom geraniums along the sidewalk, the calendar of events posted on the bulletin board by the main door, and the grand Sunday buffet. But many of the faces and boats had changed. There were new dock neighbors, new people on the barstools, and some unfamiliar families with small children playing by the pool. Miranda learned that the Howells retired from boating and moved to a tropic port in Honolulu. The Peuterschmidts won the lottery and bought a coastal mansion in Rhode Island. And Charlie Fine's notorious *Hook* was nowhere to be found. Miranda was grateful that she might have a chance at a fresh start. The club was under new management, there was a different chef, and all the former valet parking attendants had graduated from high school and moved on. No one seemed to notice that she was back. In fact, no one even remembered her! Could it be that her importance among the members was overrated? Were the tales of infamy simply a myth? Did she concoct all that drama in her own mind so she could feel special? And what about the pirates? There were no signs of their treachery anywhere. She wondered what Charlie Fine was really up to…

Linda Lewis

John Stark

First Lieutenant John Stark was a U.S. Army infantryman during World War II, and later, a police officer for the City of Detroit. Miranda signed up to volunteer with Hospice by the Bay and was assigned to provide respite care every Wednesday afternoon while his wife went into town to shop. John Stark's Parkinson's Disease had advanced to the point where tremors, a shuffling gait, and stooped posture were overtaking his frail body. Miranda knew he would soon be in a wheelchair and need more care than she was trained to give. John had peace about his condition and talked openly about his relationship with the Lord. In story after story he described how God protected him in the trenches when he was sure he would end up dead. In a way, Miranda could relate. As a volunteer, she wasn't permitted to administer medication, but at the appointed time she was allowed to place a small plastic cup containing his pills and a glass of water on the table beside him. She helped him to bed and gave him a hug goodbye, knowing he'd be asleep when his wife returned home.

One rainy Wednesday when John was sleeping, Miranda picked up his copy of the Charlevoix News Courier. The headline was about a Gala Opening at the new lighthouse museum in Leelanau. Apparently, an anonymous donor gave the local association $10M to develop a parcel out on the Peninsula. The article described the $5M structure, with the balance of the funds set aside to maintain the 124 lighthouses remaining in the state of Michigan. It was an astonishing donation. She couldn't imagine who in the little town of Charlevoix had that kind of money to spare! The museum's exhibit hall was touted by the Chamber of Commerce to be the area's biggest and most beautifully appointed space for travel and tourism expo's in the entire Up North region. The opening night party would showcase vintage boats of the Great Lakes.

When Miranda returned to Mallard Point late that afternoon there were police in the parking lot and paramedics on the dock. The flashing blue lights reminded her of all the times the police were in her driveway after a bloody incident with her husband. Wouldn't it be ironic if this time they were there to see him? Miranda parked the car, moved closer, and saw that the paramedics were gathered around a man in a huge pool of blood. It was Dominic. In an accidental fall, he hit his head on an upright and was dead.

Shoes for an Imaginary Life

Linda Lewis

Dominic's Grave

Miranda watched as tears fell from her cheeks onto a long chiffon skirt. It's crimson and wine folds moved silently as she took her place beside the casket. Although surrounded by the ashen faces of mourners-for-hire, Miranda was all alone. Men in black suits lowered the lifeless body, primped and styled for the occasion, into an unstylish hole in the ground. Greece was a magical place to visit, but a bad place to spend eternity.

The pontiff in his formal vestments turned to face the crowd, which included Dominic's lawyers and a few employees who stood smoking and looking at Facebook. The carpenter who installed the blue dome on Dominic's villa came to the funeral hoping to finally get paid. The service began with the recitation of the Trisagion, known also as the "Thrice-Holy," The pontiff looked down at the casket and cleared his throat; a lawyer looked down at his watch and noted the time.

"Holy God, Holy Mighty, Holy Immortal, have mercy on us.

Holy God, Holy Mighty, Holy Immortal, have mercy on us.
Holy God, Holy Mighty, Holy Immortal, have mercy on us."

"Here lies God's faithful servant, a man whose kindness and generosity were known to all." Father Leonidas was most likely a hired pawn, a man of God on Dominic's almighty payroll, a hypocrite paid to whisper his stained glass lies. Dominic always said that someday when he died, an armored truck would follow the black limousines to the cemetery so he could take his money with him to heaven. What irony that the same fortune was recently seized in accordance with U.S. Forfeiture Laws after Charlie Fine gave up Dominic's name to Federal Agents. All property, real and personal— the homes, the jet, the yacht, and his business assets were frozen as well, pending an investigation. While some men might have cursed God for such misfortune, Dominic Manos did not believe in religion or spiritual things. Had he not already been dead, the crumbling of his empire would have killed him.

Miranda reached into her Louis Vuitton Speedy 30 Cherry Cerise. It was a cheerful bag for an occasion marked by sorrow, but also a time for celebration. Wherever he was going, Dominic would finally be free from his crippling addiction to alcohol, the anger, and a childhood with an unrelenting grip that bound him to the horrors of his past. Miranda imagined that the only thing worse than those years of abuse and neglect, was knowing that his mother could have protected him, but didn't.

To be clear, Miranda was not at her husband's funeral to dwell on the past. She did wonder, however, whether it was his secrets or his guilt that let loose his demons night after night. She wondered if he hated God and blamed him for allowing such bad things to happen when he was young. Miranda was frequently vexed about that, too. She poured over her Bible looking for answers, praying that *other* famous short prayer... *Why God, why?*

"... everything works together for the good, for everybody who loves God, and are called according to his purpose." Romans 8:28

Miranda didn't see how that could possibly be right! How could the trials of an orphan tossed between foster care and reform school possibly work for *anyone's* good? In a well-known Bible story, there was a man named Job. He had every possession you can imagine— even more than Dominic. Job endured years of suffering and lost his entire family and all his worldly possessions. But in his case, all his trials worked together for good by demonstrating his deep faith, and his trust in God to sustain him through a harrowing time. It not only strengthened the faith of those around him, but has given reassurance and hope to every generation since. God also gave him back twice as much as he had before his trials began. No matter how bad things got, Job never cursed God. Among all the characters in the Bible, Job even made the short list of men who God called his friend.

Dominic's suffering achieved nothing, or so it seemed. Job was a grown man who knew God and trusted him. Dominic was an impressionable kid whose only exposure to the church was at the hands of a deviant priest who traded his car keys for sex. When Dominic really needed a Father in heaven, a predator at a church on earth killed his chance. Is there any place in the depths of hell deep enough for that priest to spend eternity? Miranda was counting on it.

"You shall not mistreat any widow or fatherless child. If you do mistreat them, and they cry out to me, I will surely hear their cry, and my wrath will burn, and I will kill you with the sword, and your wives shall become widows and your children fatherless." Exodus 22:22-24

A well-loved pastor and author wrote about a similar experience. When he was a boy around Dominic's age, a man in his neighborhood offered to take a group of kids camping. This was at a time when people were trustworthy, and the parents said it was okay. Before the night was over, the man had been inside every boy's sleeping bag. The experience was so horrific, so damaging, that he never told a soul. In his book, the pastor gives an account, for the first time, of what happened that weekend, and the remarkable choice he made after he came home.

The boy had been to church with his parents, and while he wasn't sure of the details, knew that communion was something important. He describes how he staged his own communion service late that night. In the absence of wafers and wine, he chose a slice of potato and some juice. He told Jesus what happened and how bad he felt, and could he please help him. Not only was he spared the suffering that was Dominic's life sentence, but a relationship that changed him forever had begun. The pastor knew the Lord— not the God of religion, condemnation, or hypocrisy— but the real, true, merciful God who even a young boy could talk to when he needed a miracle. With the burden of that abomination lifted, that pastor has helped millions of people with his books and ministry. Everything worked together for good.

Miranda's prayer life was exhausting. Over and over she pleaded on Dominic's behalf for healing and peace. She wrote his name in the margins of her Bible till there was no more room to write. She asked for wisdom, and swore that according to a verse in James, her single-minded faith entitled her to some answers.

"If any of you is lacking in wisdom, ask God, who gives to all generously and ungrudgingly, and it will be given you. But ask in faith, never doubting, for the one who doubts is like a wave of the sea, driven and tossed by the wind; for the doubter, being double-minded and

unstable in every way, must not expect to receive anything from the Lord." James 1:5-8

Though in her haste she might have seemed bossy and impatient, God liked her enthusiasm and spunk. He would provide answers when she was ready to listen.

"To everything there is a season, a time for every purpose under heaven." Ecclesiastes 3:1

"But do not forget this one thing, dear friends: With the Lord a day is like a thousand years, and a thousand years are like a day." 2Peter 3:8

Miranda touched the well-worn Bible in her bag. The white cover with gold letters was now wrapped in packing tape. And when some of the pages got loose, she carefully glued them back into place, including one she went back to again and again:

"But whoever causes one of these little ones who believe in me to sin, it would be better for him to have a great millstone fastened around his neck and to be drowned in the depth of the sea." Matthew 18:6

But did the priest drown? No he did not, at least as far as she knew. Instead, he stayed at the church where he abused how many boys after Dominic?!

"Woe to those who call evil good and good evil, who put darkness for light and light for darkness, who put bitter for sweet and sweet for bitter!" Isaiah 5:20

Miranda considered the snake in the Garden of Eden. He was a predator, too. It was his lies that convinced Eve to eat from The Tree. How is that any different than a man of God instructing a boy to do as he's told, and keep it a secret. Darkness for light, and light for darkness.

"For I know the plans I have for you, declares the Lord, plans to prosper you and not to harm you, plans to give you hope and a future." Jeremiah 29:11

Dominic had all that money and not a moment's peace to enjoy it. He had prospered but never lived. Miranda's conversations with God about Dominic's cataclysmic existence were a chess game she knew she couldn't win. He was Nea Kameri, a natural disaster that could spew enough molten lava to destroy anything in its path, but mostly her.

There were two criminals who hung next to Jesus on the cross. The man on the right was the good thief; on the left, the unrepentant one. The man on the left insulted Jesus and taunted him, saying, *If you are who you say you are, then you should get us all down from here!* The man on the right, however, sensed something different about Jesus and acknowledged that the Christ had done nothing wrong. If ever there was a soul hovering on the brink of hell, it was this criminal—

nobody special or noteworthy, but an ordinary man who chose to believe. He said, *"Jesus, remember me when you come into your Kingdom."* And Jesus replied, "Today you will be with me in Paradise." Luke 23:42-43.

The story of the good thief means it's never too late! It was this man's faith that Jesus recognized, not a formal prayer or an alter call in a fancy church. Miranda knew from experience that Lucille's famous short prayer was also enough. She wondered if at some point, Dominic might have prayed that, too.

"God help me, Hanna killed herself and it was my fault," he might have said. "God help me, I married a wife and beat her into submission." "God help me, I'm falling off my boat and I'm about to die." If the faith of the good thief had a place waiting in Heaven, then Dominic did, too.

Miranda wondered if Dominic saw the love of Jesus in her. Selfish girls who marry for money are not who you would typically find in a nursing home praying with someone on their last day, telling the story of the good thief, cleaning up vomit or changing diapers. What source so powerful could replace vanity with a kind and loving heart? What would cause such a dramatic change? Some might say, well, she just made up her mind to be a better person. But for all the years Miranda counted on sparkle and fizz to make her happy, the truth had now been revealed.

When she knelt at the foot of his bed praying at night, did Dominic notice a difference? Or all the times she put a pillow under his head when he was passed out on the floor… could he sense she had changed? She read her Bible while he read his newspapers. If there was a way to reach God through osmosis Dominic would surely know him by now!

"Draw near to God and he will draw near to you."
James 4:8

It's the easiest thing in the world for anyone who is willing and desperate enough to try.

"This is good, and pleases God our Savior, who wants all people to be saved, and come to a knowledge of the truth."
1 Timothy 2:3

She reminded God of those verses. If he wanted Dominic to know the truth, might he have helped him along? Given him a nudge to draw near? Miranda felt guilty about her husband's lack of faith and sometimes asked herself, *what's my part in it?* It was a tool frequently used by AA members as they worked on the dreaded Step Four.

"Made a searching and fearless moral inventory of ourselves." Followed by Step Five, *"Admitted to God, to ourselves, and to another human being the exact nature of our wrongs."* From *The Big Book of Alcoholics Anonymous.*

371

And so Miranda confessed. There were so many things she had done wrong, she could write a book about it.

As a hospice volunteer there were a lot of rules, and justifiably so. You don't want some loose cannon coming in and creating chaos in the spiritual construct of someone who may not wish to hear about Jesus. On the other hand, Miranda questioned whether it was right to hold back information that would change not just someone's life, but someone's eternity. Moreover, she knew that visiting the sick and the dying was God's work, and that she never, ever, could have done this without an anointing from her Father. Nursing homes and old people were never her style, but now they were her heart. What were the odds she would be caught talking about Jesus alone in the dark on someone's deathbed?

Miranda whispered the story of the good thief to hospice patients who were alone and afraid, with no family present to hold their hand, stroke their hair, and comfort them. There were many like Karla, and Sophie, and Francis Peck, whose adult children were too busy, too far away, or just not interested. Hearing is the last sense to go; that's a fact. However heavy their burdens in those last days and hours, what an opportunity they had to change their minds even at the very last second! They didn't need a church, a priest, or even a Bible. They only had to make a choice to believe!

"I'm telling you this because you are my friend, and I love you," Miranda would whisper. "Everything it says in the Bible... all the stories about Jesus and forgiveness... that's all true! You can do what the Good Thief did, and just say a prayer in your head that you're a sinner, and you're sorry, and you know in your heart that Jesus can forgive you right now. Just ask him to forgive you and tell him you want to see him in heaven." For Sophie she added, "You better be in heaven when I get there or there's gonna be trouble. Don't piss me off, you hear me?" A brief flutter of her eyelids and a half smile told Miranda she'd gotten through. Miranda never got fired because she never got caught. Her hospice volunteer work paid more than any assignment she had accepted before or since.

The priest at Dominic's grave continued, emotionless and bored. He adjusted his hat and concluded with a prayer of petition to the Lord, to grant rest to the deceased and ask for the forgiveness of sins. The hired mourners, the attorney, and the man who made the blue dome mumbled the response, *May your memory be eternal.* Miranda looked beyond the casket to the headstones on the hill. They were crowded, crooked, and poorly maintained, as if the inhabitants wouldn't be staying long. City life had encroached on every piece of vacant land, and more space just wasn't available. There was literally no place for the dead to go. But for now, this would be a quiet and peaceful spot for Dominic, at least for a while. Greek cemeteries were built on sacred ground. When they became crowded and no space remained, the plots were *recycled* to make room for more. A deluxe package could be purchased for the sum of $500,000 (U.S.). Dominic used to brag that he spilled that much in a season at Mallard Point.

Miranda considered her dilemma— half a million dollars was a lot of money. Even the most lavish funeral and burial amenities in America were far less. She had already spent a considerable sum to transport the remains. The cost was based on the weight of Dominic's embalmed corpse packed inside a shipping container, which cost extra. The container was placed in the cargo bay of a Boeing 747 for the twelve-hour flight. Dominic loathed the idea of flying commercial, much less beneath a class of people who didn't own their own planes. Miranda considered the irony. She didn't know that every check she had written to cover these costs would soon bounce like a boat on a raging sea.

The details of the burial package worked like this: The deceased would lie in a "rented" grave for a maximum of three years. After a mandatory waiting period, a family member of the deceased is required to return to the grave where a cemetery worker exhumes the body, not yet fully decomposed. The contents are moved someplace else after that. The paperwork didn't exactly say where; it was complicated. There were "family members" popping up all over the Midwest and Florida, claiming to be Dominic's sons, daughters, ex-wives, and lovers. Everyone wanted a piece of him. The legal process to sort things out would be a doozy.

As she tossed in a ceremonial shovel of dirt, Miranda imagined her husband trapped below, listening to the cold soil hit his coffin, wishing he could breathe, and scared half to death— just the way she felt hiding in her room all those nights. It was hard not to be bitter. She checked her phone and retouched her lipstick. *Rest in peace, my husband... rest in peace.*

Linda Lewis

Goodhart's Farewell

The night of the gala reception at the Leelanau Lighthouse Museum arrived. Miranda put on a floaty dress, bought a ticket, and spotted Drew Becker standing beside a beautifully restored HackerCraft; his grandfather's pride and joy! He looked impossibly handsome yet somehow ridiculous dressed in a tuxedo and entertaining the crowd. Miranda ducked her head, grinned, and moved closer. Guests were having drinks and nodding as he spoke, the way rich people do. Miranda sipped her champagne, wishing she could twirl and spin to get his attention, but now was not the time. She listened in as the women whispered among themselves.

"He's Hank Becker's grandson..."

"And he's very handsome... single as far as I know," she said to the young lady standing beside her. Another guest chimed in insisting it was high time they finally knew the truth about the old man.

"I wonder if Drew is the anonymous donor who paid to restore the lighthouse and build this museum,"

377

speculated the secretary-treasurer of the Bridge Street Garden Club.

"But where would a boat mechanic get that kind of money? This had to have cost millions, and Drew Becker is not a wealthy man," noted her friend.

The young lady didn't know whether to flirt or faint. Drew Becker was dreamy.

Miranda circled past a vintage Chris Craft and a gleaming restored Garwood, then spotted a plaque beside a row of tall windows overlooking Lake Michigan. It said, "This museum is dedicated to the men of the Great Lakes and the women who loved them. *Always follow your heart.*"

"Look here... there's a name on the boat," said one of the husbands as he stepped to the stern of the old Hacker. Drew was chatting it up with a man about doing some work on his 1938 Trumpy. He had little use for silly women in ball gowns, with stupid comments and foolish grins.

One of the women said a little too loudly, "I wonder who the lucky lady is! He named the boat *Miss Hattie.*"

"Hattie. Hmmph," replied another. The name didn't ring a bell. "She must not be from the area." They looked to each other for an answer.

"Hattie was Drew's grandmother," said Miranda, over the voices of the crowd. "Her name was Hattie, and she was beautiful." Drew knew the voice, but could it be? Miranda smiled; Drew did a double take and grinned. Maybe it would be like The Kiss on the dock all over again, or maybe even better. This time they would take a chance and find out.

In all the excitement, Miranda overlooked the most important detail of all. Everything worked together for good in the story of Job. And for the pastor things turned out well, too. Though it appeared that Dominic's trials failed to produce anything but violence and hate, Miranda's life— and Miranda's heart— had been radically changed forever.

Made in the USA
Middletown, DE
25 March 2021